Raging
Heart

First paperback edition April 2023

Published by WRLMorris Publishing
Book design by Whitney Morris

ISBN 978-1-916935-04-4 (paperback)
ISBN 978-1-916935-05-1 (hardback)
www.wrlmorris.com

For Faye

My beautiful force of nature,
You bring joy to all those around you

Prologue

Radius

In the briny deep the current swirled gently picking up sand from the ocean floor. A winter chill spread through the waters but rays of sunlight from above still reached even the deepest trenches. All was calm but a storm was brewing. Radius could feel it in the pit of his stomach. He wasn't sure how he knew but ever since he had bonded with the moon crystal, he could sense the oncoming of a storm. He sighed deeply, placing his hand on the cold window as he stared out at the city from the tower of his throne room. A multitude of colours glimmered illuminating the bustle of the underwater city. He clutched his trident tightly in his right hand as he watched his citizens' casually swimming about. Market holders were hollering their latest deals, customers perused the shop's wares and children swished about playing games of tag. The king's heart felt heavy like his chest was being restricted. The storm wouldn't affect him, tucked away safely in the luxury of his throne room. The room with its high ceilings and large windows felt so cold. The walls were draped in grand artworks, with a portrait of his late father the last king hung in the centre. His golden throne sat upon a raised platform so he would always be higher than everyone else. All these luxuries he had and what had he done to earn them? These storms were becoming more frequent. They now occurred at least once a week. Something was wrong in his waters, but he couldn't figure out what. Even worse were the fits of madness that plagued his people. This was the doing of a spirit creature, but he had no idea how to vanquish it. His forehead creased as he frowned deeply.

The throne room doors opened and in swam his wife, Harmony. Her fiery red hair flowed behind her. Her pale skin was flawless and her sapphire eyes sparkled in the bright light entering the room through the large windows. The sight of her warmed his heart. "My love," she said, her lips tightly pressed together, "I'm afraid I bring terrible news."

Panic rose from his stomach as he crossed the room to meet her halfway. "What has happened?"

"There has been another citizen hit by a fit of madness." She said, "This spirit creature is getting out of control."

The King's shoulders sagged as he shook his head. "I'm afraid I no longer know what to do." Radius looked at the Moon crystal encased in the centre of his trident. The crystal's glow reminded him of Queen Mellissa. She had been the one to retrieve the lost crystal. Something no one in the ocean had managed to do in over a thousand years. Radius jaw tightened as he clenched his fists. Thinking of the young crystal keeper always made him feel inadequate. He still felt like a complete novice at this. He may not know anything of the Sun crystal keeper but had fought beside Queen Mellissa, keeper of the Heart crystal. She was on a whole other level to him. Her abilities had amazed him when they had last met. She wouldn't have this much trouble defeating a mere spirit creature. It was only because one of her advisers he knew what they were dealing with. He was failing the ocean as the keeper.

Harmony placed her hand on his cheek. "I know that look. None of this is your fault. Spirit creatures are practically unheard of. Not even the Land Queen would know how to defeat them."

"I know but this thing has been plaguing us for too long now and we are no closer to stopping it."

"Maybe we should meet with the Land Queen again. I am sure she would help us."

Radius stood tall and puffed his chest out. "No. The sea is my domain. This is my responsibility."

"When Humarya was terrorising the land, did you not go and fight beside Queen Mellissa? She has a good heart just like you." Harmony placed both her hands on the centre of his chest. "She would be here in a heartbeat. All you have to do is ask."

"This is different. Humarya was a threat to the land and the sea. This is simply a spirit creature. We can't let the land folk think we are weak."

Harmony frowned. "The Queen would never think you weak."

"Queen Mellissa wouldn't but that council of hers, they are another story." Radius turned away from his wife, looking back out at his kingdom. "We will overcome this." He rolled his shoulders back and held his head high. Radius had been a king long before receiving the Moon crystal. He had been raised from birth to rule this kingdom. He would protect his people himself.

Winter

Gregory

Greg marched back to his office with his chief of staff Mary. Snow crunched beneath their feet. Mary was only a couple of inches shorter than him so had no problem keeping up with his fast pace. Her short blond hair was neatly tucked away under a black woolly hat. Greg wished he had thought to wear a hat as the tips of his ears now felt like icicles. He rewrapped his navy scarf, attempting to cover his ears with it, as he gazed around the city centre. All the shop's roofs had a thick layer of snow covering them. A fresh layer of the powdery stuff had fallen while they had been finalising the preparations for the evening's celebration of Winter solstice. So far things were going according to plan, even if Greg was now frozen to the bone. Despite the winter chill, the city was alive with anticipation. Fairy lights lined the streets creating a direct route towards the lake, where stalls for the evening fair were having the final touches put on them. Orbs and lanterns were all carefully placed in the area ready to be switched on after nightfall. Twinkling lights shaped like snowflakes lined the stage that had been erected beside the lake for the speeches. This was Greg's first winter solstice as an Elder. Everything needed to go well, especially after the little hiccup at the coming of winter celebrations. Greg sighed as he thought of the disaster that event had been. There hadn't been enough fireworks ordered and the lights had blown when switched on. As a child, he had always preferred the coming of winter festival in early November to the winter solstice. His father always seemed to have more time to spend with him during that festival. Greg now understood why. Solstice was a much grander celebration and the planning had taken up a lot of his time. He was determined to make the solstice spectacular for his people especially after he messed up so badly in November.

"Sir, you're not thinking about the coming of winter festival again?" asked Mary.

"Of course not," Greg replied nestling his face further into his scarf.

"What happened in November wasn't that bad and as a team, we have learnt from those mistakes." She turned and smiled at him; her blue eyes shone with excitement. "This evening is going to be wonderful."
Greg nodded, his ginger hair falling into his eyes. "Your right. This winter Solstice will be great."

They hurried onward. A small smile crept onto Greg's face. All they had left was a few bits of paperwork at city hall, then everything would be set up, and he would be free to meet Mellissa and Samson at the train station. It was weird that Samson was not already in Novosvillas at this time of year, but with his recent promotion to the Queen's chief of staff, Samson's absence at home was something Greg would have to get used to.

This would be Mellissa's first Winter solstice in the magic world. Greg's grin grew as he thought of his girlfriend and his heart skipped a beat. It was also their first solstice as a couple, which added to the pressure he felt for everything to be perfect. With all his preparations for solstice and Mellissa's for Christmas, they hadn't seen each other for three weeks. Was it weird to miss her this much? Greg had never felt this strongly about anyone before. Sometimes the intensity scared him, worried if she knew how much he loved her, she would run a mile. Greg shook his head. Everything was going to go exactly as planned and he would enjoy his time with Mellissa. Unfortunately, they would be chaperoned by her guardians and his cousin. Neither of their positions left them much alone time.

They arrived at city hall and made their way down the corridor towards the offices. As Greg removed his thick winter coat, his assistant Tom came running up to him. "Sir these forms just arrived from Lady Gabrielle." He handed over some papers. Greg flicked threw them. It looked like more council stuff. He turned to Mary. "We can add these to the pile, they won't take us long."

Tom rolled back and forth on his heel. "One more thing sir, Queen Mellissa is waiting in your office."

"What?" Greg said. His heart stopped; she was going to kill him if he had forgotten to meet her. He flicked his wrist over and looked at his watch. Her train wasn't meant to arrive for another two hours.

Mary took the papers from him. "I can handle these by myself, sir." She flicked her short blond hair back and smirked. "You shouldn't keep the Queen waiting."

"Thank you, Mary." Greg straightened his shirt and flattened his hair.

"I'm sure she won't care how you look." Mary winked. "Say hi to Mellissa for me. I'll make sure no one bothers you." She walked off down the corridor towards her office beckoning Tom to follow her.

Greg took a deep breath, smoothing his shirt out and walked into his office. Mellissa sat at his desk. She was wearing a dark green dress that showed off her curves perfectly. Her dark curls hung freely down her back. She smiled as she saw him, making him want to walk straight over and embrace her but he could play along for now. "Your early," he said, "I had intended to meet you at the train station."

She interlaced her fingers as she leaned on his desk. "Well, we have a lot to discuss. This is the first time the elves have witnessed winter solstice."

He raised an eyebrow. "Exactly how many elves are coming?"

She shrugged, swinging side to side in his chair. "Quite a few I believe. Novosvillas is the closest city to us celebrating and this is all so new." She gestured for him to sit across from her. "We have much to confer."

He shut the door looking around his office. He had the biggest office in the building. His large oak desk would overrun a smaller room. It was Mellissa's usual choice of place to sit when she visited as if she were purposely trying to stop him from working. But she sat in his office chair this time, as if the space was hers. Both walls were lined with perfectly organised books. She had been here for some time as he spotted a few out of place. She had also been flicking through the papers on his desk. The guards wouldn't have allowed anyone but her in here while he was out. He sat across from her. "You do remember this is my office. We really should be sat the other way round."

"I'm pretty sure I outrank you." He could tell she was trying to keep a straight face, but a smile crept through.

"Where are the others?"

She placed a finger on her lip as she looked up at the ceiling. "How did Victoria put it? Oh, I remember. We were at the train station, and she demanded I fly ahead, as it's been three whole weeks since I had seen you." She looked straight at him, her big brown eyes full of mischief. "Apparently we were going to be unbearable to be around with all that sexual tension and to get it all out of our system before they got here."

Greg was on his feet in a flash leaning over the desk and kissing her. Mellissa's lips never left his as she pushed herself out of the chair and climbed onto the desk. He slid her across the desk on her knees as he wrapped his arms around her waist. Heat radiated between them. Even in the middle of winter, she smelled like cherry blossoms on a spring morning. It was a scent unique to her. She giggled as he trailed kisses along her neck. He rested his forehead on hers. "I missed you."

She exhaled heavily; her breath warm on his lips. "I missed you too." She pressed her mouth to his, kissing him passionately. Her fingers snaked up the back of his neck and through his hair. Her body stiffened and she poked him in the chest, making him step back. "What?" he asked.

Her eyes narrowed as she frowned. "You cut your hair."

Greg ran his hand over his head. "Oh yeah. It's meant to look more professional like this."

She pouted, still kneeling on his desk. "But I liked the messy mop it was."

Greg took her hand placing a kiss on her palm. "It'll grow back."

She tugged him closer running both her hands through his hair. "I guess it is neater."

He kissed the tip of her nose, causing her to giggle, then her cheek and then her neck. She shifted position on the desk placing her legs on either side of him. She pulled his face to hers and their lips met. He leaned into her. Her hands ran along his shirt slowly unbuttoning it. With one hand he tugged at the ribbons at the back of her dress, while the other slid along her thigh.

A loud bang sounded outside. They both froze. "Do you not know who I am?" yelled a shrill voice.

"Oh crap," said Greg. His stomach rolled as he recognised that high-pitched voice. He quickly buttoned his shirt as he walked to his office door.

Mellissa hopped off his desk awkwardly retying the back of her dress. She pouted. "What's wrong?"

Before he could respond, the door flew open. In marched a burly older woman, with grey hair and thick-rimmed glasses. Her lips were pursed like she had a lemon in her mouth. Tom hurried in after her. He had coffee all over his shirt and looked like he was trying to hold back tears. "I'm so sorry sir. I tried to tell her you were busy, but your aunt wouldn't listen. She threw my drink at me."

Greg grimaced. "I'm sorry Tom".

His aunt scowled at him. "Why are you apologising to him?" She pointed a chubby finger at Tom. "He shouldn't have got in my way."

Greg glared at her. "I'm apologising because you threw coffee at my assistant for doing his job, Aunt Josephine." He turned back to Tom. "How about you finish up early so you can get home and change your shirt."

Tom bowed. "Thank you, sir." Tom left in a hurry. Greg wished he could get away from Josephine as easily.

Josephine crossed her arms and curled her top lip. She always looked like she had smelt something bad. "I think that boy needs firing."

Greg pushed his fringe to the side. He looked up at the ceiling and exhaled slowly. "What did I do to warrant this delightful visit?" Greg asked while forcing a smile.

She pushed past Greg and plunked herself in the chair opposite his desk. She sat up straight and pursed her lips. "That assistant of yours lied to me, Gregory. He said you were in a meeting but instead, I find you covered in lipstick, hooking up with some random elf girl." She looked Mellissa up and down, then turned away sticking her nose up. "What would your poor father think?"

Greg clenched his jaw, wishing he could make her disappear. Why hadn't he locked the door? He always made sure to lock the door, especially after the time Mary had walked in on them. It's because it had been three weeks since he had seen Mellissa and she had surprised him by turning up early.

Mellissa cleared her throat behind him. "I will have you know that Steffen loved me."

Greg nodded. "That's true. Also, auntie, she isn't some random elf." He walked to Mellissa's side and held her hand up, in the formal way of greeting someone of her rank. "Meet Queen Mellissa Hail, keeper of the Heart crystal. Mellissa, this is my aunt Josephine."

Josephine pointed at Mellissa with her stubby finger. "That girl is the elf Queen everyone keeps talking about? But she is so tiny."

Greg stepped in front of Mellissa. "What are you doing here, aunt?"

"I came to spend Winter Solstice with your Aunt Tilly. Cynthia was there with her mother, but Samson was not. I came to complain to you, but I guess I should be complaining to her." The chair rattled as she stood and jabbed another finger in Mellissa's direction. "How dare you steal my nephew away from his home." She wagged her chubby hand in Greg's face. Her bejewelled rings almost took his eye out. "And you. How could you let her take him away to that ridiculous elf city?"

Greg gently pushed his aunt's hand away. "It was Samson's choice to leave. Nobody stole him. He was offered a job and from what he tells me he is quite happy in his new position."

Josephine pursed her lips. "You would say that. The floozy has also gotten her claws into you as well."

Mellissa's eyes flashed green as she clenched her fists. "I should go. The train will be here soon."

Greg grabbed her hand. "Wait, I'll come with you." He

turned to Josephine his jaw tense. "If you don't like Samson's life choices take it up with him, but I will not have you insulting my girlfriend."

Her eyes widened. She looked like her eyebrows were about to fly off her face. "Your what? How long has this been going on?"

Greg tilted his head. "That depends on how you look at things. Somewhere between six months to a year."

"Well, it obviously isn't serious if you have been keeping it secret." She glared at Mellissa's hand in his.

"It isn't a secret." Greg snapped, "Everyone important knows including my entire staff. Now we have somewhere to be." Greg turned his back on his aunt. Holding Mellissa's hand he walked out his office, leaving his aunt with her mouth ajar.

Solstice

Mellissa

Greg and I sat on a bench at the train station waiting for the train from Urbem Folium. It was quiet and the few people that walked by didn't take much notice of us. There was no doubt they all recognised Greg; he was their elder after all, but he seemed to have a rather casual relationship with his people. I was wrapped up in my scarf and hat, with my big winter coat hood up in the hope I wouldn't be recognised. To the people of Novosvillas, I was more of a novelty than their own elder. While his people liked him, they seemed to adore me. It was nice to be loved but sometimes I just wanted to pretend to be a normal nineteen-year-old. My disguise also helped keep me warm in the icy winds of the winter. Lucky we were sheltered from the snow in the station but its high ceiling and wide opening allowed the cold air to fly through.

I huddled closer to Greg as I glanced up at the big clock in the station. Thanks to his aunt's interruption we were early. I made a mental note to have a similar clock put in at our train station back home. Compared to our newly built station, the Novosvillas train station was a lot grander. It had multiple lines coming in and out connecting Novosvillas to many cities. Whereas we simply had the one line that came here but I had been so happy when the train line was finally built. It had made things so much easier, especially now I couldn't teleport. I shivered as the warmth of Greg's body was replaced by a cold breeze. Greg leaned forward resting his elbows on his knees, what was left of his red hair fell over his eyes. With the rest of his face nestled in his scarf, I could hardly see him. "I'm sorry about my aunt," he said, "She is a handful."

"She is something," I said.

"She is prejudiced, a bigot and so many other things. I'm so sorry."

I took his hand and pushed his fringe from his face. There was a lot less hair to move. I gently tugged his scarf away and ran a finger along his jaw. I bit my bottom lip. While I had liked his longer messy look, the shorter hair showed off his chiselled jawline better and those emerald eyes of his just sparkled. Shuffling closer to him, I kissed his cheek. "You have nothing to apologise for."

He let out a heavy sigh. "I feel responsible because I'm related to her."

"As my dad is constantly telling me, we are not responsible for the actions of others." Greg laughed. I drew a circle on his hand with my finger. "So, is it just elves that Josephine hates or everyone who isn't a changeling?"

"Everyone who isn't a changeling." He leaned back on the bench and nudged me with his shoulder. "To be honest she would probably like you if she hadn't walked in on us like that."

"Right so elves are okay as long as they aren't sleeping with her nephew."

"Or giving her other nephew a job that means he has to move away from changeling territory." Greg looked up at the sky and his shoulders sagged. "Oh, gods she is awful."

"I am so glad you said it." Just thinking about that woman

had anger bubbling back up inside me. I placed my hands in my lap tangling my fingers in my skirt. "There is something she said that got me thinking about us."

Greg looked at me forehead creased. "Please don't let her scare you off. I promise you the rest of my family is nothing like her."

"Please, I have faced worse than her and I know at least two of your cousins are decent people." I turned towards him so my knees were touching his leg and interlaced my fingers with his. "What I meant was, we should take our relationship public. Pretty much everyone knows anyway."

"But you said you didn't want the publicity. You're the Queen and I'm an Elder, it'll be big news."

"I know what I said but I don't care anymore. Enough rumours are flying around about us anyway. Let them have their gossip." I tugged at his scarf, pulling him towards me so his lips were only inches from mine. "I want to be free to kiss you whenever I want."

A big grin spread across Greg's face. "You are always free to kiss me." I felt my face heat. He wrapped his arm around my waist pulling me into him. Gently cupping my face, he tilted my head towards him. "I guess Winter Solstice can be our first official outing as a couple." He closed the small gap between us, kissing me.

"Argh" Came Victoria's voice. "The whole point of sending you ahead of us was so we didn't have to watch you two make out."

We had been too busy talking we hadn't noticed the train pull into the station. Trains on this side of the veil were so quiet. I looked up at her. She had her hands on her hips and her top lip curled. She looked like a snow princess in her long navy coat and knee-length boots. Her golden hair was pushed back by a pair of fluffy baby blue earmuffs. "Where's Samson?" I asked.

She leaned on the extendable handle of her suitcase. "He is getting the rest of our luggage."

"How much more stuff did you bring?"

"I brought your gown for this evening and a few spare dresses because you plus snow is bound to end in a disaster." I rolled my eyes at her. She waved her hand around gesturing to the whole of my body. "That hat and coat are a big no for your rank. Luckily, I have your fur-lined cape. Then of course there's all the stuff I need for getting ready this evening. Oh, you also forgot your tiara." She produced a gold tiara encrusted with emeralds out of nowhere.

I grabbed it putting it under my coat. "The whole point of the big coat and hat is so I don't stick out as royalty."

Greg took my tiara and pulled off my hat. Causing my wild curls to spring to life. He placed my tiara on my head. "Tonight everyone will be looking to you as Queen."

I pouted as I crossed my arms. "Do you know how long it took me to get all my hair inside that hat?"

He twirled one of my curls around his finger. "I love when your hair is its natural wild curls."

Victoria pretended to hurl. I glared at her. She snatched my hat. "I hate to say it but Greg's right. It's time to let me work my magic as you need to be looking the part this evening." I groaned as I got up from the bench and followed Victoria.

Laughter sounded behind us as a group of children ran past. The smell of toffee and cinnamon floated by from the nearby food cart. I was sat at a wooden table making a lantern with Victoria and Samson. All sorts of papers, ribbons and glitter were scattered in front of us. The cold chill in the air was offset by the heaters on either side of the benches we had sat on. We were under a gazebo lined with examples of ready-made lanterns. There were loads of different stands set up along the street leading down to the lake. Greg had gone to formally open festivities. He would be back to let off the lanterns with us but as an elder, he had responsibilities. There was a temporary stage, that had been erected in the middle of the field by the lake. This was where Greg had made the opening speech. I hadn't listened to a word he had said. I had been too busy gazing at all the twinkling lights that lined the path. When Greg had described everything to me on the communis, it had sounded amazing but seeing it in real life was even better. In the darkness of the night the lights, illuminated the city perfectly making it look magnificent. By the lake, the trees and bushes had also been lined with twinkling lights. I was going to have to up my game for Christmas, and I only had a few days to do it.

Victoria sat playing on her phone, while Samson and I carefully decorated our lanterns.

"Are you two done yet?" Victoria asked sounding irritated.

"Not yet," replied Samson.

"Is something wrong Victoria?" I asked.

She rested her arm on the table. "I didn't get all dressed up to spend the night hidden in a stall with you two." She looked fabulous in her dark blue dress. It was form fitting around her torso, with lacy sleeves. The skirt fluttered down to just above her knees. She wore a black cape, lined with fur. The dark colours made her long blond hair, even more eye-catching. It was no wonder people kept glancing her way as they walked past.

I looked over to the stall playing music, where people were dancing. "You can go join the other celebrations if you want," I said.

"I can't leave you." She pointed to Samson beside me. "He is not adequate protection."

"Hey," Samson said, "I would give my life for the Queen."

Victoria stared at him blankly. "I know. Mellissa will then be in tears beside your body, giving her attacker an opening to kill her, taking advantage of her emotional turmoil." Samson's jaw dropped.

"Harsh much?" I said.

Victoria rolled her eyes. "Whatever. I'm gonna get some hot chocolate. Want some?"

"Yes please," I said. The lights made her hair shimmer as she walked over to the drinks stand.

Samson frowned. "I'm not that much of a liability to you, am I?"

I looked up at him. With his neatly cut brown hair and in his dark grey suit with a green striped tie he looked like every bit the businessman I knew he was. "It's okay, I'm perfectly capable of protecting the both of us," I said turning back to my creation. I finished cutting out a bunny. Now all I had to do was put all the pieces together.

"Oh, gods no," Samson said. He stood looking over me, his brown eyes wide.

"What?" I looked in the direction Samson was staring. My heart sank. "Oh no."

He ran his hand through his hair. "I guess you have already met her."

"Unfortunately." I groaned.

"Samson, darling," Josephine said opening her arms wide to Samson.

"Aunt Josephine." Samson's smile was rigid and cold. He cringed as she hugged him. It was painful to watch. Samson took a step back when she finally let go of him. He straightened his tie. "Aunt Josephine I would like to introduce-"

"We've already met." She glared at me. "At least this time you are properly attired but in green of all colours." Her lip curled, "Don't you know the colours of Novosvillas are royal blue and gold."

Samson walked around the table we had been crafting at, to stand next to me. "She is the elf queen of course she wears the elvish green."

Josephine surged forward grabbing Samson's tie. Her eyes looked like they were about to pop out of her head. "I see you wear the same green. So quick to abandon your heritage." She pushed him aside. "This is your doing. At least Gregory seems to have lost interest in you."

I gritted my teeth. "Greg will be back once he has finished making sure everything is on schedule for the ceremony."

"Yes auntie," Samson said. "Queen Mellissa will be releasing the first set of lanterns with Greg."

She jabbed her finger at me. "She's not a changeling."

Samson frowned. "So what?"

Josephine poked me in the chest. I clenched my fists stopping myself from slapping her finger back at her. She poked me again. "You have corrupted both my nephews with your wicked ways." Suddenly Josephine dropped to the floor. Victoria had hold of the older woman's arm and had twisted it around her back forcing her down. Anger burned in Victoria's blue eyes. She leaned in close to Josephine. "If you touch Mellissa again, I will break you."

"Guards," yelled Josephine, "Help me. Do you not know who I am?"

Victoria pushed Josephine away. "I don't give a crap who you are. Do you not know who I am?" Victoria's hand glowed with power, ice forming on her fingertips. "I am the Queen's guardian, and I am nowhere near as nice as she is."

Two guards appeared. "Are you all right your majesty?"

One of them asked me.

"Everything is fine," I said, "Just a little misunderstanding my guardian has everything under control."

Samson took Josephine's arm. "It appears my aunt has had a little too much to drink. I will take care of her."

"I have not been drinking." Josephine tried to pull away from him, but he held her arm firmly.

"Whatever you say, auntie." Samson was gentle but firm when he tugged her away. "Let's go find Cynthia."

The guards bowed, then left. Victoria slid beside me. "That's his aunt?" I nodded. "I'm going to have to have a strong word with Gregory about his disgraceful aunt."

"Trust me I already know," Greg said behind us causing us to jump.

Victoria spun round and jabbed his chest. "Then why haven't you done anything? Your aunt assaulted Mellissa."

Greg walked around her to me. "Are you okay? I'm sorry I wasn't back sooner. Set up for the lantern release took longer than planned."

"I'm fine and she didn't assault me just got up in my personal space."

"She laid hands on the Queen." Victoria snapped, "She should be arrested."

"That's a bit much," I said.

Greg shook his head. "No, it isn't. Victoria's right." Victoria looked as shocked as I felt that he had agreed with her. Her shock didn't last long as she folded her arms and nodded in agreement. The two of them could always be counted on to agree when it came to being overprotective of me.

Greg interlaced his fingers with mine as he sat beside me. I looked him up and down and pouted. His suit was dark blue, and he wore a gold and blue striped tie. Thinking back, he wore these colours a lot. How had I never noticed before? I was an awful girlfriend. Greg tugged me closer. "What's wrong? My aunt didn't say something horrible again."

I looked up at him. His stunning green eyes made my breath catch. The colour of his eyes matched the royal elf colours a lot better. I smiled up at him. "Everything is absolutely fine."

Mary zig-zagged her way through the stalls. She wore a dark blue dress with a smart gold jacket. I cringed, even she was wearing the colours of the city. Mary curtsied to me, then turned to Greg. "Sir it's time to start." He nodded.

Greg stood pulling me up with him. "Wait," I pointed back at the lantern stall. "I haven't finished my lantern."

He gave me a carefree smile. "You can share mine." My heart fluttered. It wasn't often he was this at ease. He was usually such a stress head. I squeezed his hand as we followed Mary. Victoria grumbled behind us as we weaved our way through the crowd.

As we got closer to the stage Mary flagged down some guards who parted the crowd for us. Once backstage I took a deep breath feeling dizzy. Victoria leaned against a post. "When is the bonfire gonna start? I have been told that's when the real fun begins."

"After the release of the lanterns." Greg replied, "The bonfire is also when everyone gets rowdy and stupid from all the drinking."

The bonfire would be when I made my leave, as that didn't sound like my cup of tea. However, I knew that was exactly what Victoria had meant by *real fun*. She was going to be one of those rowdy revellers. Harkura would be furious if he found out about us splitting up but luckily, he had stayed behind in charge of protecting Urbem Folium for the night. Greg and Mary went on stage and greeted all the people gathered. The front of the stage was packed full of people. My stomach was full of butterflies. I took a deep breath. All I had to do was go up there and release a lantern. There was nothing to it.

"Try not to trip on your dress as you walk up those stairs." Victoria pointed at the stage steps.

I scowled at her. "Maybe if you hadn't insisted, I wore this ridiculous thing we wouldn't have to worry about me potentially tripping over it."

She gave me a dismissive wave of her hand. "Oh shush, it's a beautiful gown. Tamara made it so it fits perfectly." She was right. It was stunning, as were all the dresses Tamara made me. This one was down to my feet with layered skirts making it extra poofy. The bodice hugged me tightly, and the short sleeves were covered with pink roses. The off-shoulder cut exposed my collar bone showing off the heart crystal. To finish off the look I had an emerald fur-lined cloak draped over my shoulders and a golden tiara.

Victoria pulled my cape open, so my dress was on full display. She fluffed out my skirt and straightened my tiara while rearranging my long curls. "There, perfect." We both looked toward the stage as Greg announced my long title. Victoria gave me a thumbs-up as I made my way on stage. Cheers erupted, and there was a roar of applause.

I waved to the crowd as I walked across the stage to where Greg and Mary stood. Their crowd fell quiet. Everyone was looking up at me, holding lanterns ready to set free. I plastered my well practiced public speaking smile across my face. "Thank you for having me. This is the elves' first Winter Solstice since returning to the magic world. It is an honour to spend it with all of you here in Novosvillas." There were more cheers from the crowd. Samson had written my speech. It was short and sweet but effective.

Mary held a button out to me. "Queen Mellissa, would you do the honours?" As I pressed it and all the lights in the area went off. All that could be seen was the glow of the lanterns everyone held.

Greg held his one out to me. I place my hands around his. "You ready?" He whispered, "Once we release ours everyone else will follow suit."

My heart fluttered as my eyes met his. The light from the lantern made the green of his eyes sparkle. I nodded. Together we pushed our lantern up releasing it. It floated upwards towards the stars. Slowly more and more lanterns were released, and the sky shimmered with light. I gasped interlacing my fingers with Greg's as I watched the lanterns float higher and higher. The night sky looked as if it had come alive, as floating lights slowly danced across it. "Amazing," I whispered. Greg squeezed my hand pulling me closer to him. The warmth from his body made my whole body tingle. His eyes met mine and before I knew it, I was up on my tiptoes kissing him.

For a brief moment, I had forgotten where we were. The sounds of the crowd cheering and whistling caused me to blush, and I knew my wish for our relationship to be public had been granted.

Press

Gregory

reg woke to the sound of banging on his front door. He looked at the clock on his bedside table. It was six in the morning. Not too early but considering they hadn't got in until two this morning and then Mellissa had kept him up an extra hour, he was exhausted. It was the day after the solstice, most people would spend the day relaxing after the festivities from the night before. The banging got louder. He groaned as he pulled on the first set of clothes he laid his hands on. Mellissa rolled over in bed. "Tell them to go away," She grumbled.

He shook his head. It didn't sound like whoever was at the door was leaving anytime soon. Greg made his way downstairs and opened the front door. In marched the head of the PR department along with Mary. Greg rubbed his head trying to remember the PR woman's name. He knew the names of everyone he worked with daily, but this department usually went through Mary. He knew her name began with an H and that she was very good at her job. Greg shut the door and looked at the two women. They were complete opposites. Mary had dirty blond hair that was only long enough to cover her ears and towered over the other woman, whose jet-black hair was tied in a tight ponytail that went all the way down her back.

Mary clasped her hands together. "I'm sorry sir but Hayley here was very insistent that we meet."

"Okay," said Greg, "Shall we go sit in the kitchen." The two women followed him down the hallway to the kitchen. They watched him as he fumbled around the kitchen making coffee. His head was pounding so decided to make his coffee with a double shot. Once they were all sitting around the table with a hot drink in hand, Hayley laid out a newspaper in front of him. Greg looked down at it. His and Mellissa's kiss had made the front page. "This is a disaster," said Hayley.

"How so?" Greg asked.

Hayley pointed at the paper and looked at him her forehead creased. "Sir, you and the queen are on the front page. If you were going to announce your relationship to the people, I should have been consulted first so we could control the story."

Greg picked up the paper and skimmed through the article. It was a pretty favourable piece. There wasn't anything negative written about him or Mellissa. He placed the paper back on the table. "I still don't see the problem."

Hayley look liked she was about to pull her hair out. "The public is going to have questions. I mean if they find out how long you two have really been dating, they are going to feel lied to."

"Why should it matter? Our private lives are not public domain." Greg shuddered as both Mary and Hayley stared at him with an eyebrow raised. He put his hands up in front of his chest. "Okay, I know I'm like public property as an elder."

Hayley nodded while crossing her arms. "And it is my job to maintain not just your image but the entire office."

Mary cleared her throat. "I think what Hayley means is that both you and Mellissa need to get your stories straight, as the press will be sniffing around, and we don't want the people losing faith in you by hearing conflicting versions of events."

Greg ran his fingers through his hair. He was too tired to be having this meeting. Mellissa walked into the kitchen, wearing fluffy cat pyjamas. She looked at the three of them sitting at the table. Hayley and Mary turned to her. Mellissa's eyes widened. "I'll just leave you to your meeting." She turned back towards the door.

Hayley stood holding her hand out. "No, wait," she said. "You should be part of this meeting too."

Mellissa turned around slowly. "And what exactly is this meeting about?"

Greg held up the newspaper with the picture of them kissing splashed on the cover. "We made the front page."

"We what?" She marched over to him and snatched the paper from his hands. Her jaw dropped as she read through it. Mellissa dropped the paper in front of him. "This is the exact reason I wanted to keep our relationship to ourselves. This is your fault."

"How?" Greg asked, "You said only yesterday you wanted to go public."

"Well not like this."

"You're the one that kissed me on that stage."

She pointed at him accusingly. "You're the one that pulled me in close, lulling me in with those emeralds you call eyes." Greg grinned. He loved the way he could mesmerize her with the right sort of stare. Her cheeks turned red. "Do not let that go to your head."

"As cute as this disagreement is," interjected Mary, "It doesn't matter whose fault this is. The story is out."

"And the press is going to want to know more," said Hayley. "The two of you need to be able to give them the same answers to their questions."

Mellissa sat beside him and shrugged. "I don't see why we

need to have a meeting about this, we both know the ins and outs of our relationship."

Hayley sat up straight in her chair, placing her hands together on the table. "Okay, how long have you two been dating? How did you get together?"

Mellissa scratched her head. "Um- I- Greg?" She looked at him with wide eyes.

Greg shrugged. "Well that all depends on how you want to measure things."

Hayley pointed between the two of them. "This is what I mean. You cannot give answers like that." She stood pushing a loose hair behind her ear. "I'm going to set up one interview. Telling them it's an exclusive. I will send Mary a list of questions for you to come up with better answers for."

Mary also stood, neatening her jacket as she did. "We will give you some time to discuss this." The two of them walked towards the door. Greg got up to follow as Hayley's head popped back around the door frame. "I suggest when asked how long you have been together you say 3 months, any more than that the people will feel cheated, even though we all know it has been longer."

"We will take that into consideration," Greg said. He saw them out and returned to the kitchen. Mellissa was staring at the kettle as it boiled. He wrapped his arms around her waist. "Well, that was unexpected."

She turned round in his arms and jabbed him in the chest. "This is your fault."

"Again, with the blame game. I recall you kissing me, it's not my fault you find my eyes irresistible."

She pushed him away as her cheeks turned red. "I do not."

He pulled her back into his arms. "It's okay because I find everything about you irresistible." His eyes met hers and she blushed.

She covered her face with her hands. "I'm not looking at you." She giggled as he tickled her. "Stop that." He trailed kisses along her neck. She groaned as her arms wrapped around his neck and kissed him on the lips. She rested her forehead on his. "You are so annoying." He leaned forward kissing her again. As he stood to his full height, he lifted her sitting her on the kitchen counter.

"Ugh," grumbled Victoria. They both turned to see her standing in the doorway. Her hair was a wild mess and she had big dark circles under her eyes. She had stayed out a lot longer than the both of them. "It is way too early for all this lovey-dovey crap. It's nauseating."

Mellissa hopped down off the kitchen counter. "I think you should have stayed in bed."

Victoria waved her hand at Mellissa, forcing them away from the kettle. "I need coffee." She pulled what she needed out of the cupboard. "I heard the door and thought the chef had arrived."

"Sorry Victoria but I gave the chef and maid the day off," said Greg.

She dropped the coffee grains she had been about to put in her mug. "You what? Your chef is the only thing that makes staying here worth it. What am I meant to eat now?" She laid her head on the worktop. "My head is pounding."

Mellissa took over making the coffee. "Is it possible you drank too much?"

Victoria put her arm up in the air. "I will never say that."

Greg went over to a different cupboard and grabbed a couple of packs of pastries. "I brought these yesterday."

He placed them down by Victoria. She sniffed at them. "They will have to do. I guess the custard-filled one is for Mellissa." Greg nodded. Victoria rolled her eyes. She plucked out two pastries. Mellissa handed her a hot cup of coffee.

"Thanks, I'm going back to bed." With one pastry hanging from her mouth, another in her hand and the cup of coffee in the other, she walked out of the kitchen, looking like a zombie.

Greg tugged Mellissa towards him and wrapped his arms around her waist. "Now where were we before she rudely interrupted."

She placed her hands on his chest. "You were admitting to everything being your fault." She said.

"No after that."

She went up on her tiptoes and her lips brushed against his. "We were also going back to bed."

A smile spread across his face. He pushed her hair behind her ear. "I love you." Her fingers interlocked behind his neck, as she pulled him to her. Heat radiated between them as she pressed her lips to his. She tugged at his shirt. Slowly walking towards the door her lips never left his. She gasped as he lifted her off her feet and carried her up the stairs.

Victoria was hurrying Mellissa along. She was dragging their suitcases and pulling Mellissa by the arm towards the door. "We will miss our train if you don't hurry up."

Mellissa pulled her arm free. "I just want to make sure I haven't left anything I need."

Victoria chucked the suitcase at the door and grabbed Mellissa with both hands. "You are wasting time." She nodded at Greg. "Anything you forget he can send to you using summoning magic."

Mellissa pouted. "I guess."

Victoria wagged her finger in Mellissa's face. "You are purposely trying to make us miss the train." She marched over to the door picked up the suitcase and tugged the door open.

"Get out now."

Mellissa frowned as she curled a piece of hair around her finger. Greg took her hand. "It's only two days, then I will be coming to Urbem folium."

"This living in different cities sucks."

Greg's chest tightened as he looked into her big brown eyes. He hadn't seen her for three weeks and she had only been able to stay one night. "It will only be two days," he said more to himself than her.

She jabbed him in the chest. "And you will be on time or I will send Harkura to come get you."

He interlaced his fingers with hers. "I haven't been late for anything in months." He leaned in for a kiss.

Victoria clutched her stomach and pretended to hurl. "Can we go now?"

"I'm coming." Mellissa placed a hand on his chest and went up on her tip toes kissing him tenderly. He felt her slowly pull away. "Two days she whispered." He nodded. She walked over to Victoria dragging her feet. As they went to walk out the door Mary crashed into them.

"Oh, I'm so sorry," Mary said, grabbing Mellissa's shoulders to steady her. "I was distracted."

"Is everything all right Mary?" Greg asked.

She stood tall and straightened her jacket. "As Hayley and I were discussing plans for your interview at a café, we bumped into your Aunt Josephine."

Greg rubbed the sides of his forehead. "I am so sorry for whatever she did."

"It's fine I can handle myself, I just wanted to warn you that she is furious with you about last night's kiss and your cousin departing to Urbem folium so soon."

Greg let out an exacerbated breath. "Why is this woman suddenly so interested in controlling our lives?"

"It's all right I brought you some time by directing her to city hall but it won't be long till she comes this way."

Melissa sucked her bottom lip in. "Well, that is our cue to leave."

"Finally." Victoria rolled her eyes.

Mellissa quickly gave Greg a peck on the cheek and whispered, "Good luck with your aunt." and sped off with Victoria dragging their suitcases behind them. Greg sighed. He was going to need more than luck to deal with his meddlesome aunt.

Christmas

Mellissa

I stood in my dressing room staring at my reflection in the full-body mirror. As I swished from side to side the emerald ball gown I was wearing shimmered. Ivy lined the top of the satin bodice, and it wrapped around the tops of my arms. The full skirt covered my toes, and the train was so long, Tamara, the royal seamstress had added a loop to the end to put around my wrist to keep it up out the way when I danced. Not that I planned to do much dancing. I still wasn't sure why I had let Harkura talk me into a Christmas Eve ball. He had convinced me it was the perfect way to introduce Christmas to the magical world as everyone loved a ball. Everyone, except me.

I sighed, my heart feeling heavy. This wasn't how I usually spent Christmas Eve. I used to spend it with my best friend, Matt. We had a tradition of doing all things Christmas together. I should be in the kitchen baking cookies or walking along the lake discussing the Christmas film we had just seen. I looked at my pedicured hands. Things were different now. Matt was trapped in the tree of time and I was queen of the elves.

In the mirror, I saw Greg walk into my dressing room. He was in a grey suit with a tie and pocket square that matched my dress. Tamara must have gotten her hands on him. His aunt

Josephine would have a tantrum at the sight of him wearing elf colours. I turned to face him. He smiled, making my heart melt. "You look amazing," He placed a hand on my cheek. "But why so glum?"

"I'm not. It's just- I don't know."

"This isn't how you usually spend Christmas Eve."

I sat on the stool by my dresser. My chest was tight. "It just doesn't feel right."

"This time of year must bring up a lot of conflicting emotions. I know it's your favourite time of year, but you also have a lot of memories tied to Matt around this day in particular."

"How is it you know what I am thinking so well?"

He shrugged. "Lucky guess. Matt would want you to enjoy yourself."

I nodded. He was right. If Matt was here, he would be just as enthusiastic as Victoria about this ball. He would be encouraging me to relax and let loose a little. Matt wouldn't want me looking to the past, instead, he would have me moving forward. The problem was this wasn't my idea of fun. I would rather be in my pyjamas with a warm mug of hot chocolate, watching a film. I picked up the sides of my dress. The fabric was smooth to the touch. I groaned. "This dress is ridiculous."

Greg knelt in front of me. "And yet you look beautiful in it. I'm happy to miss the ball if that's what you want."

I bit my bottom lip, tempted to hide away from everyone with him. I took his hand pulling him up as I stood. "Harkura would kill me if I missed it. He has put a lot of work into planning this ball."

"You have to remember that you're the queen, not Harkura."

"I know but for some crazy reason I agreed to this months

ago." I held my hand out to him. "Shall we go?"

Greg picked up my tiara from the dresser. "You have to stop forgetting to put this on."

I crinkled my nose. "I'm not really a fan of tiaras." He placed it on my head. My hair had been twisted up into a neat bun with a few curls neatly hanging by the side of my face. Greg smiled as he gently stroked my cheek. Matt hadn't been Greg's biggest fan, but he would have wanted me to be happy. I wrapped my arms around Greg's neck. "Everything is going to be okay, isn't it?"

He rested his forehead on mine. "As long as I've got you with me, I know everything will be just fine."

We both jumped as the dressing room door flew open. Harkura marched in dressed in a black suit and jade shirt. "Mellissa you should have been down ages ago. The guests are all waiting on you to make your entrance."

"Why did I agree to this ball?" I grumbled.

"Because it is a symbol of the elves' prosperity and how we have been integrating your culture into the magical world," replied Harkara

"Right." I kissed Greg on the cheek. "I guess I will see you down there."

Harkura held up his hands. "You will be making your entrance together now that your relationship is out. The press will be waiting to get a shot of the two of you, so make your arrival a grand one."

My stomach churned at the thought of the press. For the most part, they had left me alone, when I wasn't saving the world, I was pretty boring compared to the other leaders. Hogan, one of the dwarf leaders was constantly in the papers for some crazy stunt he had pulled. I grimaced. "I really don't want to do this."

Greg took my hand and smiled. "Don't worry we've got

this."

"Come on," said Harkura. We followed him out of my room, along the hall and down three flights of stairs to the bottom floor of the castle. Harkura chattered into his communis as we walked. We stopped at the ballroom doors. Harkura turned back to us. "Samson is about to announce you both. You will walk in together, hand in hand but make sure you lead the way, Mellissa."

I nodded. Harkura opened the large double doors. I took a sharp intake of breath as I took in the sight before me. The ballroom had been transformed into a winter wonderland. White drapes hung around the grand windows, crystal chandeliers twinkled above, and fake snow scattered through the air. The room was full of finely dressed men and women, who had all turned towards the open doors. Samson's voice boomed above us. "I present the keeper of the Heart, Queen Mellissa Hail and Lord elder knight Gregory Ainsworth."

Greg held his hand out to me. I softly placed my hand in his. My eyes met his and I instantly felt at ease. Together we walked down a long runway to the centre of the ballroom. All eyes were on us. "Would the Queen care to dance?" Greg asked.

I looked up into his green eyes. "With you, always."

Greg flashed a smile making my heart flutter. He bowed to me and held his arm out. I placed my hand on his forearm. Soft music began to play. Greg pulled me towards him, causing my breath to catch. Clasping my left hand in his and placing his other hand on the small of my back, he gently guided me through the dance. Everyone was staring and I could feel my face heat. He leaned in close and whispered in my ear. "It's just you and me, forget about everyone else." His lips briefly brushed mine and then his hand left my back as he spun me away causing my dress skirt to fan out in a twirl. With the hand that still held mine, he tugged me back spinning me into him. I rested my free hand on his chest as his eyes locked onto mine. We glided around the dance floor as I lost myself in his stare.

I woke bright and early. Yawning I stretched in bed. The ball hadn't been as bad as I thought it would be. The people of the city had loved it and so had the few others who had travelled to celebrate with us. It had been good for community spirit and getting everyone it to the festive season.

Pulling on my big fluffy dressing gown, I walked over to the balcony doors. The windows were frosted over but I could see the treetops covered in snow. I slipped on my slippers and pushed the doors open. I shivered as the cold air prickled my cheeks. Stepping out onto the balcony I took in the sights of the city. The view from up here was amazing. I could probably spend hours sitting out here. A scattering of snowflakes danced on the wind. The forest surrounding the city had been beautiful during summer, but the snow made it look truly magical. I squealed as I ran back over to the bed and jumped on Greg.

"What are you doing?" He yelled. His hair was a mess and he still looked half asleep.

"It's snowing," I said.

"Seriously?" He said, "You know it always snows at this time of year."

I frowned. "Not where I'm from. It like never snows on Christmas."

"I guess I missed the part where snow was a big deal."

I sat on the edge of the bed and looked away from him. "You are such a spoilsport."

"Don't be like that. You know this is only my second Christmas." He sat up and tried to pull me towards him, but I didn't budge. "I'm sorry."

"Then come out onto the balcony." I grabbed his hands and pulled him up.

He grumbled as he wrapped himself up in one of the blankets. "You know I don't have a fluffy dressing gown."

"I'm pretty sure that's because you said they are too warm and make you sweat."

"That was before I knew you were going to make me stand on the balcony in the snow." He tugged the blanket tighter as we walked out onto the balcony. He looked down at the snow. "It's very nice, now let's go back inside."

"You are looking at the wrong thing." I pointed out to the horizon where the sun was peaking above the trees. The sky was pale pink, and the light made the snow glisten. When the wind blew, it made the trees gently sway shifting the light causing a rainbow of colours to appear. "It's beautiful," I said.

"I will admit that Urbem Folium suits the snow well." Said Greg.

I sighed. "You are such a grouch." I went back in and he followed close behind shutting the doors behind him. My room used to be a massive open space, but I hadn't liked it. It had felt too big, so I had it redesigned. I also hadn't liked the way Victoria and Harkura always let themselves in. My privacy had felt lacking. This is why I had divided the room up. This gave me a separate living room and bedroom. It made this room feel cosier and like home. I'd chosen to have the balcony in my bedroom as I liked looking out over the city and into the forest. Something Greg didn't seem to appreciate. He threw himself back on the bed.

"Hey what are you doing?" I said pulling at the blanket he had wrapped himself up in.

"Going back to bed, you kept me up late," his head popped out of his blanket cocoon. "Since when do you get up so early?"

"It's Christmas."

"Right, thinking back I remember you doing something like this last year. I wish you would just write all these traditions down for me."

I stomped my foot. "You take the fun out of everything. I got way more it to your winter solstice than you are being for Christmas."

He sat up. "Your right I'm sorry. I did remember the tradition of presents though."

I sat beside him on the bed. "You got me a present?" I asked more excitedly than I had meant to.

He swished his hand around. In a sprinkle of lights, a red gift bag appeared. He handed it to me. "Merry Christmas." I pulled the tissue paper off the top and scowled at him.

"A packet of crisps," I yelled.

He burst out laughing. "I was just replacing the pack I owe you from over a year ago." I grabbed the packet and threw it at him. He put his hands up in front of him. "You know it's hard to come up with a gift for a Queen, right?" He flicked his wrist, producing another present. "But that wasn't all I got you."

I reluctantly took the present and slowly opened it. It was a black fabric. I shook it out holding it up. It was an oversized hoodie. A smile spread across my face. "I love it. I'm going to have to hide this so Victoria doesn't throw it out. She hates when I wear this sort of thing."

"Check out the hood."

I flicked the hood over. "Oh my god, it's got cat ears." I threw my arms around him kissing him. "You are so annoying."

He raised an eyebrow and smirked. "What about my gift?"

"All my presents are under the tree downstairs." I tapped my bottom lip. "But I did get you a special something you can have now."

"And what's that?"

I pushed him down on the bed. "The gift of me. Care to unwrap it?"

My dressing gown was flung to the floor in a flash. Greg flipped me onto my back, pinning me down with kisses. My heart hammered in my chest and my body tingled with every touch. My room's door creaked open. I squeaked pushing Greg away. He fell off the bed with a thud. I scrambled about finding my dressing gown and throwing my bedding over Greg. The problem with my redesign was I hadn't put a door between the living room and bedroom. There was just a pretty archway, which didn't give me a lot of time to compose myself. I tied my dress gown tight and was on the end of the bed just as Victoria, Harkura, and my dad appeared in the archway. My dad was holding a tray of hot drinks.

Greg pulled the blankets from his head. "What was that for? Oh." His face turned as red as his hair as he looked up at the people now in my room.

Victoria took one of the drinks. "We thought we would start the day with your dad's famous hot chocolate, but I see you had other ideas." My face felt like it was on fire, it was probably as red as Greg's had gone. I knew she was smiling behind her mug of hot chocolate.

Sweat dripped down the back of my neck. Leaning against the kitchen worktop I fanned myself with my hands. My dad and I had been out here for the past couple of hours cooking Christmas dinner. The smell of turkey and roast potatoes filled the kitchen. Cooking with my dad felt like the good old days before I got swept up in magic. We had taken over the third kitchen for the occasion. It was the smallest of the three in the castle and it was boiling now we had all three ovens on. Pot and pans bubbled away on the stove. Dad put the turkey he had been checking, back in the oven. "It should be ready soon." He came and leaned against the same worktop as me. "It is just a waiting game now. I will make the gravy just before we serve everything up."

"I've missed this." I said, "You know cooking. It's nice having a royal chef but also really weird."

"I would love to have a chef." Dad gave me a sideways glance and fiddled with the tea towel in his hands. "So how are things going with you and Greg?"

I covered my face with my hands. "We do not need to talk about that dad."

He placed the tea towel he was holding over his shoulder. "I accepted a while ago that you're an adult now and you are going to do what you're going to do." He pulled my hands from my face. "What I mean is are you happy?"

I looked up at my dad. We were opposites, his complexion was pale, and he had sandy straight hair, which contrasted my warm brown skin and wild dark curls. Our brown eyes were the only thing we shared. "Yes, I am," I said.

"Good so will I hear wedding bells anytime soon? I'm not getting any younger and I would like to give you away."

"What no." I nudged him with my shoulder. "You are only like forty Dad and I'm nineteen, a bit young to be thinking about these things."

"Me and your mother were only a year older than you when we married, and we had you a year later."

"Dad," I narrowed my eyes at him. "Harkura hasn't been going on about heirs to you, has he?" Harkura had been obsessed with the concept a few months ago and had tried to push me into marrying a random stranger. He even talked about it being like a business transaction.

"No, but now that you mention heirs." He rubbed his chin.

"How does that work? Won't you and Greg both need an heir?"

I walked over to the cooker pushing my arms out to the side. "No, just no. I am not having that conversation." I checked on the veg and then began making gravy.

"Interesting," said Dad. "From your reactions, I would say marriage is on the table, but kids is a no."

I pointed the spoon I was about to stir the gravy with at him. "Stop it, Dad."

He put his arm around my shoulder. "You know I would like to be a grandfather one day in the future."

I pushed away from him and pretended to busy myself with something on the other side of the kitchen. "Maybe in the far, far future, if you're really lucky."
My dad hummed to himself as he took over making the gravy I had abandoned.

Laughter filled the room. The smell of the roast we had just eaten still lingered in the air. After our awkward wake-up call, the rest of the day had gone amazingly. We were in the second dining hall. It was still twice the size of the dining room at my dad's house but felt a lot cosier than the main dining room. The gorgeous fireplace was lined with fir tree garlands, two seven-foot trees stood tall on the opposite sides of the room, their lights twinkling. The walls, ceiling and windows were littered with gold, red and green decorations. It made the place feel truly festive. Victoria's parents had joined us for dinner and so had Greg's cousins, Samson, and Cynthia. This was their first Christmas and like Greg last year, they were completely in awe.

My dad stood, getting everyone's attention. He looked down at me beside him. "I guess now is time for presents. I'll start." He pulled an envelope out of his pocket and handed it to me. "Here you go, sweetie."

I opened it. Inside was a folded piece of paper. I frowned as I read what it said. "I don't understand. It says you're taking early retirement."

My dad shrugged. "With you gone, there's nothing left for me in the human world."

I slowly rose from my chair. "Wait you mean…"

"I'm taking you up on that offer of a nice cottage in the woods."

I hugged my dad tight. "Oh, Dad this is the best present ever."

As everyone else began handing out presents amongst themselves, I looked down at the piece of paper I'd been given. I turned to my dad. "Are you sure about this?"

"Of course, I am." His forehead creased. "Do you not like your gift? Should I have spoken to you about it first?"

"No, I'm happy to have you here. I miss not seeing you every day, it's just I don't want you to give up your life in the human world for me."

He took my hand. "Honey, you were my life and I've been a little lost since you've been gone. I need to start over. Urbem Folium seems to be the perfect place to do it. My life won't centre around looking after you anymore but at least I can visit you more easily while I figure things out."

My heart felt heavy. I hadn't realised the effect my leaving had on him. It had been a big change for both of us, but I was constantly surrounded by people. My dad was alone. I squeezed his hand. "I can't wait for you to move here."

New Year

Gregory

*G*reg lay on the plush sofa and flicked through his messages on his tabular. He was alone up in Mellissa's living quarters, which he was sure she had redecorated again. He was almost certain the walls had been turquoise the last time he was here but now they were a pale shade of pink. The tree painted on the wall was new and it looked like Mellissa had done that herself. She was currently in a meeting downstairs about the elves' New Year's celebration. The humans had a lot more holidays than in the magic world. The elves all having grown up in the human world and a lot of them being part human, still wanted to celebrate them. While the changelings did mark the new year, it was generally a quiet dinner with the immediate family. Last year they had been too busy dealing with Kadon for him to learn about how humans celebrated the new year. From what Mellissa told him, the elves would be having a huge New Year's Eve party, with fireworks set to go off at midnight.

He sighed as he found nothing interesting in his inbox. His father used to not have much work during the last week of the year, after winter solstice, it was the one time of year he used to have his father's full attention. Greg's heart felt heavy. It had been almost a year since he had lost his father. They hadn't had the easiest relationship, but he missed him. So much had happened since then. Things that he wished his father had been around to see, things that he wished he could get answers from his father for. Greg ruffled his hair as he leaned back in the chair. He sighed not sure what to do with himself. He was used to everyone turning to him to make decisions, but here that was Mellissa's job. A part of him felt lost but at the same time, a part of him was relieved. He could have a lie-in. He had come to understand why Mellissa liked doing it so much.

His tabular pinged, alerting him to a new message. He swiped his finger across the devices screen opening the message. Mary had forwarded him a document from Hayley in PR. An exclusive interview had been set up. He groaned as he read through the questions they were going to ask. They were along the lines of what he thought but he knew Mellissa wouldn't like them.

His communis rang. He picked it up activating it as he did. "Mellissa, are you calling me from downstairs?"

"So, what if I am? The meeting's over, come join me for lunch."

"Okay, I'm coming." He deactivated the device chucking it on the coffee table. With his tabular in hand, he went downstairs. They may as well discuss the questions over lunch.

Greg found Mellissa in the smaller dining room, sat with Laxus. He frowned at the sight of the blue-haired pixie. Mellissa smiled when she saw him and gestured for him to come to sit by her. "My dad made steak pie but don't worry I made a mini vegetable one for you." She pushed a plate in front of him with a perfectly shaped pie on it. A pastry heart had been cut out and placed on top of it. He glanced at Laxus. "I didn't realise you were in Urbum Folium.

Laxus flicked his curls from his eyes. "I arrived early this morning. I'm gutted to have missed the Christmas festivities, but I'll be here to celebrate new year's."

"What he means is that he is gutted to have missed out on my dad's Christmas dinner." Interjected Mellissa.

Laxus nodded. "Your father is a marvellous cook."

Mellissa pushed Greg's plate of food closer to him. She looked at him with eager eyes. He picked up a fork and took a bite. "It's really good." He said. The vegetables were soft and juicy, and the pastry was perfectly crisp.

She flicked his arm. "Why do you sound so surprised?"

"I'm not surprised. You just haven't cooked in ages. I forgot how good you were at it."

"Well, the steak pie is even better." Said Laxus stuffing his mouth.

Mellissa glared at him. "How would you know; you haven't tried the veg one."

"Your father is the best cook ever." Laxus pointed his fork at her. "He may have taught you but it's not the same."

Mellissa scowled at Laxus and then shook her head. "Anyway, while I have you both here, I have something for you." She bent over pulling two boxes out from under the table. She handed one to each of them. Greg opened it. Inside was what looked like a smaller version of his tabular.

"You got us human mobiles." Said Laxus turning the device over in his hand.

"Not quite." Mellissa took the phone from Laxus. "It is an adapted mobile phone that links up to a communis. Like so." She placed her sphere-shaped communis on the table and turned the phone on. Its screen lit up. She pressed a few buttons and the communis glowed and an automated voice said, connected to Laxus' phone. "Okay now turn your phone on Greg and ring Laxus. He should already be in your contacts along with me." She smiled at Greg, and he did as requested.

As he pressed call and the phone's camera turned on and he was looking at his face. Laxus' phone rang, and when Mellissa answered, a projection of Greg appeared from the communis. "Pretty cool right?"

"So if my phone was connected to my communis I would be able to see a projection of you?" Greg asked.

"Yeah. It's like video calls but levelled up. The phone also does everything your tabular does."

Greg ended the call and turned the device over in his hands. It looked pretty much the same as the phone Mellissa had given him in the human world. "How have you managed to get the human tech to run on magic."

Mellissa lent back in her chair. "I haven't it was all Josh. Turns out he has a degree in computer science and his hobby back in the human world had been integrating technology with magic."

Josh had taken over as her advisor when Samson had been promoted to chief of staff. He was meant to advise her on all the elvish traditions she had missed out on growing up hidden from magic. Greg had no idea he had these sorts of skills as well. "So do you think there is a market for these phones?" asked Mellissa, "We plan to launch them in the new year?"

Greg nodded. "Definitely. Looks like the elves have found themselves a unique export."

"Wait until you see some of Josh's other ideas. He has completely upgraded everything in the castle."

"Maybe I should hire him to upgrade city hall for me. Which reminds me," Greg pushed his tabular towards Mellissa.

She pulled a face at him. "Not work stuff."

"It's not work." He swiped along the screen bringing up the interview questions. "It seems Hayley has set up that interview she mentioned, for after the new year."

Mellissa picked up the device and looked over the

questions. "Some of these questions are ridiculous. Why do they need to know this?"

Laxus knelt on his chair so he could get a look at the tabular over Mellissa's shoulder. "An interview about your relationship, that should be interesting."

Mellissa placed the tabular on the table. "Why is our relationship interesting?"

"For me, it's interesting because I know how awkward you are." Laxus sat back in his chair properly, pulling the tabular towards himself. "For the general public, it's because they are nosy and you're both public figures."

Greg rested his arm on the table laying his head on his hand. "Hayley wants us to answer the questions together and then send them back for her to check."

"Practicing is also a good idea. I'll be the interviewer." Laxus cleared his throat. "Everyone is excited about the news of the Queen and an Elder knight as a couple." He flapped his hands around while putting on a fake exaggerated voice. "So how long have you been dating?"

"Three months," said Greg.

Mellissa grabbed his arm. "It's been longer than that."

"I know but Hayley said not to say anything longer than three months".

She crossed her arms. "I'm not lying."

Laxus looked between the two of them. "Shall we try a different one? Where was your first date?"

"Um, I don't know." He looked at Mellissa. "What would you class as our first date?" She shrugged.

"Okay moving on." Laxus's eyebrows arched as he looked back at the tabular. "Who asked who out?"

Mellissa pointed at Greg. "He asked me."

Greg rubbed the back of his neck. "I told you I loved you, but I don't actually remember asking you out."

She frowned. "You asked me to the circus."

"Equally you asked me to play hooky from work and go to a theme park with you."

"You kissed me after the circus, so that was closer to a date."

Greg tilted his head from side to side. "You kissed me in the December before that."

Mellissa's jaw dropped. "Are we even dating if neither of us asked the other out?"

Laxus pushed the tabular along the table back towards Greg. "You two have a lot to figure out. I'm gonna go do something away from here." Laxus got up from the table and swiftly left, taking his pie with him.

Greg took her hands in his. "Of course, we are dating. Our relationship just isn't the conventional sort. Those questions are just so people can squeal and have something to gossip about."

"I guess." She bit her bottom lip. "I just thought the questions would be easier to answer than that."

"We have time to figure them out. Take a day to think then message me with how you want to answer them."

"Why do I have to message you? Can't we figure this out together in person?"

Greg ran his fingers through his hair. "I'm going home tonight and aren't you returning to the human world with your dad for the new year? I thought that was why you had to get the new year's preparations out of the way this morning."

She traced a circle on the table with her finger. "About that. With my dad deciding to come live here, he has decided not to go back until after the new year celebrations. He plans to only return to pack up and sell the house."

"You're staying in Urbem Folium."

She placed her hand on his thigh. "And I was hoping you would stay with me."

"I can't just change my plans like that."

She pouted looking up at him. Her brown eyes sparkled. "You can't have much work on at the moment and you were going to come to see me on New Year's Eve anyway."

She was right, he didn't have much to do. He would just be going home to that big empty house to be alone. "I can talk to Mary. It isn't busy at the moment so it should be easy to coordinate things with her from here."

She slipped onto his lap and pressed her lips to his. His arms wrapped around her back pulling her closer to his chest, taking in her sweet cherry blossom scent. She rested her head on his as she caught her breath. "I guess I should go unpack." He said breathlessly.

She nodded and played with the collar of his shirt. "Definitely and about this whole packing and unpacking thing we do when we visit each other, I don't think we should do that anymore."

"Okay, what do you suggest we do instead?"

"Just leave stuff like clothes and whatnot at each other's. My dressing room is big enough to spare a shelf for you."

"Right and I guess you would want a whole wardrobe at mine."

She placed her finger on his lips. "I was thinking a whole room."

"I might be able to make that work but just because it's you." Her face lit up as she smiled, making his heart melt. He ran his finger through her hair and pulled her in for another kiss. She tucked her fingers between the buttonholes on his shirt. Just because they had struggled to answer those silly questions it didn't mean anything. They had each other and that's all that mattered.

Music blared throughout the castle. Greg could hardly hear himself think. Even out in the corridor away from the main hall, he found no peace. This New Year's Eve party was nothing like the Christmas Eve ball. There was tons of drinking and rowdy untamed dancing. Multi-coloured flashes of lights almost blinded him. It was no wonder Mellissa had disappeared from the main party. She had first been swept away by Victoria but then he had spotted her in the middle of the dance floor, without Mellissa. According to, her Mellissa had been called on by the chef. Greg had made his way out of the hall and was walking down the corridor towards the kitchens.

"Gregory," shouted a shrill voice making the hairs on the back of his neck stand up. Greg turned to see a tall blond, in a short tight dress, staggering toward him. Greg groaned on the inside as he recognized her. Her hair was in pigtails and she had glow sticks sticking out of them. She had another hanging around her neck. What was she of all people doing in Urbem Folium?

She placed her hand on his chest, fluttering her eyelashes which looked to have been painted with charcoal. "Imagine seeing you here. It's been like forever."

It had been over a year since he had last seen his ex, Lucy and even then, her presence hadn't been welcomed. "What are you doing here, so far from home?" Greg asked.

"I could ask you the same thing." She wiggled her finger at him. "You are our elder you should be in Novosvillas."

Greg frowned. "Me being here is not the same as you. Who exactly do you know here?"

She held her arms wide turning on the spot. "Loads of people. At least I do now. When I heard about this party, I knew it would be better than what we had going on back home."

She stumbled forward wrapping her arms around his neck

and pressing her lips together. "Hey, let's dance."

Greg stepped back leaning his face as far away from her as he pried her arms off of him. "No thanks, I'm looking for Mellissa."

"Oh yeah, I heard about that." She ran her fingers across his shoulder and down his arm. "I'm sure your queen won't mind if we dance. I saw her going to the kitchens with some guy. They looked pretty cosy."

"I said no Lucy." He turned to walk away, and she shoved him.

"You are such a tease."

"What are you on about?"

"Your aunt said you missed me."

Greg scowled. "Which aunt?" he asked through gritted teeth.

"Your aunt Josephine. She said you and the queen weren't serious it's just a PR stunt." She stepped closer to him and pouted. "She said you missed me."

"Well, she lied." Greg's blood boiled. This was low even for Josephine. He took a deep breath. He couldn't take his anger out on Lucy. She was just his aunt's pawn.

Lucy tugged at his arm. "Don't be such a stick in the mud. Let's just dance."

"Excuse me, madam, is this man bothering you?" asked Mellissa. She looked so regal with her head held high, her gold tiara encrusted with emeralds sparkling atop her perfectly curled hair. In her forest green dress that hugged her hips perfectly she was a vision to behold.

Lucy quickly tucked her hands behind her back. "Not at all. He is just being boring."

Mellissa walked around him, placing herself between him and Lucy. "I find he can be a bit of a grouch, but he has other charms."

Lucy sucked in her bottom lip looking Mellissa up and down. "Your look has improved from the shabby commoner you were last time I saw you."

Mellissa interlaced her fingers with Greg's and tilted her head to the side. "I'm sorry have we met?" Lucy's jaw dropped. Mellissa patted Greg's chest. "Come along Gregory, I tire of this conversation." She walked down the corridor and Greg followed, trying not to laugh.

Once they were out of sight, she pinned him against a wall, narrowing her eyes at him. "What is your ex-girlfriend doing in my castle."

Greg put his arms up. "I thought you didn't recognize her."

"Your aunt seems to think you miss her."

"How long were you listening?" he asked.

"Long enough to know she is lucky I didn't snap her fingers off."

Greg stroked her cheek. "I think you handled it well."

Mellissa tilted her head. "You do?"

"I'm sorry Lucy turned up and I'm sorry about my aunts meddling. I will sort this out somehow."

She poked him in the chest. "You better." Her nose scrunched as she glared at him.

He smirked. "You're cute when you're jealous."

She folded her arms over her chest and looked away from him. "I'm not jealous."

He pushed her hair behind her ear and stroked her cheek. "You have nothing to worry about. You're the only girl I'm interested in." She blushed. He held his hand out to her. "Do you want to return to the party?"

She shook her head. "This party is way too stressful. The things I do to make my people happy."

He cupped her face in his hand. She leaned into his touch as he gently stroked her soft skin with his thumb. "What would make the queen happy?"

"Sitting on my balcony with a nice cup of hot chocolate." She took his hand and smiled sweetly. "Looking at the stars snuggled with my boyfriend."

He gently pressed a kiss to her forehead. "Then that's what we will do." Hand in hand they left the party behind, forgetting about the evening's events.

Stolen

Mellissa

The moon was high in the sky shining light off the surface of the water. Sand crunched under my feet as I shifted my feet back and forth. I wrapped my arms around myself as a cold breeze sent a shiver down my back. Waves crashed against the shore causing me to jump. Someone chuckled behind me.

I turned to see a tall blond boy standing behind me. "Matt," I said frowning. My best friend who had been sealed away in the battle against Kadon stood in front of me.

He smiled his blue eyes shimmering in the moonlight. "I see you're still not fully comfortable with the water."

"I can be near it now, but I still-" I shook my head, pushing the images of almost drowning out my mind. My brows drew together. "Matt, I don't understand how you are here?"

"I have been reaching out for months, but it hasn't been easy."

I extended my hand out and gasped as I wrapped my fingers around his arm. He was solid. "You're really here."

"In a sense."

"How did you get out of the tree? I'm sorry I failed to free you."

He took hold of my shoulders, bending to look me in the eyes. "You haven't failed me but Mellissa, I'm still in the tree. However, I'm also here talking to you."

"That doesn't make sense."

Matt looked up at the moon. His blond hair shone in the light. "It's like the tree and I have become one. It has opened my mind. I have seen so much." He looked down at me his eyes full of worry. "So much that I had to warn you."

I wrapped a curl around my finger as I tugged at my hair. "Warn me of what?"

The light shifted creating a shadow across his face. "Hard times are coming Mellissa." The waves raged against the shore and the wind picked up almost blowing me over. Matt grabbed hold of my arm. "Things are not what they seem. The darkness is returning." Matt shouted over the wind.

A mist rolled in from the ocean. I couldn't see Matt anymore. A strong gust threatened to knock me off my feet. "Matt" I yelled.

"You must be able to overcome the water." He shouted from within the mist.

I woke with a start, gasping for breath. My hands reached out to my bedside table, fumbling along the surface trying to reach the lamp. Warm hands grasped my shoulders. "Mellissa, what's wrong?" Greg asked. I pulled away stretching over the bed, finally reaching the lamp. The sudden light made me see stars as my heart pounded in my chest. I gazed around my room. Everything was quiet except for the ticking of the clock. It had all been a dream. I pulled my knees up to my chest wrapping my arms around them. Of course, it wasn't real. It had been months since I had visited the tree of time. My attempts to free Matt had all been ineffective. Humarya had told me only a dark stone could do it. Something with the opposite kind of power to my own. I couldn't use dark magic like that so I had given up. But why was I dreaming of Matt now?

Greg slid across the bed gently putting his arm around me. "What happened?"

I shook my head hiding my face in my curled-up arms. He gently pulled my arms away and cupped my face in his hands. His green eyes shimmered as his forehead creased. "Talk to me."

I gave a small shrug trying to downplay things. "It was just a dream."

"A dream that startled you. Have your nightmares come back?"

I relaxed under his touch as he stroked my cheek. This hadn't been one of the nightmares that had plagued me not so long ago but it had panicked me. Letting out a long breath I calmed myself. "I saw Matt in my dream. We were by the sea. He was warning me of something." I rubbed the side of my head. "I didn't hear what as a strange mist blew us apart."

Greg leaned back against the bed's headboard. "A more insecure guy would be jealous hearing his girlfriend was dreaming of another guy."

I shoved his shoulder. "You know it's nothing like that."

"I know I'm sorry." He took my hand kissing my knuckles. "Was it the warning that spooked you?"

I dug my fingers into the bed bunching up the sheets. "The warning was strange, but it was the way the mist and wind suddenly changed. It felt real. As if something was trying to stop Matt from telling me what he knew."

"It was just a dream. You're probably just stressed, from all the work you put into Christmas and New Year."

I shook my head pulling my hand from his. "You don't

understand. I felt some ancient magic at play." I bristled as I saw the pity in his eyes. Gritting my teeth, I shoved off the bed and marched into my dressing room. I filtered through my clothes finding my training gear.

"What are you doing?" Greg shouted from the bedroom.

"Getting dressed." I pulled on a pair of leggings, a baggy t-shirt and my blue running trainers. I bumped into Greg as I walked back into the bedroom.

"Where are you going?"

I wouldn't meet his gaze. "For a run."

"I'll come with you." I put my hand on his chest as he went to get dressed.

"No, I need to clear my head." I was out of the room before he could say anything else.

I was dripping with sweat and in desperate need of a shower when I returned to the castle after my run with Harkura. I grabbed a drink of water before parting ways with him and heading up to my room. As I opened the door, I found Greg packing his bag. A pang of guilt sliced through me. "What are you doing?" I asked.

He turned, his face lacking any emotion. "Getting ready to go home."

"You're not leaving because you're mad at me? I'm sorry I stormed off."

Greg was in front of me in two long strides, brushing the strands of hair that had fallen out of my ponytail from my face. "I'm not mad at you, I understand why you went off without me. Although I did notice you took Harkura with you."

"He is my guardian, he would go crazy if I left the castle

without him." I pointed at his bag. "Why are you packing then?"

"I was already returning home today, remember?"

My heart sank. "Yeah of course." I looked down at the floor as I walked over to the coffee table and placed my drink on it. Pulling my hair out of its bobble I stared at myself in the mirror above the sofa across from it. My curls dropped limply down my back.

I saw him approach in the mirror. He wrapped his arms around me from behind and rested his chin on my head. "Don't look so glum."

"I'm not glum." Looking up at him in the mirror I pouted.

"Even you pouting at me like that won't change the plan. I already stayed longer than I should have."

"I know, I was lucky to keep you this long." I leaned back into him. "It's just you're going today. My dad and Victoria are returning to the human world. It just seems like everyone is leaving me."

"Why is Victoria leaving?"

"She is visiting her parents and escorting my dad back at the same time."

He gently twirled me around in his arms. Tilting my head up so our eyes met. "It's only temporary. They will both be back soon."

I ran my fingers along his arm. The hairs on his arm always stood up when I did, making me smile. "And what about you?"

He stepped back, rubbing the back of his neck. "I don't know."

I pushed down a lump in my throat. "So, I'm meant to wait another three weeks before I see you again?" He went to talk but I cut him off. "Don't you dare say I will see you in a week once the council recess is over?"

"I wasn't going to say that." He tried to hold my hand, but I crossed my arms. "I don't know when work will allow me to come back. You can come to Novosvillas whenever you want."

"It's not that simple for me to leave either. I also have to go pack up my stuff at my dad's house at some point."

Greg's posture stiffened. "Oh, packing up your old bedroom is more important than the running of my city."

I felt like pulling my hair out. "I didn't say that." I threw my arms to the side. "God is it so wrong that I want to be with you?"

His shoulders dropped. "No, it isn't." I turned away from him. I hadn't meant to say that. It had just burst out before I knew what I was saying. I felt the warmth of his body close behind me. "I don't want to argue with you."

"It's a bit late for that," I muttered.

He walked around me, so he was facing me, placing his finger under my chin. "I want to be with you too but we both have complicated schedules. It's a balancing act we haven't quite got figured out yet but will eventually."

"How can you be so sure we can do this?" I asked.

"Because I love you and plan for us to be together for a long time."

I looked up at him. His green eyes sparkled making my heart melt. "I was thinking along the lines of forever."

He smiled resting his forehead on mine. "I like the sound of that." My heart fluttered as I placed my hand on his chest. I looked over at the bag he was packing.

"What happened to leaving your stuff on a shelf in my dressing room?" I asked.

"I figured I would do that next time when I have planned what I want to leave here properly." His thumb brushed across my bottom lip. I leaned towards him. *Bang!*

We both jumped as my room door burst open, slamming loudly into the wall. Samson stumbled in, his usual calm demeanour gone. His shirt was ruffled and he panted as if he had run all the way here.

"I'm sorry to barge in like this but I have some terrible news.

My stomach churned. "What's happened?"

"Someone has broken into the council vault." He licked his lips as his brows drew together. "The air stone is missing."

I gasped. My heart pounded as the room spun. Greg spoke but I didn't hear him. All I could hear was the ringing in my ears. Nausea rose in me. I dropped to my knees clutching my chest. My breathing became harsh as it felt like a hand tightened its grip around my lungs.

Greg grabbed my shoulders. "Mellissa it's okay. Just take slow breaths."

He took deep breaths in and out. I nodded syncing my breathing up with his. I shut my eyes as I curled into myself. The air stone was gone, which meant she was back. This is what my dream had been warning me about. The return of the darkness. Humarya was back.

Interrogate

Gregory

reg trailed behind Mellissa as Lady Gabrielle lead them down to the lower levels of the council building. Harkura and Samson had been made to stay on the upper levels. Lady Gabrielle had stated only Greg and Mellissa were permitted in the cells. Greg's stomach had been in a tight knot the whole journey here, and the closer they got to their destination, the tighter the knot grew. Samson had been a stuttering mess, trying to calm everyone's nerves on the train journey over. Whereas Harkura had been unnervingly calm. Greg was glad they hadn't been permitted down with them. They would have just made the tension lingering in the air unbreathable. Mellissa was convinced this was all Humarya, but Greg had his doubts. If his suspicions were correct, then this was his fault. His stomach churned and he thought he might throw up. Mellissa was going to hate him and Harkura would end him.

"You know you didn't need to come all this way," said Lady Gabrielle. "Everything I have found out will be presented at tomorrow's emergency meeting."

Mellissa shook her head. "Tomorrow isn't soon enough. I need to know what your prisoner does?"

Lady Gabrielle sighed as she removed her glasses and

massaged the bridge of her nose. "He insists he is innocent. He claims to have no memory from last night."

Greg straightened his jacket and let out a long breath. He needed a level head. He stood tall forcing his inner turmoil down. "Can I talk to him?" Greg asked.

Lady Gabrielle looked him up and down and nodded. "Keep it brief."

Mellissa spun around and glared at him. "I want to talk to him too."

Lady Gabrielle frowned and her forehead creased. "I'm not sure that's a good idea."

"Why does he get to talk to the prisoner and not me?"

"Do you think you could hold your temper?" Greg asked.

She folded her arms. "I don't have a temper." Lady Gabrielle looked at the floor.

Greg rubbed the back of his neck. "Mellissa, you have to admit your mind is not clear at the moment?"

"And yours is?"

"Clearer than yours. Just trust me, okay?"

"Fine," she said through gritted teeth.

Lady Gabrielle placed a hand on Mellissa's forearm. "It's okay we can watch from outside. Lady Gabrielle led them past the guards. She opened the door letting him enter the room. Mellissa's stare bore into him as the door was closed behind him, leaving him alone with the prisoner. It was a small room with just a table with two chairs on either side. The prisoner sat in one, his hands shackled in chains.

Greg locked the guard over. He was a similar age to him. His eyes were red and puffy as if he had been crying. On the train journey over, Greg had read all the crime scene notes and thoroughly looked over the photos. He had looked up the guards' records. He hadn't been working here long and would have only recently had a background check. Either someone had messed up in their checks or he was very good at deception.

Greg sat across from the guard. "What did you do with the air stone?"

The guard pressed his hands together as if praying. "Like I told the others, I didn't do this."

Greg tilted his head to the left raising an eyebrow. "Then help me to understand this camera footage of you with the stone. The way the vault was breached would have taken inside knowledge, like that of a guard."

"I promise you sir I have no idea how they got that footage. I have no memory of last night. It is like I have hopped through time."

Greg leaned back in his chair tapping his fingers on the table. "There were a lot of other items locked in that vault. Some are worth a lot of money. Whoever hired you must have paid you a lot for you to take nothing else."

"Please believe me. I know this looks bad, but I didn't do it. Check my accounts I haven't received any payments."

Greg had already checked the man's accounts. No unusual transactions had taken place. "You could have been paid in cash."

The man looked around the room. "Then check my house. Check everywhere I have ever visited. You won't find anything because I didn't do this."

"Investigators are already searching your house."

"Good, then you will all see. You will have to believe me when they find nothing." The guard lowered his head as his bottom lip began to quiver. "I don't know how this happened. I was meant to be meeting my girlfriend last night to go out for dinner, but I don't even know if I saw her."

"She has already given a statement saying you didn't

show up."

The man looked up at Greg his eyes full of tears. "I don't know what happened. I have no memory of last night, I feel like I'm losing my mind."

Greg jolted upright as a memory from a few months ago flashed through his mind. The sea king had told them of his people experiencing temporary fits of madness and having no memory afterwards.

Greg rubbed his chin. "What's the last thing you remember?"

"Leaving work at around five. I was going to my girlfriend's house. The next thing I know I'm waking up at home and it's already ten in the morning."

"Can you remember anything else? Something hazy even. Like a dream maybe. Was there a woman with you, telling you what to do?"

The guard shook his head. "I'm sorry sir, it's all a blank. I wish I knew what happened, then I could clear my name."

The chair screeched along the floor as Greg pushed it back and stood. He placed a hand on the table and looked down at the guard. "I believe you. Someone did something to you and I'm going to figure out what."

The guard's eyes sparkled with hope. "Really?"

Greg nodded. He walked over to the door and knocked on it. He looked back at the guard who was looking down at his shackles. "Something weird is going on," said Greg, "and I'm going to get to the bottom of it." The door opened, and he walked out.

Mellissa was waiting on the other side of the door, her hands on her hips. "What was that? You didn't get any answers out of him. I'm going in myself."

Greg grabbed her arm as she went to push past him. "He told me exactly what I needed to know. He didn't do this

Mellissa."

She pulled her arm from his grip. "They have him on camera."

Greg rubbed the sides of his head. "Let me rephrase. He wasn't in control of himself when he took the stone."

Her forehead creased as she crossed her arms. "You think someone was controlling him? You told me mind control wasn't a thing."

"Remember all those months ago when the sea king came to ask for help as his people were suffering random fits of madness?"

She nodded. "You said it was a spirit creature." Her jaw dropped as her eyes went wide. "You think this spirit creature is now on land." Greg nodded. She narrowed her eyes at him. "There is something else you're not telling me."

He held his arms up in front of his chest. "I have told you everything I know, promise." He took her hand. "I'm going to tell Lady Gabrielle what I learnt, you go back upstairs and fill in Harkura and Samson."

She yanked her hand from his. "Fine." She stormed off, her long curls trailing behind her.

Greg let out a long breath. Lady Gabrielle's eyebrows rose. She had been stood against the wall, to the side of the two of them. "You know perfectly well I heard everything you just said. What are you not telling her?

Greg's shoulders sagged as he made his way over to her. He leaned against the wall looking down at the floor. "I also think my mother is involved."

She gasped. "You believe Gwendolyn to have returned?"

Greg's jaw tensed as he slammed his fist against the wall. "Yes, and if she has, this is all happening because of me."

Sorrow

Mellissa

The cold air stung my cheeks. I pulled my hat down making sure my ears were covered. Not that it did much to stop the chill spreading through me. Harkura walked a few steps in front making sure our route through the capital was clear. My head was spinning as I recalled the council meeting, I had just left. An emergency meeting had been called to discuss the missing air stone. Yet somehow it had become like every other council discussion where Lee made everything about him. How the theft affected him. Were the witches now in danger? Of course they were, we all were! I had held my tongue. But he had set something off in me, some sort of intuition. My gut was telling me the capital was not where we needed to be. As soon as Lady Gabrielle adjourned the meeting I shot out of there and grabbed Harkura. My chest felt tight. I hoped this pit of terror inside me was wrong and there was nothing dangerous about to occur.

Harkura turned to look at me. The moonlight flickered off his pale blue skin. "Are you okay?" he asked, "The snow is pretty bad. Maybe we should wait till morning to travel."

It had been snowing nonstop all week. Tomorrow wouldn't be any different. "No," I said, "That council meeting was a waste of time, but it did make me sure of one thing, we need to protect everyone. That means getting Victoria and my dad back to the castle as soon as possible."

Harkara's indigo eyes shone as he rose a single brow. "Are you sure you're not overreacting? So far all we know for sure is that the air stone is missing not who has taken it."

I clenched my fists, my whole body trembled with anger. "Oh come on Harkura. Who are you kidding? We both know this means Humarya has returned."

Rubbing the bridge of his nose Harkura sighed. "Yes, it's very likely her but Humarya's goal has always been the dark stones. We should focus on keeping Laxus safe. Those two visiting the human world should be fine."

I shook my head clasping my hands to my chest. "I can't explain it Harkura, but I can just sense something is wrong. They are not safe, no one is."

Harkura frowned as he placed a hand on my shoulder. "Is it the nightmares again?"

I pulled away. "Harkura no." I threw my hands down beside me. "Yes, I've had weird dreams, but they are not my nightmares. They are telling me something. Matt is trying to warn me, like when I used to dream of Queen Freya."

Harkura straightened, placing his hands behind his back. "If you feel this strongly about it then I will trust your instincts. We shall travel straight from the train station to the human world."

I took Harkura's hand and gave him a small smile. His blue eyes were full of worry. Swallowing the lump in my throat I marched onward, with Harkura by my side.

We stepped through the tear in the veil that separated the

two worlds and were instantly plummeted by rain. I put my hood up over my hat. Of course, it would be raining on this side. Harkura put his arm around me while searching the trees. I smiled as I sensed Victoria's presence. An umbrella was placed over my head. "I thought you might need this," she said.

I hugged her and took the umbrella. She brushed my hug off. "It's just an umbrella, no need for this touchy-feely stuff."

Harkura nodded at Victoria. "It is good to see you are in good health. How are your parents?"

She forced a smile. "They are good considering." Victoria had gone back to the human world with her parents after the new year's party. This time of year was hard for the Street family. This was when their son, Victoria's twin, Matt had been trapped in the tree of time. They didn't blame me for what happened, but I did. Kadon had tricked me, tricked us all but it was still my magic that had sealed Matt away and I was yet to find a way to break it.

Harkura grasped her hand. "I am glad you are doing well." He pulled me into a hug squeezing me tightly. "See all is good. Victoria is fine."

"Harkura," I pushed away from him. "Focus. We need to get my dad as well."

Harkura rolled his shoulders back and nodded. "Of course. Your resolve worried me earlier so I was just very relieved to see Victoria well."

Victoria put her arm around me, squeezing my shoulder. "I understand your worry but I'm all right and so was your dad when I checked on him last night."

"I won't be satisfied until I see him." Victoria and Harkura glanced at each other but didn't say anything else. We walked in silence to Victoria's car. We piled into the small vehicle and were at dad's house in five minutes. I glanced out at the large semi-detached house that used to be my home. It was deadly quiet, and all the lights were off. My stomach churned as I got out of the car. Harkura grasped my hand, his indigo eyes narrowed on dad's car parked in the driveway. He could sense it too. A dark aura was cast over the area. Pulling my hand from his grip, I ran up the drive, the gravel crunching under my feet. I banged on the door. There was no response, so I knocked again, shouting for dad.

"Don't you have a key?" Victoria asked.

"Yes," I said, "Somewhere." I rummaged through the small bag I had brought with me.

"I'll check round the back." She clicked her fingers and then pointed to the left. "Harkura you try the garage." He nodded and the two split up, leaving me at the front door.

A dark pit of dread filled my stomach. Something was wrong, I could sense it. I peered through the front window. It was pitch black. Squinting I glimpsed a figure laid on the floor. I screamed Harkura's name. He was by my side in a flash. He peered in through the window and gasped. My pulse quickened as I ran back to the front door. Magic surged through my body. Light energy exploded out of me as I blasted the door off its hinges. The smell that assaulted my nose, had me gagging. It was freezing inside and eerily quiet. The dark aura hit me like a sledgehammer. As I stepped inside Harkura grabbed my wrist trying to pull me back, but I shoved him away. He said something to me, but my heart pounded so hard it was all I could hear. I kicked the living room door open and stopped in my tracks. The sight before me chilled me to my core. "Dad" I croaked. There was no response. I took a slow step forward. "Dad," I said again. Silence. My eyes filled with tears. I kept repeating the word "no" with every step I took toward my father's pale body lying on the floor surrounded by black feathers. The smell was stronger in here, it was coming from him. I dropped to my knees beside his lifeless body.

"Dad," I whispered touching his cheek. He felt like ice. I looked into his eyes. The same brown eyes I had, frozen in fear. My heart shattered. Screaming I let out a wave of light energy. I laid my head across his chest, tears streaming. Where I should have heard a heartbeat there was nothing. He couldn't be gone. He just couldn't.

I heard a gasp. I didn't bother to look up at the source. "Mellissa," Victoria said. I didn't respond. My whole body was shaking. I should have been here to protect him. The ground began to tremble. The more I cried the stronger the tremors got. This wasn't right. I clenched my fists and screamed at the top of my voice. The heart crystal began to glow frantically. My lungs ached as I struggled to breathe through my tears.

Victoria's arms wrapped around me and she pulled me into a strong embrace. "I'm so sorry Mellissa" she cried. Why was she sorry? She hadn't done this. The Heart Crystal shuddered. There was a dark pit in my stomach. I was empty inside. Whoever had done this would pay. I held on tight to Victoria and cried on her shoulder. I'm not sure how long we stayed like that, but Victoria held me until I no longer had any tears left to cry.

Murdered

Gregory

s soon as Victoria had called, Greg made his way to the human world. At first, he thought he hadn't heard her right. It couldn't be true but then she had repeated herself and the quiver in her voice had him moving. He hadn't been sure what to expect when he arrived, but it hadn't been this. A glamour charm had been put over the house to stop any unwanted attention from the humans. From the outside, the Hail's residence looked the same as the last time he had been there. A brick semi-detached house, with a gravel driveway. A normal house where nothing untoward could have occurred. Once Greg stepped through the glamour charm, he saw the place was cluttered with people. The guards at the front nodded him in. Investigators, illusionists and techs went about their business. People were in and out of the house investigating or covering up what had happened here. Greg shuddered at the thought of a cover-up. He knew why any evidence of magic needed to be hidden from the humans, but it seemed wrong to be thinking about something like that when a man had just died.

Greg made his way into the house and quivered. It didn't feel like Mellissa's home anymore. Something dark had touched this place and the sweet family home was now a crime scene. Furniture had been moved, frames dislodged, and cupboards searched all in the hope to find one tiny clue. He tensed as he entered the living room. The body had been moved but he was told this was where Chris Hail had been found. Where Mellissa had found her father dead. He clenched his fists. This wasn't right. Mr Hail was a human. With Melissa gone, magic shouldn't have come for him. Dried blood was splattered on the carpet. Black feathers were scattered throughout the living room. Greg picked one up turning it over. It couldn't be one of hers. Humarya was gone.

"Lord Gregory." Came Harkura's voice behind him.

Greg stuffed the feather in the back pocket of his jeans and turned to face him. Harkura's eyes were red and puffy. His forehead was creased. His blue skin was paler than usual. Greg had never seen the fire nymph look so pained. "Where is she?" Greg asked.

Harkura pointed out the door. "Upstairs in her father's room. I have never seen her like this."

Greg nodded to Harkura and then ran up the stairs. Victoria stood by the door of Mr Hail's room. Shadows rested below her eyes and her shoulders sagged. She looked just as miserable and stressed as Harkura. When she saw him, she gave him a weak smile. "She isn't speaking but maybe she will talk to you." She stepped aside letting him in the room.

Mellissa sat on the bed with her legs pulled up to her chest. Her eyes were red raw and her hair had fallen half out of its braid. She had a vacant look on her face as she stared out the window. The room looked like she had pulled everything out. The bed was covered in her father's clothes and she clasped to a shirt as she rocked back and forth. She looked like a shell of herself.

Greg closed the gap between them, pulling her into a hug. At first, she seemed shocked as if she hadn't realised, he was in the room, then she buried her face in his chest. "Mellissa, I'm so sorry," He said.

She looked up at him. The usual sparkle in her eyes was gone. "Why does everyone keep saying they're sorry?"

His heart ached as he took in the hollow look she wore. He pushed the stray hairs from her face. "Because this shouldn't have happened. Your dad-"

"He's gone, Greg." She said interrupting him. She pushed away from him as a shadow covered her face. "He was just lying there, so cold." Her eyes drifted back to the window as she curled back in on herself. Her eyes were dark and puffy. She squinted into the distance almost as if she could see something he couldn't.

He went to touch her shoulder, but she flinched away. Moving more slowly this time, he stroked her cheek. "What can I do?"

She shook her head. More strands of hair broke free of her braid as she did. "You can't heal the dead Gregory."

Her words struck him, he felt like he had a vice around his heart that someone was slowly tightening. She was so obviously broken but he didn't know how to help her.

Mellissa suddenly stood. "I have to sort things." She looked around the room manically. "My dad. I can't just leave him lying there."

Greg took her hands in his. "You don't have to do anything. Everything is under control. Your dad's body has already been moved."

"Moved where?" Her voice broke as tears slowly rolled down her cheeks.

"There will be an autopsy, then they will prepare him for a funeral."

"A funeral." Her legs gave way. Greg grasped hold of her as she crumpled.

"You don't need to worry about that just now." He held on to her as she sat back down on the bed. "Take all the time you need. Everyone is here for you."

She nodded, grasping his arm. "You won't leave me, will you?"

The panic in her voice shook him. She was holding on to him so tight her nails dug into his skin. He tried to keep his face calm. "Of course not."

She wrapped her arms around him tight nuzzling her face in the crook of his neck. "Promise you won't leave me."

"I promise." He said. Pulling her arms from his neck, he got her to lie down. He curled up beside her on the bed, stroking her hair until she eventually fell asleep.

Greg quietly slipped out of the room, shutting the door gently. As he turned, he came face to face with Victoria. "How is she?" she asked.

"Asleep," replied Greg.

"Good, she was a mess." Victoria frowned. "What are we meant to do now? How will she ever recover from this?"

Greg placed a hand on Victoria's shoulder. "We just all need to be there for her. I don't think this is something she will get over, but she will find a way to keep going." He knew all too well the pain of losing a parent. He still thought about his father and sometimes wished for his guidance. Mellissa wasn't like Greg, she felt things stronger than he did. She also had a close relationship with her father unlike him. If he still occasionally felt his loss, he was sure this was something she would feel for the rest of her life.

Victoria looked pale and her blue eyes had lost their usual icy glow. "I'll keep watch, just in case she wakes."

Greg nodded. If watching over Mellissa would help her feel better, then who was he to stop her, but he couldn't stay put. Greg needed to find out what had happened to Chris Hail. He headed downstairs and located the head investigator. He was a tall slender man with a pointy face.

"Lord Ainsworth, I'm chief Lars." Lars held his hand out to him. Greg shook his hand. "I had expected you sooner."

Greg narrowed his eyes at the chief. "I went to see Queen Mellissa first. So, what have you found?"

"Cause of death is still unknown but it was magical."

"I assume you took pictures and documented everything before moving the body."

Lars's face tightened. "Of course, we did."

"Can I see them?" Greg held his hand out. Lars snarled as he handed over his tabular. He opened up the documents that had been loaded into it.

Greg scanned through the photos of the scene when the investigator first arrived. The body was clean. No markings left, no wounds of any kind. "By the looks of it, he can't have been dead more than twenty-four hours."

Lars nodded. "That is what our coroner said."

Greg zoomed in the eyes. "His eyes are bloodshot."

"So?" asked Lars

"It could mean several things." He looked back through the photos until he got to the last one. It showed the whole room and exactly how the body had been placed. Mr Hail's body had been in the centre of the feathers. Greg narrowed his eyes as he looked at the feather's placement, they were too neat. Perfectly placed around the body after death. Greg gritted his teeth. The feathers were a message. "What else have you found?" he asked.

Lars pulled a notebook out of his pocket and flicked through it. "We have spoken to neighbours."

"What have you told them has happened?"

"Don't worry no mention of magic or death. This isn't my first rodeo. We have informed them Mr Hail has been reported missing by his daughter and asked if they had seen anyone suspicious around."

"Right." Greg rubbed his chin. "Did they have any useful information?"

Lars shook his head. "Not really. The old lady next door whittled on about the strange boys Mr Hail kept taking in. From the descriptions given they sound like, you, the keeper's guardian, and a little boy. The only other person she noticed around recently was Mr Hail's new girlfriend."

"Wait what?" Greg asked. "Mr Hail didn't have a girlfriend. Mellissa definitely would have mentioned that."

Lars shrugged. "Maybe it wasn't serious, so he didn't mention it to his daughter. Of course, there were all those black feathers. If you ask me, with the recent theft at the council and then this. I'm thinking Humarya has returned."

Greg shook his head. This wasn't Humarya. That was what the perpetrator wanted everyone to think. "Did you get a description of the girlfriend?"

Lars flipped his notebook shut. "No, like I said all evidence points to the return of Humarya. Who else would have the power to cross the veil unnoticed?"

Greg turned his back on Lars. All this so-called evidence was circumstantial. This was all too neat. Humarya had not been in this house. Greg pulled the feather he had picked up earlier from his pocket. This was a bird feather, not a Valkyries. He turned it over in his hand, some sort of blackbird, a raven maybe. Lars was right about the veil. It would take someone powerful to cross without alerting Mellissa's stone guards. Whoever had done this had the air stone or was working for them. Greg couldn't disregard the possibility that Humarya had done this. But it was more likely she helped the murderer cross the veil, even ordered them to but she hadn't been the one to end Mr Hail's life.

Greg marched out of the house and knocked on the neighbour's door. An old lady opened the door. She glared at him. "I've already told you lot everything I know. Now go away."

Greg held his hands up. "Wait, I'm not one of the investigators."

She looked him up and down. "Oh, it's you. You're the boyfriend, right?"

He nodded. "Right."

She jabbed a wrinkly finger at him. "What do you want?"

"You told the investigators you saw Mr Hail's girlfriend round recently."

"Yes, she was round two nights in a row."

"Mellissa didn't know her dad was seeing anyone. Can you tell me what she looked like or better yet a name?"

"I don't know a name, but she was a redhead. Must be a family kink." The old woman rubbed her chin, looking him over. "Come to think of it she looked a bit like you. You have the same striking green eyes. The sort of emerald that you can still see the shine off in the dark."

Greg took a step back. His mouth went dry as a lump lodged in his throat. Gwendolyn. The description sounded just like her, but she couldn't have done this. His mother couldn't have killed Mellissa's father. If she had, it was all his fault.

Failure

Victoria

ain poured from the dark grey sky, soaking Victoria as she made her way up the steps to her parent's house. Her eyes were still sore from crying. She had failed in her duties as a guardian. She fumbled for her keys to open the door when it flew open.

Her mother stood in the doorway, her features creased with worry. "Oh darling get in out the wet quick."
Victoria was ushed inside, her mother closing the door behind her. She pulled off her wet coat and hung it over the radiator in the hall. She turned towards the stairs to go up them but her feet didn't move forwards. Victoria clenched her fists as she took slow breaths. Her mother placed a hand on her shoulder. "I heard what happened at the Hail residence. Are you okay?"

Victoria shook her head. "I failed her mum." She shouted. "I failed Mellissa. I'm the worst guardian ever."

Her mother pulled her into a hug and pattered her head as tears streamed down her face. "This is not you're fault. You checked in with Chris only yesterday, how were you to know? Your powers are incredible, but you cannot predict the future."

Victoria pushed away from her mother. Her face was warm and wet. "No mum. I should have been there to protect Mr Hail. I was here only ten minutes away and yet I sensed nothing." Victoria threw her arms out to the side. "Mellissa was on the other side of the veil in the Capitol, and she sensed something was wrong. I should have sensed the dark magic when it crossed the veil."

"Neither I nor your father sensed anything was wrong."

"You're not the Queen's guardian," Victoria yelled punching the wall in the hallway. Ice spread from her fist along the corridor. Her mother gasped covering her mouth with her hands. Victoria quickly pulled her magic back and the ice stopped spreading. Her shoulders sagged as all the fight left her. "I'm sorry Mum. It's just- you should have seen her, Mellissa, she's a mess and there's nothing I could do."

Her mother pulled her into her arms and hugged her tightly. Victoria felt the tears welling up again. "I love her mum."

"I know you do honey."

Victoria rested her face on her mother's shoulder. "I couldn't guard her. I should have protected her."

Her mother gently cupped her face in her hands. She wiped her daughter's tears with her thumbs. "Vicky there are some things you can't protect someone from. The pain of loss is one of them."

"I know. I just wish I could have done something." She sniffled as she wiped her eyes on her shirt sleeve. "Thanks for listening to my ramble."

"Of course honey. That's what I'm here for." She gave her daughter's shoulder a squeeze. "You keep so much locked away in that heart of yours. I will always be here to listen when you need to offload." Her mother gave her a small, tender smile. "I assume you just came back to collect a few things and will be staying with Mellissa."

Victoria nodded. "Yeah, I just need to grab some stuff from my room." She exchanged a look with her mother and then headed upstairs. Her room was the first on the right. She stopped outside her bedroom door and looked down the corridor at her brother's room. Matt would have sensed the danger. He had always been more in tune with nature and the vibes of the universe than her. She shook her head and went into her bedroom. Grabbing a duffle bag from under her bed. She opened it wide, placed it on her mattress and started throwing things inside. As she opened her wardrobe, the memory of walking into the room and finding Mellissa crying over her father flashed through her mind. She froze on the spot, gripping the door handle. Her heart ached as she thought of how Mellissa had cried in her arms. She hadn't realised it was possible for someone to cry that much. It didn't matter what her mother said she was a failure. Mellissa was her world and she had let her down.

The last time Victoria had ranted at her mother like this was when she had been trying to protect Mellissa from the heartbreak that was Greg. She had said the same thing. 'There are some things you can't protect her from.' But that had been a matter of the heart and Greg had actually stepped up in the last few months. This was different. If she had been there when Mr Hail was attacked, she could have done something. She would have fought and maybe he would still be alive. And Mellissa wouldn't be the empty shell she currently was.

She tugged random items of clothing out of her wardrobe walked back over to her bed and stuffed them in the bag. Something shiny on her dresser caught her eye. She grabbed it. It was a silver bracelet with a heart-shaped charm that said 'best friend'. Victoria's eyes filled with tears again. It was her Christmas gift from Mellissa. She didn't know when it had happened. It was her mother that had made her realise it. She had fallen for the girl she was meant to be a guardian for. She knew Mellissa would never feel the same way she did. She had never told her how she felt and didn't plan to. Being her best friend was enough, but she was terrible at that too. She was an awful guardian and friend. She placed the bracelet on her left wrist, put on a fresh, dry jacket, then zipped the bag up and slung it over her shoulder. She would make up for her shortcomings by being there for Mellissa now. She would let her cry on her shoulder as much as she needed. She would see her through her grief.

Victoria grimaced as Mellissa's grip tightened in her hand. They had just entered the castle in Urbem foilum and all the staff were in the entranceway. Samson was the first to come over and offer his condolences. He placed his hand on Mellissa's shoulder. "I will take care of everything for now. Take all the time you need." But then person after person had come over to do similar. Mellissa had grabbed Victoria's hand and now her grip on her felt like she was trying to cut circulation off to the limb.

Victoria stepped in front of Mellissa, while still holding her hand. "Queen Mellissa appreciates your well wishes but it has been a long journey home. I will be escorting her to her quarters so she can rest." They all stared at them, some nodded but they all moved back creating space for them to get through.

Victoria led Mellissa through the corridors and up the three flights of stairs to her living quarters. She opened the door and ushered her inside. As soon as Victoria had shut the door Mellissa fell to her knees. Victoria hurried to her side. She knelt beside her placing a hand on her shoulder. "What's wrong? Are you hurt?"

Mellissa dug her fingers into the carpet. Her chest rose and fell unevenly as her breathing became harsh. "I don't know what's wrong with me. All those people. It's just- I can't-" Her words were cut off as she took a sharp breath. Her eyes filled with tears.

Victoria grasped both of Mellissa's shoulders tight. "I think you're having a panic attack." Victoria gritted her teeth as she looked around the room. She should have waited for Harkura and Greg to come back with their luggage from the carriage that had brought them back. Harkura would have made sure the entrance had been clear for them and Greg would know what to do now. Victoria bit her lip. "Okay just breathe with me." Victoria took a deep breath and counted, "One, two, three…" and out "for seven, eight, nine, ten."

Mellissa clutched her hands to her chest but counted along. Her breathing became less manic, and she rubbed her eyes with the palm of her hands. It didn't stop the tears from rolling down her cheeks. "I'm such a mess," Mellissa croaked.

Victoria pulled her cardigan sleeve over her hand and dabbed at Mellissa's tears with it. "With everything that has happened, I'd be concerned if you weren't."

Mellissa snorted as more tears fell. "I'm sorry."

"Do not apologise for feeling like this. You can be as sad as you need to in front of me."

Mellissa gave a weak smile under all the tears and snot covering her face. Victoria looked up as she heard the door click open. Greg and Harkura walked in carrying all there belongings. As soon as he saw them on the floor Greg dropped everything he was holding and was on his knees beside the girls in an instant. "What happened?"

"Nothing, it's just..." Mellissa started but her words seemed to fade. She rubbed her eyes with the back of her hand and Greg pulled her into a hug, resting her head on his chest.

Victoria placed her hands on her knees. "It was just a bit much seeing everyone and them all wanting to give their condolences."

Harkura stepped forward and thumped his fist on his chest. "I'm so sorry I should have been there to clear the way for you both."

Victoria shook her head. "I should have held back and waited for you, instead of rushing ahead." She placed her hands on the ground and pushed herself up to standing. "We'll give you two a minute. Harkura and I will see if there is any ice cream or cookies in the kitchen." As she went to walk away, she felt a hand tug at her sleeve.

Mellissa had hold of her. She was still wrapped up in Greg's arms but she looked up at Victoria, her eyes wide and glossy. "Thank you."

Victoria smiled down at her. "It's what I'm here for." She turned to Harkura and he held his arm out to her. Linking arms with him they left the room leaving Mellissa and Greg alone. Victoria swallowed a lump in her throat. Harkura pattered her hand that was linked to his arm. She rested her head on his shoulder. Even though she was taller than him this position worked. They stayed like this as they walked back downstairs and towards the kitchens.

The Prisoner

Gregory

reg followed the guard closely. Down they descended, further and further into the depths of the infamous prison of Magnus. This was Lady Gabrielle's city and home to the warlocks. The warlocks were well known for their expertise in battle magic, making them the perfect people to guard their world's biggest prison. It had taken a lot of persuasion for him to get access to this particular inmate. This person wasn't meant to have visitors. He was locked away from the others for his own safety. Due to his previous position in life, riots would have broken out and the rest of the inmates would have wanted his head.

They finally reached the bottom of the iron steps. The guard led Greg down a long corridor. They stopped at a metal door. The guard turned to Greg, his face a stoic wall. "Lord Ainsworth keep one meter from the glass at all times. I will be right outside if you need anything."

Greg nodded. "I understand." The guard bowed and opened the door. As Greg walked in the smell of bleach flared his nostrils. The door clicked shut behind him. A red line was taped across the floor marking a meter in front of the glass. The glass panel spanned the width of the room and behind it smiled Emerson.

His hair had grown out and was a matted mess. He now had a bushy beard, and his dark hair was now almost all grey. He looked nothing like the posh, snob of an elder knight that he used to be. Somehow, he seemed to have aged years in only a few months. He looked at Greg with wild manic eyes. "It's so good to see you, Gregory. How long has it been months, years? Time moves differently down here. Have you missed me?"

Greg walked forward, stopping at the red line. "I haven't come to exchange pleasantry."

Emerson tilted his head leaning forward. "Why are you here Gregory?"

Greg stood tall, steeling his facial features. He couldn't give anything away to Emerson, but he needed to see if he knew anything. When he had first been arrested Emerson had refused to talk. Maybe now he had been down here for six months he would be more talkative. "There has been an incident."

"You can't possibly think it was me." He gestured to his surroundings. "I have been in here the whole time." He pointed to the camera behind Greg. "They are always watching me. Always watching but they never let me see anyone."

Greg looked at the camera and then back at Emerson, whose eyes had gone wide as he pressed closer to the glass. Greg straightened his shirt. "I think your queen has returned."

Emerson slammed his hand against the glass and snarled. "I have no queen." `

Greg didn't move, keeping his face blank. "Your attitude seems to have changed."

Emerson stalked to the back of his cell. He faced the wall with his arms neatly behind his back. "I have had a lot of time to think down here. My father served Humarya before I was even born and raised me to do the same. I never had a choice. At least that is what I thought." Emerson looked back at Greg. His forehead creased. "You and I are similar. We are both products of terrible parenting. Yet somehow you turned out better than I." Emerson's top lip curled. "Humarya is not a queen. A real queen is not cruel. A queen cares for her subjects and fights for them." As Emerson tilted his head his eyes narrowed on Greg and a wide toothy smile made him look even more manic. "Like your queen. Does Mellissa know you're here?"

Greg swallowed. "I will be the one asking the questions."

"So, she doesn't. What is so important you have come to see me behind your beloved's back?"

Greg pulled the black feather from his pocket. "Do you recognize this?"

Emerson came back toward the glass and peered at the feather. "It is a raven's feather as you should know."

"Do ravens have any meaning to Humarya? Do you know what she could be planning?"

Emerson shrugged. "The only bird she ever kept was your mother, and as far as I know Humarya's plan remains the same. Get the dark stones and revive her dead husband."

"The feathers couldn't have been some sort of message?"

Emerson leaned on the glass his eyes boring into Greg. "Why is the raven feather so important? What has she done?"

Greg tucked the feather back into his pocket. Straightening his posture, he placed his hands behind his back. "They were at a crime scene, but it was nothing significant."

"You're a terrible liar Gregory." Emerson tapped the glass. "If those feathers were left behind it wasn't by Humarya but a changeling." Emerson began to laugh. "And we both know she only has one changeling left working for her." Emerson pulled at his hair as he laughed. He walked to the back of his cell. Leaning against the wall he slipped onto the floor and sat laughing.

"Emerson," Greg said but he didn't get a response.

Something in Emerson seemed to have switched off as he just continued to lean against the wall and laugh. Greg left the room his heart heavy as lead. Emerson had confirmed Greg's fears. Gwendolyn was the prime suspect in Chris Hail's death. Greg's mind swam with flashes of what he had seen of the investigation so far, wondering how long it would take the investigators to make the connection. He looked at his watch. He needed to get back; Mellissa would be upset if she realized he had left. His chest tightened as a lump lodged in his throat. How long until Mellissa's grief turned into hate and that hate was aimed at him?

Laid to Rest

Mellissa

I laid in bed staring up at the ceiling. Alone. Greg was gone but I couldn't find the motivation to get up and see if he is somewhere in the castle or actually gone. I should move. Get dressed and leave this room but I couldn't. Something inside me was broken. I was numb. It was like there was a giant cavern had opened inside me as if I would never be whole again.

There was a knock on the door. It creaked open and a few moments later Harkura appeared in the archway to my bedroom. He was dressed in his skin tight black training gear. He smiled at me, but his indigo eyes were full of worry. "Good, you're awake. I thought we could go for a run."

Rolling onto my side, I pulled the cover over me. "I don't feel like running."

The mattress shifted as Harkura sat on the edge of the bed. "I know you don't feel like doing much of anything, but the fresh air may do you some good." He pulled the covers from my head and pushed my wild hair from my face. "You haven't left this room in days. You don't talk to anyone but Gregory and Victoria. I am worried about you."

"I talk to you too," I whispered.

"When was the last time you brushed your hair?"

My fingers caught on knot after knot as I ran them through my tangled mane.. I knew I was a wild mess, but it didn't matter what I looked like. No one was going to see me as I didn't plan on going anywhere.

"How about we just go for a walk? We don't have to run." I shook my head. Running wasn't the problem. The idea of leaving my room made me clam up. Greg had tried to get me to leave yesterday, and the resulting panic attack had me sitting on the floor gasping for breath. I didn't know why it was so hard to pull myself together. I had made it back here from the human world. Kept it together long enough to get into the castle but then I saw everyone. The looks of pity on their faces. They all offered their condolences. I knew they were trying to be kind, but I couldn't take it. It was almost like something else had snapped inside me and I hadn't thought that possible after what I had seen. My dad lay there, pale, and lifeless, and the smell. My breathing became harsh as I thought about finding my dad's body.

Harkura grabbed the top of my arms. "Just breathe. In and out, slowly." He breathed along with me helping me to set a slower rhythm. "That's better."
Harkura stepped back looking down at me with concern. I hung my head. "I don't know what's wrong with me. It just seems wrong that the world keeps spinning even though my dad isn't in it anymore."

"There is nothing wrong with you. We all grieve differently but shutting yourself off won't do you any good."

"I'm just not ready to face the public yet."

"You don't have to. How about we just walk around the empty corridors up here? It'll just be me and you." He held his hand out to me. I slipped my hand in his and I was pulled to my feet. As we approached the door my chest tightened. Harkura gave me a gentle pat on the back. With my arm linked with Harkura, we walked out of the room.

My pulse quickened and the hairs on the back of my neck stood up. Harkura patted my arm that was linked with his and hummed. As we walked around the loop of corridors, my pulse began to calm. It wasn't as bad as I thought. I may not have left the building or even gone downstairs, but I was out of my room. By the time we were back at my door, I was smiling.

I opened the door to the smell of freshly baked croissants. Greg was sitting on the sofa. Across from him was a tray of croissants, a pot of tea and two glasses of orange juice. He stood when we walked in. "Imagine my surprise when I returned with breakfast, and you weren't here."

"Harkura convinced me to go for a short walk." I looked at the food on the coffee table and then up at Greg, narrowing my eyes on him. He was dressed in a shirt and tie like he was ready for a day at work. His hair was ruffled, and he was smiling at me a bit too much. "Where have you been?" I asked.

"Just walking around the castle. I had to wait for the chef to make these fresh." He pointed at the tray of croissants.

Harkura placed his hand on my back. "Why don't you eat your breakfast and stop worrying."

Maybe I was being paranoid, but I was sure Greg had been out of the castle. I sat down taking a croissant. It was still warm and when I bit into it, I groaned. It was flaky, soft, and buttery. Chef Dean was getting good at making these. Greg poured the tea. "I'm sorry I didn't bring enough cups."

Harkura waved his hand at Greg. "I don't need anything." Harkura turned to me. "When you finish, I suggest you get a shower and wash your hair, then I will brush it out for you and put it in a braid."

I nodded unable to talk due to having stuffed another croissant in my mouth. The anxiety was still lurking beneath the surface. A short walk around the top floor of the castle wasn't going to cure me. I didn't think this was something I was going to recover from, but I needed to be able to leave this room. I was the queen and I couldn't let myself be consumed by this grief. Even more important than that, I needed to be at my father's funeral. No matter what I was feeling, or how messed up I was, that was more important than anything.

An icy wind blew rustling the leaves on the trees. Snow covered the ground except for the small clearing where everyone stood. I'm not sure how many people had spoken to me. How many had offered me their condolences? Had told me what a good person my dad was. People spoke to me, but I didn't hear them. I felt hollow. Like a part of me was gone forever. It didn't feel right, to have a funeral when I still didn't know what had happened to him. He had been murdered and no one could tell me who the culprit was. I wasn't even sure how we got to this day. Council investigators had swarmed my dad's house and covered up all use of magic. In the human world, he was simply missing. His friends and colleagues didn't know the truth. None of them were here. Harkura took over arranging everything for me. I felt awful for relying on him to sort things, but I just couldn't handle it. The fact I was outside the castle and not locked away in my room was massive progress. How had things become so terrible? I wrapped my arms around myself as I shivered watching my dad's body lowered into the ground.

"Your majesty," Someone said. "Would you like to spread the earth?" Everyone was staring at me. They wanted me to bury my dad.

Victoria placed a hand on my shoulder. "You don't have to do this."

"Yes, I do," I said stepping forward. The handful of dirt

I picked up from the mound, felt heavy. Numbness spread through my body. I had to be the one to do this, not someone else. Tears threatened to fall again. Closing my eyes, I clenched my fist full of dirt and in one movement, lifted the entire mound of distributed earth with my magic and filled the hole where my dad lay. When I opened my eyes, the tears began streaming. He was gone and all that was left was this mound of earth I had created. My legs threatened to give way. I felt warm arms wrap around me.

"You don't have to stay here," said Greg holding me close.

"I can't leave him," I whispered in between sobs. "Not yet."

Greg gestured to someone over my shoulder. Victoria and Harkura began gathering people up and sending them back to the castle, with Samson leading the way. Eventually, only the two of us remained. We sat at the edge of my dad's grave. I placed my hand on the soil. This wasn't meant to happen. My dad was supposed to move here to Urbem Folium. He was meant to live well into old age, enjoying his retirement with the elves. But instead, he was to lay here beneath the earth. "I don't know what to do next." I said, my voice cracking as I spoke.

"You don't have to do anything yet," Greg replied.

"Yes, I do. I'm the queen. I can't just crumble but that's all I'm doing." I covered my face with my hands. "I'm falling apart."

Greg gently pulled my hands from my face. "You're allowed to fall apart. Everyone will understand. You have Samson and the rest of your staff to keep things together for now."

I looked at the freshly disturbed soil. "But what if I can't ever pull myself back together again?"

"You don't have to do it alone." Greg placed a finger

under my chin, carefully turning my head. "Come back to Novosvillas with me. Stay for a week or two. I have already checked with Samson and Josh. They will run things while you take time to grieve. You can come back when you're feeling better."

"I don't think I will ever feel better."

"It may seem that way. The pain won't go away but you will find a way to continue because it's what your dad would have wanted for you. If you keep going his memory will live on in you."

My heart felt like it was about to burst. Greg was right. I couldn't let myself be destroyed by grief. My dad wouldn't want that for me. He would want me to keep moving forward, but I just couldn't. At least not right now.

"I'll come to Novosvillas, but I can't leave him, not like this." I crawled over to my dad's grave and placed my hands on the earth. Magic surged through me. I could feel roots taking hold as a small tree began to grow. It shot up from the ground, branches forming. Leaves burst forth. With my hand engulfed in light, I engraved my dad's initials into the tree. "Now he will never be alone."

Greg put his arm around me as we walked back to the castle.

Planning

Mellissa

"What do you mean you are going to Novosvillas?" Laxus asked. He was standing in front of the suitcase I was trying to pack with his arms folded.

"Laxus I just need some time to process everything," I said.

Laxus sighed. His wings dropped as the usual shimmer his skin held dwindled. "I understand that you are still mourning but we need to act."

"And what do you think we should do?"

He threw his arms in the air and growled. "Find Humarya before she strikes again and end her." His young face looked so serious. In that moment you could tell he was much older than he looked.

I stared blankly at him "We are not sure who is behind this."

"Really Mellissa? The air stone was stolen and then your father was found dead surrounded by black feathers. It is obvious his death was no accident."

I threw the dress I had been folding down. "Of course, I know." I glanced at an envelope on my bedside table. Laxus looked in the same direction.

"You still haven't opened it."

"I couldn't do it."

"Then let me." He picked up the envelope and I

snatched it from his hands.

"No" I yelled.

He put his hands up in front of his chest. "I'm sorry, I didn't mean to overstep but don't you want to know."

I shook my head. "No" I squeaked looking at the floor. The envelope crumpled as my fist tightened around it. Samson had brought me this envelope days ago, but I hadn't been able to open it. My dad was dead, reading a report of how it happened wasn't going to bring him back. But I needed to know. To have my suspicions confirmed. That it was Humarya.

Laxus gently took my free hand, stroking the back of it softly. He looked up at me with his pink eyes wide. "Let me read it for you."

I swallowed a lump in my throat and nodded. Taking a deep breath I handed him the envelope. My head throbbed and everything moved in slow motion as Laxus ripped the envelope open. There was a deafening silence as I watched him unfold the letter and read it.

When Laxus looked up from the paper my heart froze. "Your father was suffocated."

"What?" My voice came out as a croak. "How?"

Laxus frowned. "Are you sure…"

"How?" I demanded.

"The air was pulled from his lungs."

The room spun and all I could hear was a buzzing sound. I dropped to my knees. "Air magic," I whispered. I dug my nails into my palms as I felt my eyes fill with tears.

Laxus wrapped his small arms around me. "I'm sorry for pushing you."

I shook my head. "I needed the push. Everyone has been so patient with me, but I can't run away from this."

"Then what are you going to do."

"Face it head-on." I wiped my wet eyes on my sleeve. "I'm done being sad. Now I'm angry."

The sky was dark, with big grey clouds. The ocean was calm as

I walked silently along the beach. "It's good to see you again." I jumped at the sound of a male's voice. Matt stood in front of me smiling. His blond hair shone in the moonlight.

"Where did you come from?" I asked.

"The tree of course," he said.

I rubbed my forehead with my finger. "I don't understand."

"You don't have to, you just need to know why Humarya had your dad killed."

I wrapped my arms around myself and looked out at the water. "Because she is evil."

"She wanted to hurt you," Matt said.

"I know," I shouted. "And she succeeded because I'm hurting. All because I had to do the right thing and stop her and now, she hates me."

"You don't understand. It was because…" A strong gust blew in, whistling around us. Dark clouds loomed above. Matt lowered his gaze. As he pushed his hands down beside him he took a deep breath. The wind slowed. He looked up, his blue eyes catching mine. "Do you remember how you were after you discovered I was trapped in the tree?"

I placed my hand over my chest as I felt it tighten. "But I…" my words cut off as his gaze intensified on me. My jaw dropped as realisation dawned on me. "I pushed everyone away and refused to fight."

Matt nodded. "I'm sorry about your dad. I wish things were different…" His words slowly faded as he stepped backwards away from me. "Wait," I shouted. A grey fog rolled in from nowhere. I reached out to him, but my hand closed around air.

I opened my eyes and gasped. Sitting up I saw the familiar surroundings of my bedroom. Greg lay beside me fast asleep. Another dream but that conversation with Matt had been real. Somehow he was communicating with me from inside the tree of time. I laid back down and stared up at the ceiling. Matt had been trying to help me. Something must be disrupting our connection, that's why our talks were so disjointed. But what was I meant to do with the information he had managed to give me?

I sat in my office looking around at the blank walls. It felt cold and lifeless. With how little I used it I had never really made it my own. Samson and Laxus sat in the two chairs on the opposite side of my desk, while Victoria and Harkura were by the door. I had called a meeting and we were just waiting on the last person. I had spent last night unable to sleep. After my weird dream, I had laid looking up at the ceiling thinking over my conversation with dream Matt and what had happened earlier with Laxus. That's when a wave of determination hit me, and a plan formed in my mind. There was a knock on the door. Harkura immediately opened it and ushered Josh in.

I looked up at the five people that filled my office. They couldn't be more different, but they were all important. "You're probably wondering why I called you all here," I said.

"Because you're going to Novosvillas," Victoria said.

I narrowed my eyes at her. "Yes, and while I'm away. I'm putting Samson in charge of the day-to-day running of things. Josh, you're in charge of the welfare of our citizens. And Harkura you're in charge of security."

Harkura stepped forward his forehead creased. "I am going with you. It is my duty to protect you."

"Victoria and Laxus will be coming with me."

"Laxus is hardly capable of keeping you safe. If anything he is more of a liability to you."

"Hey," said Laxus.

I put my hand up quietening them. "Victoria is more than capable of acting as my guardian alone while in Novosvillas. I need to know the city is safe in my absence. There is no one I trust more than you to do this."

Harkura clenched his fists. "Very well, your majesty." He bowed and stepped back. He leaned against the wall looking sullen.

I turned to Josh and Samson. "I am relying on you two to keep everyone calm and keep things running smoothly."

"Does that include the launch of our new elf tech?" asked Josh.

"Of course. But you're going to have to do it without me."

Josh fiddled with his shirt collar. "I'm not sure."

I smiled at him. "I believe in you."

Samson nodded. "Don't worry, I'll have his back. But what is it you will be doing?"

I stood up turning my back on them. "I thought I needed to clear my head." I dug my nails into my palms to try stop myself from shaking. "Humarya made this personal when she murdered my dad. At first, I thought it was revenge for ruining her plans but then I realised she wants me to crumble, to be so distraught that I'm out of her way." I slammed my hands down on my desk. "Well, she messed up because I'm even more determined to stop her. I'm going to Novosvillas to use their extensive library to get ahead of her."

"What do you think you will find there?" asked Samson his nose scrunched.

"Her plan is what it's always been," I said.

"To get the dark stones," finished Victoria

I pointed at Laxus. "We know where the Land stone is. My guess is that's the reason she hasn't attacked us already…"

"Is because her target is the Sea Stone," Said Laxus finishing my sentence. "If she gets that first, overpowering Mellissa and taking my stone will be a walk in the park."

"So you intend to discover the Sea stone's whereabouts and get it first?" said Samson.

I sat back in the office chair and interlaced my fingers. "Exactly."

He rubbed his chin. "That's a good plan."

"Why are you so surprised?" I asked

"I'm not, it's just with everything that's happened."

"You thought I would be a simpering mess." He grimaced. I waved my hand dismissively. "Well I was, up until last night, and I still sort of am but a more focused mess." I stood. "So does everyone know what they are doing?" They all nodded. I smiled and dismissed them. My heart was still heavy, and a pit of despair was within me but there was a rage bubbling deep within me. I needed to focus and force myself onwards, otherwise, I would be consumed by it.

Keeping it Together

Victoria

Victoria carefully folded her jeans and added them to her suitcase. The case laid open on the end of her bed, already half full. The rest of the large four-poster bed was covered in clothes, toiletries and makeup, all of which Victoria planned to take with her. She had also pinched one of Josh's prototype TVs that streamed films from the human world. After the meeting earlier she had followed him back to his office and persuaded him to hand it over. Victoria sighed. Going to stay at Greg's wasn't her idea of fun but the plan made sense. At least Mellissa was doing something other than hiding away in her room. Most of the top floor made up Mellissa's living space but Harkura and herself both had large bedrooms with ensuites, up here too. Victoria didn't mind not getting her own place in the elf city. It meant she was always nearby for when she was needed. It also helped that her room in the castle was giant compared to back home with her parents.

Victoria pouted placing her hands on her hips. She looked over everything she still had to pack. It wasn't going to all fit. She marched over to the large cupboard in the corner of the room and heaved a larger suitcase out. She turned around to see Harkura was sat on a stool next to her bed. She jumped and dropped the suitcase on her toes, crying out in pain. "Harkura what the hell." Victoria picked up the fallen suitcase and dragged it over to her bed. "How many times have I told you not to sneak up on me like that."

Harkura's forehead creased. "I didn't sneak. I simply walked in, pulled the stool from your makeup table over, sat down and watched you rummage through that cupboard."

"Yeah, but you did it without making a sound." This was constantly happening. Ever since they had moved into the castle, Harkura was always catching Victoria off guard. His movements were always so silent and as he lived next door to her, she was used to having his magical presence close by. She narrowed her eyes at him. "I may have to insist Mellissa get you a bell."

"I am sorry I startled you. I will try to remember to announce myself when I enter." He held a hand over his chest and looked at her sternly.

Victoria pushed the clothes on her bed to the side and sat in the small space she had created. She crossed her legs on the mattress and rested her hands on the clothes beside her. "Okay, what's wrong?"

Harkura folded his arms and frowned causing the sides of his eyes to crease. "I don't like being left behind. Mellissa keeps doing this. Making me stay and watch over Urbem Foilum when I should be by her side."

"You heard Mellissa. You're the only one she trusts to protect the city."

He stood and paced the length of the bed. "My job is to protect Mellissa not this city."

"Protecting this city is protecting her." Victoria pushed her hair out her eyes. "I have learnt that being the guardian to the keeper isn't as simple as staying by their side all the time."

He stopped pacing and looked at her, with his arms folded. "Then what exactly is our role."

"To be there for her in the way she needs." Victoria waved her hands about in the air. "Like how we train her to defend herself or the meditation techniques you have taught her. Those are things that have helped way more than us constantly trailing her."

"That makes sense." Harkura sat back down on the stool and pouted. "I just don't like her going off alone."

Victoria placed her feet on the floor. While still leaning on the bed she placed a hand on Harkura's shoulder. "For your information, Mellissa will not be alone, I will be with her. I will kick anyone's butt that dares cross our Queen, and I will look damn good doing it." Victoria winked and sat back on her bed.

Harkura chuckled. "Yes, you will."

"You staying here will allow Mellissa the space to heal and focus on stopping Humarya," said Victoria, "She wouldn't be able to do this if she didn't feel secure in the fact everything here was taken care of."

Harkura stood and patted Victoria on the arm. "I'm sure I have said this before but you are wise beyond your years."

"You have but I am happy for you to repeat it." The two guardians grinned at each other.

Harkura picked up a dress off the bed. "I see lots of clothes but no weapons. Are you not at least taking a dagger with you?"

Victoria chuckled. "I am the weapon remember."

Harkura smirked. "That you are but I just mean that we need to make sure Humarya is finished properly this time." He bent over and pulled a knife from his boot. He held the handle out for Victoria to take. "Here have this, I can spare one of my blades for you."

Victoria gently pushed his hand away. "I don't need it. I find creating weapons out of ice more convenient. And if I stab someone with an icicle it leaves very little evidence behind once it's melted."

"Very well." Harkura flipped the blade round and returned it to his hiding spot. He gently placed a hand over Victoria's. He stared at her, his indigo eyes serious. "But you will kill Humarya when our queen's gentle soul cannot?"

Victoria squeezed Harkura's hand. "I know what is expected of me and when the time comes, I will not hesitate to take the killing blow."

Harkura nodded, seemingly satisfied with her response. He began folding her clothes on the bed. "I will assist you with your packing."

"That would be nice." Victoria stood next to Harkura and together they folded her clothes and got them packed into her suitcases.

Victoria sat eating a custard-filled doughnut while she flicked through a magazine. Greg had gone out and brought all of Mellissa's favourite foods. Which was great because they were all things Victoria also liked. This stay might not be too bad if Greg was going to keep running around to every whim of Mellissa's. They had arrived just after six yesterday evening. The journey had been uneventful. Victoria had been given the largest of the guest rooms at the end of the corridor and Laxus was in the room opposite. She had unpacked, done a security sweep and gone to bed. Now she sat in Greg's kitchen at the table waiting for Mellissa to get dressed. Laxus sat across from her with a cup of coffee and a book he had borrowed from Greg's personal library. He may be over 200 years old but it seemed wrong for him to drink coffee when he looked 12.

Mellissa walked in with two hairpins in her mouth as she tried to tie her hair up in a ponytail. Victoria rolled her eyes. "Come here." She stood up and waved Mellissa over. Mellissa walked over to her and handed her the hair bands and pins. Victoria swiftly pulled Mellissa's curls into a high ponytail and slid the two pins in the front.

"Thanks," Mellissa pointed at the bag of doughnuts on the kitchen table. "Any of those left for me?"

"Yeah, and I made you a tea in a to-go cup." Victoria grabbed a travel mug off the kitchen counter and handed it to Mellissa, who had already stuffed a doughnut in her mouth.

Laxus got up from the table. "Are we off to the library then?"

Mellissa nodded. "Sorry for taking so long."

"What about Greg?" Victoria asked.

"He has just popped to city hall for work stuff." She shrugged. "He said he won't be long as he plans to work from home while we are here."

"Well, we better get moving," replied Victoria.

Laxus and Mellissa walked ahead out the house nattering about the book he had been reading. Victoria followed behind. She was shutting the front door when she heard the commotion. A crowd of people shouting Mellissa's name and the scream of her best friend. Victoria spun around magic forming in her hands. Mellissa was crouched on the ground her hands over her ears. Laxus stood in front of her arms wide as a group of people flashed their cameras at the gates to Greg's house. Victoria lunged forward her hands glowing. Ice shot forward and surged up the gate creating an ice barrier. She ran back to Mellissa and crouched beside her. "Common let's get back inside." Victoria scooped Mellissa up in her arms dragging her up onto her feet. She pulled Mellissa towards her wrapping her arms around her friend's back and supporting her weight. They managed to get back in the house before Mellissa crumpled back onto the floor in the foyer. Victoria shoved the door shut and locked it.

Mellissa sat on the floor her legs pulled up to her chest. "What was that?"

Victoria marched over to a window pulling the blinds back slightly and glared out the window. "The paparazzi."

"But why? They have never been like this before."

Laxus put his arm around her and patted her back. "You're relationship with Greg wasn't public knowledge before."

"Oh please," snapped Victoria, "they just want to get pictures of the grieving Queen." She flexed her fingers as magic surged through her body. "I should show them what happens to people who upset Mellissa."

"Victoria no." Mellissa grabbed her arm and looked up at her with wide eyes. "Please just stay here with me."

Victoria clenched her fists letting her powers fizzle out. "Fine but can we sit somewhere more comfortable than the floor."

Mellissa nodded and rubbed her eyes. Taking both her hands Victoria pulled Mellissa to her feet.

"I'll make tea," said Laxus. He went down the corridor to the kitchen while the girls walked into the lounge. Mellissa curled up on the sofa snuggling in between the pile of cushions, while Victoria worked on lighting the fire. She cursed a couple of times but then the fire took. She turned to join Mellissa on the sofa when she heard the front door open. She held her up hand in front of Mellissa. "Stay here." And was out of the room in a flash. The lounge door slammed behind her and ice was forming in her hand.

Greg dropped his keys as he put his hands up. "What have I done now?"

Victoria fired her ice at the floor. "It's just you. I thought one of those reporters was trying to get in."

"Oh, I've already contacted the authorities. They should be removed shortly." Greg picked up his keys and checked the front door was locked. He turned back around slowly his brows drawn together. "Nothing happened while I was out, did it?"

Victoria crossed her arms as she jutted her hip out to the side. "Only your vulnerable girlfriend having a bunch of cameras thrust in her face when we tried to go for a walk."

"Is she okay?"

"I'm not sure she will ever leave the house again but other than that she is fine."

Greg frowned. "That doesn't sound fine."

"You think." Victoria stepped forward jabbing a finger at him. "You better get the people of this city in line otherwise I will take matters into my own hands."

"Don't worry I'm on it. I'm pretty sure your ice wall on the gate will make people think twice. I had to shift into a bird to get in."

Victoria rolled her eyes. "Oh poor you."

Greg gave a dismissive wave of his hand. "Where's Mellissa?"

"Lounge."

"Thanks." He walked past her into the living room and Victoria followed. Greg kissed Mellissa's forehead and sat beside her. Victoria slumped down in the armchair closest to the door. A moment after Laxus came in carrying a tray with a teapot, cups and a plate of biscuits. Laxus placed the tray on the coffee table and began pouring everyone a drink. The four of them sat in awkward silence sipping tea. This morning's incident had shaken Mellissa. Victoria knew this meant their plan for library visits was ruined. If they were going to be stuck inside the whole time they were here, it was going to be unbearable.

Fragile

Gregory

Greg rushed around his office filling his bag with files and books. He didn't want to leave Mellissa alone for too long. If he was quick enough, he could be back before she woke up never knowing he had left the house. He paused looking down at the file in his hand. He didn't know what to do and he hated it. Sometimes Mellissa seemed like her old self, chatting and laughing with Victoria. Routing through his library and discussing books with Laxus. But then there were times he would catch her alone staring off into the distance looking lost. She didn't want to be left alone but kept sending Laxus and Victoria into the city. He tried to comfort her, but her mood was all over the place. He had asked her here, hoping to help her recover but sometimes it felt like she was pulling away from him. Greg shook himself back to reality and began packing his bag again. He still had work to do but he could do it from home. He would be there for her but wouldn't push too hard. Hopefully, if he acted as normal as possible, it would help her find her way back.

There was a knock on the door. "Come in," he said. In walked a tall but plump woman with mouse brown hair. Greg smiled at her. "Aunt Tilly, what are you doing here?"

She beamed at him. Her grey-blue eyes glowed. "I came to see you of course."

"You have never come to city hall before."

"Well, no, I don't like how formal this place is. It

reminds me too much of my big brother." Greg frowned at the mention of his father. Her hand shot to her mouth. "I'm sorry dear, I didn't mean it like that."

"It's fine. I was just grabbing a few things to work from home. Would you like to come to the house and talk over a cup of tea?"

She shook her head waving her hand at him. "Oh no, I heard about what happened to Queen Mellissa and I wouldn't want to intrude." Of course, she knew Mellissa was in town. Mellissa had been in Novosvillas less than 24 hrs before the whole city already knew she was there. Having such a spotlight on her wasn't going to make dealing with her grief easy. It was probably why she hadn't left the house all week. He had planned to get her away from the pressure of being queen. However, his people loved her and were massive gossips. His aunt touched his cheek. "It is lovely to see how much you care about her. That's actually why I'm here."

"It is?"

"Yes, all this gossip flying around about death is awful, but it got me thinking life is too short." She reached into her coat pocket and held a small box out to him. "I wanted to give you this."

Greg raised an eyebrow as he took the box from her. "What is it?"

"Open it." She smiled eagerly rolling back and forth on the balls of her heels.

He opened the box. Inside was a gold ring with an opal at its centre, with three small sapphires on either side of it. It sparkled in the light. Greg's jaw dropped as he looked at his aunt. She was looking up at him her eyes filled with hope. "It's very nice but why are you giving me this?"

"It has been in our family for generations, always passed down to the eldest child. When your father proposed to your mother, she rejected the ring saying she wanted something new, not some old granny's ring." Aunt Tilly put her hands on her hips frowning as if she could see his mother. She put her hand under his pushing the ring toward him. "Anyway, he gave the ring to me, as he wanted it to stay in the family but that was before he had you."

A bitterness rolled through Greg's stomach. His aunt's story showed just how selfish his mother was. Greg removed the ring from the box holding it up to the light. How could she have rejected something so beautiful? He shook his head; he didn't need to think of his mother right now. Greg carefully placed the ring back in the box. "Why give it to me now?" Greg asked, "Surely you want to give it to Cynthia or Samson."

"Rightfully, the ring should have been passed to you. Besides, I could be waiting years for them to have someone to give it to. Admittedly now may not be the best time or maybe now is exactly the time."

Greg put his hand on his aunt's shoulder. "Wait, what are you talking about?"

"You and Mellissa of course." She looked like she was about to start bouncing with excitement. "I'm giving you the ring so you can propose."

"What no- I mean-" Greg ran his finger through his hair. "We haven't been dating that long. It's too soon for all that."

"You love her, don't you?"

"Of course."

"Then what's the problem? When you know you've found the one why wait? Then when you have kids, you pass the ring on."

Greg waved his hands out in front of her. "Now you are moving way too fast."

"Oh, but I long for grandkids. As neither of my children seems inclined to give me some anytime soon, I will just have to fawn over yours." A big grin spread across her face. "I have no doubt the queen will make beautiful babies." Greg's face was on fire, he was sure the colour of his cheeks currently matched the red of his hair. His aunt wrapped him in a big hug. "Just think about it." She practically skipped out of his office having completed her task. Greg turned the ring box over in his hand. Aunt Tilly was getting ahead of herself, but she had been right about one thing, Mellissa was the one.

The walk home from city hall had seemed longer than usual. Greg's head was still spinning from his aunt Tilly's unexpected visit. As much as he loved Mellissa, now wasn't the right time. He patted the left side of his jacket and felt the box tucked away in the inside pocket. He would find a good hiding place for it later. As he walked through the door, Mellissa flew into his arms almost knocking him over. He stroked the back of her head. "I thought you would still be in bed."

She shoved him her face tight. "I woke up and you were gone. I came downstairs to find the house empty. Where have you been?"

"I just went to get some stuff from my office."

"Of course, it's always work with you."

"Can I please get in the house properly before you start shouting at me?"

She moved over to let him pass. "I'm not going to shout."

Greg shut the door. Taking her hand he led her from the foyer into the living room. "I'm sorry I went to the office without telling you, but I also went to the bakery on the way back." He held up a bag of pastries to her.

She snatched the bag and looked inside. A small smile crept onto her face. Sitting on the sofa she curled her legs up and glared at him. "This doesn't make everything okay. I was worried. You practically never walk with a guard."

Greg sat next to her. "Where are Laxus and Victoria?"

She plucked out a pastry and began pulling it apart, exposing its gooey apple centre. Flakes scattered all over the sofa. "They went to the library."

Greg sat beside her taking the one and only cinnamon swirl from the bag. "Why are they at the library?"

She made a clicking sound with her tongue. "For books."

"I have plenty of books here…"

Mellissa jabbed him in the chest with her finger. "Back to the topic of you walking around with no guard."

Greg sighed. "I have a guard. You know Luke."

"I don't see him much except when he is trailing you before and after council meetings."

"He still acts as my personal guard while I'm working." Greg shrugged. "When I'm not working I'm just me."

Her brows arched as she tilted her head. "What is the point of a personal guard that is only around when you're in the office? This whole house needs to have more security. It's huge and you're here all alone."

"My father didn't walk around with a fleet of guards so neither will I."

She dropped her food on the coffee table. "The first time I came here there was way more security. You had that fancy intercom on the gate. Now anyone can just walk on up." Greg went to talk but she held her hand up cutting him off. She looked at him her expression turning serious. "In addition, your father wasn't dating a person with a massive target on their back putting everyone they care about in danger."

Greg gulped. She sure knew how to make him feel guilty. He took her hands in his. "Don't think like that. You have not put me in any more danger than I would be in just being elder."

She shook her head. "Tell that to my dad."

"Okay if it will make you feel better, I will start having Luke escort me to and from work."

"What about the house?"

He kissed her cheek. "There isn't anywhere safer than by your side."

She poked his chest. "Don't sweet talk me and that is debatable. What about when I'm not here?"

"How about you always be here? Or at least we always be in the same place."

She pulled back, sitting up straight. "What?"

"I know this is random because I only just thought of it. You should move in here and I should move into your castle."

She ran her fingers through her curls as she bit her bottom lip. "How would that work with our respective responsibilities?"

Greg shrugged trying to look nonchalant about it, when inside he was relieved, she hadn't outright said no. "I don't know exactly but we would both be living between the two places. We could work out some sort of schedule. With our two cities now connected by a train line, it wouldn't be hard to travel back and forth. Flying would be even quicker."

"It sounds like it could work in theory, but I don't know if it would be so simple in reality."

Greg interlaced his fingers with hers, kissing her hand. "Wouldn't you feel better knowing I was always coming home to you?"

She narrowed her eyes at him. "Yes."

"Then isn't it worth a try?" He stood and kissed her on the head. "You don't have to decide now. Just think about it. I'll go make some tea." Greg walked out of the room. Asking her to move in hadn't been his intention, he had just blurted it out before he knew what he was saying. It was his aunt Tilly's fault. She had gotten into his head. As he walked into the kitchen, he froze looking at the back door. His stomach felt like it was in knots as he remembered what he had done. All those months ago after Humaraya's defeat, his mother had come to him and he hadn't got her arrested. He had let Gwendolyn go. Worse still, he had never told Mellissa about it. If it was revealed that his suspicions about his mother's involvement in Mr Hail's death were right, there was no way Mellissa would be moving in. His Aunt would have given him that ring for nothing, as he would lose Mellissa forever.

Greg stood in the sunroom looking out at the garden. He watched Mellissa running from Victoria. Even here she couldn't escape from training. Thick snow covered the grass. Greg shivered at the coldness creeping in threw the open door. Ice flew across the garden at Mellissa. She dived into a roll. As she rose, Greg felt the earth shake. Mounds of earth had sprouted all over his pristine lawn. Greg rubbed the bridge of his nose. They were going to destroy his garden.

Laxus walked out holding tightly to a book. His blue curls bounced as he strode over to Greg. "Have you seen Mellissa?"

Greg pointed out the window. Victoria had just been thrown into the air by a giant vine created by Mellissa. "Oh," said Laxus, "When Victoria is done crushing her, let her know I have something I'd like to discuss."

"Mellissa is doing pretty good." Just as Greg finished his statement, Mellissa went flying hitting the ground with a thud. He winced. Laxus turned to walk away. "Wait," said Greg, "What is it you want to discuss with Mellissa?"

"I'm not sure if I'm permitted to reveal that to you."

"Why wouldn't you be permitted? Mellissa and I don't have secrets."

Laxus raised an eyebrow. "Don't you? I know there are things you are keeping from her."

The back of Greg's neck prickled with sweat as he frowned. "Like what?"

"Things to do with Gwendolyn."
Greg gulped. He narrowed his eyes at Laxus. But the boy just smiled at him.

"Hey what are you two talking about?" Greg jumped at Mellissa's question. She stood in the doorway.

Laxus beamed at her. "Oh, nothing." He skipped out of the room leaving a shimmer of pixie dust behind.

Mellissa walked in and kissed Greg on the cheek. "Everything all right? You look pale."

"Yeah, I'm fine," Greg said. Mellissa tilted her head looking up at him. He took her hand. "Really I'm fine." He looked at her properly and his eyes widened. "I'm more concerned about you. Victoria is your guardian she isn't meant to beat you up." Greg cupped her chin with his hand and examined the big purple bruise down the side of her face.

"She needs to learn how to block," said Victoria coming in from the garden. "Other than that she did all right." She pointed at Mellissa. "Same time tomorrow." Mellissa nodded and Victoria walked further into the house leaving them alone.

"Sanum quid fit," said Greg. His hand glowed green

and he placed it over Mellissa's bruised face.

"It's not that bad," she said, "Victoria's right, I messed up and should have blocked."

"It will be healed in a few seconds." When he removed his hand her skin was back to its perfect soft brown colour. He kissed the side of her face he had just healed. She sat on the rattan sofa and curled her feet up beside herself.

Greg cleared his throat as he sat beside her. "How about we go out for something to eat later?"

Her gaze didn't move from the window. "I'm okay eating whatever your chef makes."

"Today is his evening off."

"Oh." She shrugged. "Well, whatever you cook then."

"We will probably end up with food poisoning if I cook."

She threw her arms down on the chair, swinging her legs round in front of her, getting up. "Fine, I'll cook."

He took both her hands before she could get away and pulled her back down to sit with him. "That's not what I meant. I just thought it would be nice to get out of the house. You've been couped up all week. You keep sending Victoria and Laxus places, but you just stay here."

"I was just outside." She pointed out the large windows of the conservatory.

"You and Victoria destroying my garden while training is not leaving the house."

"I'm not exactly some anonymous face in the crowd Greg." She cuddled a cushion tight and looked out at the garden. "I know everyone knows what has happened. I don't need them all staring at me. Pitying me. The poor broken queen."

"You're not broken."

"But I am Greg." Tears filled her eyes. "This isn't what I came here to do. I planned to go to the library, read books, and do research." She clutched the cushion tighter and growled in frustration. "Instead I'm sending Laxus and Victoria out to look things up on my behalf and hiding away here. I'm also panicking about every little thing you do. Because what if-" The tears burst through, streaming down her face. "What if you're her next target." She covered her face with her hands as she coughed threw her tears.

Greg pulled her close to his chest wrapping his arms around her tightly. "You don't need to worry about me. You are just in pain right now and its putting you in a heightened state of anxiety."

She buried her face in his chest. "There is a hole in my heart, and I don't know how to fix it.".

Greg stroked her hair. "You don't need fixing. You just need time." He kissed the top of her head. "How about we order in instead?"

She nodded as she wiped her wet cheeks with her sleeve. "I'll go see what menus I have." Greg got up and walked out of the sunroom to the kitchen. His heart ached but there was also a giant knot in his stomach. As he pulled open the kitchen drawer he felt nausea. What was it Mellissa had Laxus researching for her and why hadn't she told him about it before? Laxus was right. Greg was keeping secrets and so was Mellissa.

The Return

Mellissa

I sat crossed legged on the end of the double bed in the guest room currently occupied by Victoria. It was a large room which usually consisted of a bed, wardrobe, and dressing table. We had been here a week and the room was now overflowing with Victoria's dresses and shoes. Makeup and hair products covered the dressing table. She had moved a large body-length mirror into the room and installed one of Josh's prototype TVs, that run on magic but could stream movies from the human world.

"So basically, we know as much as when we started our research," said Victoria slumping down on the bed beside me.

"Not exactly." Laxus fluttered his pixie wings, reflecting colourful rays of light around the room. "I have a theory. We can't find much information on the dark stones because they were meant to be kept hidden from the world."

"Isn't that something we already know," I asked.

Laxus rolled his eyes. " Let me finish. Instead of looking for information about the dark stones, I looked more into the life crystals."

"We already know about the life crystals and how they are opposites of the dark stones," I said.

"To be precise the life crystals and dark stones are each other's balances." Laxus pulled a blue marker out of his trouser pocket and began drawing on the mirror.

"Hey don't ruin that." Victoria went to get up but I placed my hand on her arm.

"Just give him a minute to explain," I said. She folded her arms in a huff.

He stepped back from the mirror. He had drawn what looked to be elemental symbols. "We know the whereabouts of the land and air stone." Victoria and I nodded. He pointed at the symbol for air. "Humarya was the guardian of the air stone and she resided above the clouds. Which is also where the keeper of the sun crystal is believed to live. These two are each other's balances." He placed his hand over his chest. "I guard the land stone and in habit..." He looked wide-eyed at us.

"The earth," I said, "and you're my crystals balance."

Laxus' wings fluttered lifting him off the ground. "Therefore, the sea stone is the balance to the moon crystal."

"It's in the ocean." I smacked my forehead. "It's so obvious."

"But how are we meant to find the sea stone in the ocean," said Victoria, "It's not exactly the Heart crystals territory."

"Enlist the help of the sea king," suggested Greg. My heart stopped as I turned to see him standing in the doorway with his arms folded.

I jumped to my feet. "What are you- I thought you were working in your study."

"I was but I thought I'd pause for lunch. I came to see what you wanted to eat." Greg walked further into the room. He looked the board over. "So this is what you've had them going to the library for. Why didn't you tell me?"

I tugged at my hair. "I don't know."

"Because she thought you would stop her." Victoria was on her feet and glaring at Greg.

"I think Mellissa can talk for herself," replied Greg through gritted teeth. "I would like to talk to my girlfriend alone."

Victoria stepped in front of him eyes glowing icy blue. "I won't let you bully her into standing down."

"That's not my intention."

I pushed in between them. "Stop it." I took Greg's hand. "Common let's talk." I pulled him towards the door. Victoria came to follow but I shook my head. "It's fine." I led Greg down the hall to the other end of the house to his bedroom. I shut the door and sighed as I tried to think of what to say.

"Mellissa, why would you be researching the dark stones like this?" Greg asked.

"To get the last stone before Humarya does." I huffed as I threw my arms in the air. "Am I just meant to do nothing, like the council is?"

Greg massaged the bridge of his nose. "That's not what I meant. Why didn't you tell me when you know researching is one of my key skills?"

My jaw dropped, my anger dissipating as quickly as it had appeared. "Oh."

"Did you really think I would stop you?"

I shrugged. "I don't know maybe. You wouldn't let me talk to the guard." I pointed at him. "And never really want to talk about the missing stone."

Greg turned away from me and ruffled his hair. He kicked the bedpost as he muttered something under his breath. He slumped down on the end of the bed with one hand over his face. I stepped forward reaching out to him. "What's wrong?"

He put his hand out to motion for me to stop. "I need to tell you something." His serious tone had me frozen where I stood. My heart was pounding so hard that it was all I could hear. He looked up at me, his forehead creased, and his lips turned down. "The reason I've been so standoffish on the subject is because I think my mother may be involved in all of this."

"Oh thank God." My hand covered my heart as I sighed with relief. "I thought you had cheated on me or something."

"What no! Why would you think that?"

"You looked so serious, and your aunt doesn't like me. Your ex was throwing herself at you on news years eve." I waved my hands around gesturing to the whole of him. "I mean common you can get like any girl."

Greg jumped to his feet and grabbed me by the

shoulders. "I would never, none of those people matter. My other aunt is a big fan of yours." He rested his forehead on mine. "Most importantly, I love you."

"Why didn't you just tell me about your suspicions?" I asked.

"Because I didn't want you to hate me."

"Why would I hate you?"

"Because it's my fault, Mellissa."

"You don't control your mother's actions."

"You don't understand. I let her go. After everything that happened in the mountains, she came here begging me to go with her. I said no and kicked her out. I had the chance to detain her and get her arrested, but I didn't. Then the next time I catch wind of her is at the scene of your dad's murder."

My blood ran cold. The room span. "When you said you thought she was a part of everything, you really meant everything." I pushed him away from me.

"Mellissa I'm sorry," he said.

"You lied to me." I shoved him again. "To protect your murderer of a mother?"

Greg tugged at his hair. "No, it's not like that."

"Then what is it like Greg," I shouted.

"I was trying to protect you."

"Liar you just wanted to protect yourself."

His shoulders sagged. He looked defeated. "You're right. The only person I was trying to protect was myself. I thought if you knew what she had done I would lose you."

"You are not your mum. I'm not angry with you for what she did. I'm angry because you kept the truth from me. Even if it was only a suspicion, I had the right to know."

He reached his hand out to me but I slapped it away. "Anything else you're keeping from me," I asked.

"I visited Emerson in prison."

"How did you have time for that?"

He shrugged. "Flying gets you places quicker."

I snickered. "And you had the nerve to ask why I hadn't told you what we were doing."

"I know I'm the biggest hypocrite." Greg knelt in front

of me taking my hands. "I know saying sorry won't make things better but I am."

I shut my eyes unable to look at him. My heart was conflicted. Seeing him upset tugged at my heartstrings but the lies he had told filled me with a rage that urged to be released. I took a slow breath my jaw was tense. "I understand why you let her go." I said, "She is your mum and she had just come back from the dead. But the rest, you should have told me."

"I know I should have said something, but I was scared of losing you. I was stupid."

I pulled my hands from his. "I can't, I need some air." I ran out of the room, along the landing and down the stairs. I heard Greg shout after me but I just continued to run through the hall and out the front door. As soon as I saw the sky, I pushed off the ground and launched myself into the air. Flying off as fast as my magic would allow.

I landed with a thud and screamed into the open air. The ground shook and light radiated off me melting the snow on the ground. I had no idea how long I had been flying. I had just let the wind take me. Now I was in the middle of nowhere, with nothing but open land around me. I dropped to my knees and punched the earth creating fissures. My heart felt like it was about to burst as I screamed into the nothingness. Tears rolled down my cheeks. As I shook with rage, so did the ground beneath me. How could Greg keep this from me? He knew how much my dad meant to me. I clutched my hand to my chest and choked on my tears. If it was Gwendolyn who had murdered my dad, there was no way Greg, and I could continue as we were before. Could we move past this?

I looked up at the clear blue sky. "Oh dad, I could use some words of wisdom right now. You always knew the right thing to say." I curled in on myself hugging my legs to my chest. "I don't know what to do anymore," I whispered closing my eyes tight.

I jumped at the sound of my phone and communis ringing in unison. I must have dosed off as the blue sky was now dark and I was shivering, no longer surrounded by the warm light of my magic. My phone stopped ringing but immediately started again. I took my communis out of my pocket and answered the call. A projection of Victoria appeared. "I know I shouldn't have run off," I said.

"Mellissa, Humarya is in Perluves," Said Victoria.

My pulse quickened. "What?"

"We have just received an urgent call from Yuko, that Humarya was spotted on the beach by their city. She said they were sending troupes to intercept her."

"She can't do that. I need to go."

"Mellissa be careful. I won't be able to get there in time to back you up."

"I'll be fine." I ended the call. With a running start, I leapt into the air flying up above the trees, heading straight to Perluves.

The cold wind whipped at my face as I flew. I zoomed past the forest and hills. All I could hear was the air as it whizzed by me. As the ocean came into view, I slowed my speed. Black smoke twirled upwards. The tall buildings of the city were only just visible through the haze of smog. I leaned towards the trail of smoke following it to its source. Screams and shouts echoed down below. Flames danced across the buildings, engulfing the city. As I got closer, I could see people running and taking shelter from glass creatures. I landed with a thud, releasing a ray of light as I did, destroying all the creatures in range.

"It's the Queen." I heard someone cry. "We are saved."

I scanned the area. The streets were in chaos with people running all over. Shop windows had been shattered. Smashed glass was scattered all over the ground. Fire burst from one of the buildings to a chorus of shrill screams. Sweat dripped down my back and my breathing became sharp. My powers were useless against flames. I needed Victoria. My body went stiff as water gushed over me. The fire dwindled against the force. A group of water nymphs stood together pushing and pulling their arms back and forth in rhythm with one another. I let out a long breath and smiled. This was a city full of Water Nymphs, of course, they could handle a little fire.

My ears twitched at the sound of more screams. They were coming from uphill. I ran in the direction of the cries, taking out any glass creatures I came across along the way. I skidded to a halt when I saw her. My heart raced as my body tensed. There she was her wings black as the night and her long dark hair blowing in the wind. The armour she wore made her look like a fierce warrior. She was surrounded by water nymph soldiers. They had water whips wrapped around her arms, legs, and wings. They closed in around her. She tilted her head to the side and that's when I saw it. Round her neck was a yellow stone surrounded by shadows. The air stone. Her eagle eyes narrowed on me and she smiled. Shadows burst from her with a gust of wind. I threw my arms up creating a barrier of light. The soldiers were caught in the gust and thrown to the ground.

I lowered my arms as the wind died down. Humarya hovered off the ground with her wings spread wide. "Hello, little queen."

My heart almost stopped. The way she had greeted me sent shivers down my spine. Her tone was dark and her smile sinister. I shook my head. She was just trying to spook me. Holding my hand out to the right, the Heart crystal glowed and shot from round my neck to my hand transforming into staff form. I ran at her. Leaping into the air, power surged through me as I fired a bolt of lightning. She swiftly countered with a flurry of shadows. As our attacks collided a massive bang echoed through the city.

Humarya flapped her wings hard, slamming me to the ground with a burst of wind. I held my staff against my chest. Gritting my teeth, I surrounded myself with light and pushed my way through the gust. Twirling my staff, I launched myself into the sky. The air was alive with static energy as I brought lightning down on her. She screeched as she was struck and dropped to the floor. The moment her feet touched the ground, I called to the earth with my powers. Swishing my arms around, vines began wrapping around her. She struggled against them, but I just kept binding her. I landed in front of her, and she stopped struggling. The dark look in her eyes made me shudder. She grinned in her restraints. "I will be honest I am surprised to see you here. I thought you would still be wallowing in grief somewhere. Too broken to fight."

Rage boiled through me. I pointed my staff at her neck. "You're a monster. My dad had nothing to do with any of this."

She faked shock. "What did I do?" She smirked. "Oh, you mean your father's murder." Her eyes flashed yellow. "You took away my chance to see my beloved again, so I had someone killed that you loved. Hurts, doesn't it? But I'm not the one that killed him."

"Liar," I yelled.

"Please child. Why would I dirty my hands killing a lowly human?" Magic surged through me, causing the crystal to glow. I pressed my staff firmly against her neck. She laughed. "We both know you don't have what it takes. Or maybe you loved your father more than your mother."

"Shut up." I lifted my arm and pushed forward. The vines around her mirrored my movements slamming her against a wall. The creeping plants seeped into the wall crushing her against it.

She burst into laughter. "You know it wasn't even my idea to kill him. I had ordered her to kill your boyfriend but that little bird of mine still has a soft spot for him."

My arms sagged beside me. "What?"

"Little Bird chose to kill your father over your boyfriend. She guaranteed me it would leave you just as broken."

"Gwendolyn killed my dad." My ears rang. The world around me began to spin. Greg's suspicions were right. It really was his mum. I yelled as something draped around my legs burning my skin. Pain shot through me as I hit the ground with a thump. Shadows snaked around me. A talon wrapped around my neck, and I was yanked up.

Two yellow eyes peered at me. "but by that look on your face maybe I should have stuck to my original plan and killed your beloved."

Rage bubbled up to the surface. I screamed as I kicked my legs into her chest, engulfing my body in light at the same time. She stumbled back. I just managed to get my hands out in time, flipping myself over to land on my feet. "I won't let you hurt anyone else," I shouted.

She fired shadow balls at me, and I dispersed them with a wall of light. I clenched my fist shaking the earth and opening up a hole beneath her feet. She swiftly took flight. Quickly spinning her arms, she created a whirlwind that took my feet out from under me, throwing me into the air. As I began to fall back down, I threw my arms out to the side stopping my fall mid-air. Before I could fully regain my balance whisps of shadows slashed into my back. I crashed onto the ground. Clutching my staff, I released a pulse of light dispelling the darkness.

Humarya's voice echoed above me. "Until next time." and then she was gone.

I groaned as I pushed myself up off the ground. Tears threatened to fall. She had gotten away. I tightened my grip on my staff as my jaw tensed. I wouldn't let myself cry. My legs almost gave way as what Humarya had told me began to sink in. She hadn't killed my dad, but she ordered his death. Ordered her little bird Gwendolyn to do it. I dropped to my knees as the realisation swept over me. Gwendolyn had picked my dad's death over killing her son.

"Queen Mellissa are you okay?" asked one of the soldiers that had been on the scene when I arrived. He held his hand out to me.

I took it and he pulled me to my feet. "I'm fine." I gasped as Humarya's words echoed through my mind. *I should have stuck to my original plan and killed your beloved.* My chest tightened. "Greg," I whispered.

The soldier frowned. "Shall I take you to the high priestess? Do you need healing?"

I put my arm up stepping back from the soldier. "No, I have to go." I ran through the city once I had enough memento going, I soared into the air heading straight to Novosvillas.

I crash-landed in the front garden of Greg's property. I rolled up onto my feet not missing a beat and ran up the pathway. My head was pounding and in my rush, I kicked the door with my foot engulfed in light sending it flying. It landed with a thud on the stairs. Greg and Laxus came running out of the living room. "Mellissa, what is going on?" Greg asked.

I threw my arms around him letting out a sigh of relief. "You're okay."

"Of course I am. Why wouldn't I be?"

"Humarya. She said -- She threatened your life."

Greg held me at arm's length. "You fought her? Are you all right?" His eyes scanned my whole body.

Victoria came running down the stairs and pulled me into a hug. "Thank god you're okay."

"A little beat up but still standing," I said giving her a half-smile.

"Come sit down and I'll heal you." Greg took my hand and led me into the living room. He made me sit in the middle of the sofa in front of the fire. Once he had a good blaze going, he came over and started looking over my wounds. He started by healing the burns on my legs.

Victoria sat in the armchair to the left of me and Laxus perched himself on the arm of her chair. "I guess this confirms that Humarya stole the air stone."

I scrunched my nose. "Yep."

"I think it also backs up my theory," said Laxus, "The sea stone is in the ocean. Why else would she be in Perluves?"

"I think she is struggling with getting underwater," I said.

"Well her powers aren't exactly compatible with the ocean," replied Laxus rubbing his chin. "Did she say anything that might give us a clue to what she knows?" asked Laxus.

"Not really." My pulse quickened and I clenched my fists. "She just gloated about my dad's death." Greg gulped but didn't look away from the burns he was healing.

"What did she say exactly?" asked Victoria.

"She killed him to break my heart. Her original plan was to kill Greg, but his mum persuaded her otherwise." I looked down at Greg, his eyes locked on mine. "To save you, your mum killed my dad." Greg's eyes darted away from mine. He looked like he was about to vomit.

Victoria launched out her chair and grabbed Greg. She had him by the scruff of his neck. Her eyes glowed with magic and an icy breeze filled the room. "Your mum killed Mr Hail," she yelled. Greg shut his eyes as she punched him in the face. He toppled backwards falling to the floor.

"Victoria," I yelled placing myself in front of Greg with my arms out wide. "It's not his fault."

"If it wasn't for him, your dad would still be alive." Her words cut me like a knife.

"He didn't know," I said.

Laxus pulled at Victoria's arm. "I think we should go for a walk to calm down."

"I don't need to calm down." She yanked her arm free.

I placed my hand up in front of her and stared at her unblinking. "I think you do."

She glared at Greg, her top lip curled, and growled. She turned so suddenly her hair almost whipped me in the face as she did, and stormed out of the room, slamming the door behind her.

"I'll keep an eye on her," said Laxus.

"Thank you," I replied. He quietly walked out of the room, gently closing the door. My whole body was shaking. I wanted to scream.

"Why did you defend me?" Greg asked.

"I wasn't going to let her hurt you." I spun around to look at him. My head swam and nausea overwhelmed me. I placed my hand on my head as I fell into the sofa.

"Mellissa!" Greg scrambled over to me. His forehead creased and his stare stoic.

"I'm fine, just a dizzy spell," I said waving him away.

"I need to finish healing you. Lay on your front so I can look at the cuts on your back."

"Fine." I did as he asked laying across the sofa. He knelt

beside me and lifted the back of my top. I felt the warmth of his magic scatter over my skin and seep into my wounds. Slowly the searing pain disappeared.

"You know Victoria is right. Your dad's death is my fault," he said.

"No, it's not. You don't control the actions of your mother."

He rubbed the back of his neck, looking at the floor. "But it's because she chose to spare me that he is gone."

I pushed up off the sofa and swung my body around so I was facing him. "And if she hadn't I would have lost you instead."

Greg shrugged. I clenched my fists as anger swirled in the pit of my stomach. Greg's gaze remained on the floor. "Why didn't you tell Victoria that I already suspected my mum?"

"Because she would have gone ballistic." I sighed as I ran my fingers threw my hair. "I understand it better now. You were scared."

"Why are you being so understanding? With how you left earlier I thought you would hate me."

I slid off the chair onto my knees, so I was face to face with him. I cupped his face in my hands. "You're an idiot. I could never hate you because I love you. I know I don't say it enough. You tell me you love me like a thousand times more than I say it. But I love you with all my heart. I was mad but hate you?" I shook my head "No." I placed my forehead on his. "When she threatened your life the first thing I did was run back here. I couldn't bear it if I lost you."

Greg shut his eyes sinking towards me. "Everything is such a mess."

"Yeah." I snickered. "It is, but we'll get through this." I sat up straight and placed my hand over his heart. "No more secrets, we need to be on the same page."

Greg nodded. "No more secrets."

No more Lies

Gregory

Greg rushed through city hall. He walked straight past his office down the hall and knocked on his chief of staff's door. Mary opened the door, her brow creased as she looked at him. "I thought you were still working from home," she said.

"I am, sort of." Greg nodded towards her office. "Can I come in?"

She stepped aside. "Of course." Greg walked in and sat in the chair opposite her desk and waited as she walked around her desk and sat down. Mary's office was a lot cosier than his. It was a similar size, but the layout was more relaxed. She had one bookcase full of books and a filing cabinet, whereas his office walls was lined with books. There were two plants with purple flowers by the window. On the wall was a silver mirror with her two-degree certificates, one in politics and the other in business management, framed on either side. There was a picture of her kids on her desk. Greg always felt odd when he looked at it as her eldest was only a few years younger than him. "What's wrong?" Mary asked. She sat across from him leaning on her desk.

"I need your help, but this needs to stay between us." Greg had thought about this all night. He had hardly slept. Mellissa may not blame him for his mother's action but that didn't change the guilt he felt. He needed to do something to correct his mistake but so far, he had failed at finding anything useful on his own.

"You know I keep everything confidential. What is the problem?"

"My mother." Greg looked down at his hands in his lap. He knew what he wanted to say but for some reason, he was struggling to say the words.

Mary reached out across her desk patting his arm. "What has she done Gregory? She hasn't returned to Novosvillas?"

Greg shook his head. "No, she isn't in the city. She is assisting Humarya again."

"It's official then, Humarya has returned?"

"Yes, I'm sure the news will be everywhere before noon today. She attacked Perluves and Mellissa engaged her in battle."

"Is the queen all right?"

"Yes, she's fine."

"What do you want me to do then?"

"This isn't about Humarya. I need your help to track Gwendolyn." Greg's heart felt like a dead weight in his chest. He let out a long breath. "She murdered Mr Hail."

Mary gasped. She sat back in her chair her eyes wide. "You mean."

"My mother killed my girlfriend's father." Greg snickered. "How messed up is that?" Greg nodded keeping his gaze on the desk. He couldn't bear to look at the shock and pity painted all over Mary's face. "I need to find Gwendolyn and stop her. I'm responsible for what she's done and whatever she does next."

"Sir that just isn't true. Just because she is your mother doesn't make you responsible for her actions."

Greg gave Mary a weak smile. Mellissa had said something similar, but their words didn't take away this pain he felt. "That doesn't change the fact she is dangerous. Capturing her also takes away an ally for Humarya. Will you do this for me?"

Mary sat up straight and held her head high. "You can count on me."

Greg stood. "Be discreet. I might be paranoid but I'm sure they have eyes and ears everywhere." He turned to leave.

"Sir," Mary called after him. Greg stopped at the door and looked back at her. Her forehead was creased again. "May I ask if Queen Mellissa knows about all this?"

"She knows what Gwendolyn did, but I haven't told her about trying to find her yet." Mary nodded. Greg walked out of her office closing the door behind him. Hopefully, Mary would have better luck tracking Gwendolyn. He knew he could trust her, and she was more detached from the situation. She would be able to think more clearly than him. Ever since Gwendolyn had revealed she wasn't dead he had been in turmoil. He had been stuck not knowing what to do but now, he was sure. His mother needed to be stopped by any means necessary.

Greg riffled through the draws in his office. They were full of all sorts of junk, but he was sure he had put it in one of these draws. This was the other reason he had come here this morning. Anna, his father's ex-assistant had ordered a new security lock for the front gate months ago before she retired but he had never had it installed. It was fancier than the old one his father had used. This one worked on facial recognition and had an alarm that could be directly linked to the Novosvillas authorities. He hadn't felt he needed it, liking the idea of being easily accessible to his people but it would put Mellissa's mind at ease. Humarya's threat yesterday spooked her. He opened the next drawer and smiled. He picked a large white box out of his drawer and placed it on his desk. It was all still neatly packaged, untouched. He hooked the box under his arm and walked towards the door of his office. Just as he reached the door it flew open causing him to flinch. His aunt Josephine almost barrelled into him. She slammed the door shut. Greg stepped back as she stamped her foot and jabbed her stubby finger at him. "You ungrateful, spoiled boy. I always told your father he wasn't strict enough with you. Gave you too many freedoms."

"What on earth are you on about?" Greg clenched his jaw to stop himself from shouting. Who did she think she was barging into his office like this? She obviously hadn't known his father very well either. Greg had spent his whole life jumping through hoops for the man trying to win his approval. Greg had loved his father, but he hadn't been perfect.

She crossed her arms and stuck her nose up, tilting her head to the side. "After I went to the trouble of making your path cross with Lucy again and you threw the opportunity away."

"Then you admit to filling Lucy's head with lies and shipping her off to Urbem Folium."

"I told no lies. Your life is missing a good changeling girl. Lucy comes from a respectable family and most importantly she is from Novosvillas. You must see the two of you are a much better match than you and that elf." Her top lip curled, and she looked like she was ill when she said the word *elf.*

Greg ground his teeth as his grip tightened on the box he was holding. Heat spread up his neck. "Get out."

She scowled at him. "What did you say?"

"I said get out," replied Greg through gritted teeth.

"How dare you." Her voice rose as she became shrill. "You should show more respect."

"Like you have? Respect is earned and you have done nothing to deserve it."

"You pick that girl over your family."

Greg snickered. "We may be related by blood but you're not my family. As a child, you ignored me whenever you visited my father. You only became interested in me when you decided you didn't like what I was doing. Aunt Tilly doesn't have a problem with my relationship. She has always been supportive of me. She is my real family."

"She didn't, did she?" Josephine snarled as she pushed passed him and began riffling through the drawers in his desk. "Where is it?"

"Where's what?" Greg asked.

Her eyes locked on his. She looked like she wanted to

burn him alive. "The ring. That sentimental fool Tilly gave it to you, didn't she? Well, I say no. I will not let your grandmother's ring be given to an elf."

Greg took a deep breath and pointed to the door. "I'm going to say this one last time. Get! Out!"

"You're a disgrace to this family." She looked at him like he was a bad smell and stormed out of his office. Greg leaned against his desk rubbing the side of his forehead.

"Do I want to know what that was about?" Greg looked up to see Mellissa leaning against the open door.

"What are you doing here?" He asked.

She shrugged. "Checking you're still alive. Getting dirty looks from your aunt as I walk down the corridor."

"I'm sorry about her. I was just about to head back when she barged in here. She should be banned from city hall. I'll tell the guards on the way out."

He pushed off his desk and gestured for her to lead the way, but Mellissa didn't move. She looked at her nails as if they were really interesting. "So, is this how you do it? Get up stupidly early so you can sneak around behind my back. At least you're still in the city and haven't flown off to visit another prisoner."

Greg wondered how early she had woken up. She looked stunning in her pale green dress, lined with roses. Her hair was loose, and her curls hung perfectly down her back. Her eyes snapped to his. The anger in them made him flinch. "I came here for this." He picked up the box containing the new security system.

"And you had to come here before I woke up?"

He rubbed the back of his neck. "I also needed to speak to Mary."

"You could have just called her." Mellissa pushed off the door, walking slowly but purposely towards him. "You came here this early because the rest of your staff wouldn't have arrived yet and I couldn't overhear the conversation you had with her. You had hoped to be back in the house before I woke. Am I right?"

Greg pushed his fringe back. Sweat lined his forehead.

"Fine. I also came to talk to Mary about capturing Gwendolyn. I didn't want to upset you by bringing her up again so soon."

Mellissa's hand flashed in his face making him blink twice. "We said no secrets," she shouted, "You couldn't even wait a full day before you started sneaking about again?"

Tom walked up to his office, saw the two of them and walked away eyes wide. Greg manoeuvred around Mellissa and shut the door. The rest of his staff were starting to arrive. "That wasn't meant to happen," he said.

She whirled round her long hair whipping over her shoulder as she did. "Right because you were going to slip back into bed and pretend you hadn't left or where you going to claim to have been getting me breakfast?"

Greg winced at her words. "No, I was going to bring breakfast and tell you everything I had done. I'm sorry, I should have said something first."

"You're only sorry because I found out and that only happened because your aunt interrupted you. What did she want? To tell you to break up with the mess of an elf queen."

"That isn't exactly what she said but_"

"Oh, so she does want you to break up with me."

"I don't care what she wants." Greg went to touch her shoulder, but she swatted his hand away.

She slunk over to his desk leaning on it with her back to him. Her curls covered her face. "You only seem to care about your own agenda. Did you even listen to anything I said yesterday?"

"Of course, I did that's why I came to get this stupid security system."

She rolled her eyes, placing her hands on her hips. "That was just to cover up the real reason you came here."

Greg forced the lump in his throat down. She was right. He kept doing these things without fully thinking of the consequences. It was hard to predict how Mellissa would respond. He should just talk to her instead of constantly worrying about upsetting her as he seemed to do that anyway. "I just thought you would want to rest after your ordeal yesterday and we could discuss things later."

She glared at him her lips pressed tightly together. "Nice words Gregory but I will believe you when you actually act them out." Her voice got quieter. "You just keep lying to me and your aunt. Why do you keep letting her in if you don't care what she thinks?"

"Come with me now so I can talk to the guards about banning her." Greg grabbed her hand but she yanked it away.

"How do I know this is real and not for show? You lie to me. Your family whisper in your ear to get rid of me."

Greg grabbed her shoulders turning her round to look at him. "I would never do that because I love you."

She tilted her head looking down at the floor. Her voice was barely a whisper. "But why? I'm not exactly a lovable person."

"Of course, you are." He stepped back looking at her properly. She was withdrawing back into herself. Her gaze remained lowered, and her usual spark was gone.

She crossed her arms rubbing the sides of them. "I'm really not. I'm paranoid, jealous and possessive. Not exactly attractive traits."

"We all feel those things at times."

She scoffed. "Right, I've never seen you act jealous and crazy like me. You're practically perfect. You always have it together."

"I have been trained my whole life to pretend. I'm good at faking it." Greg pulled her towards him and curled a strand of her hair around his finger. "You are so much more than you think. You are sweet, funny, courageous and strong."

"I am not strong. I'm a mess. An angry mess. I'm mad at you, at your aunt." She paced the width of his office. "I'm in a fight with Victoria over you. I'm furious with what Humarya has done and Gwendolyn-" Her breathing became harsh. "Most of all I'm angry with myself for being weak."

"Mellissa-" She put her hand in front of his mouth stopping him from talking.

"Everything is too much. My feelings are too much. I feel like I'm about to burst. I just want to rage at the world." She shoved him but he barely moved. She did it again. He stepped back just to satisfy her. "You better stop all of this because I refuse to let you go."

She looked at him her eyes filled with tears, but they weren't tears of sadness but of the rage burning inside her. How hadn't he noticed this anger in her before? Greg frowned. "I don't want you to."

"Good because I won't. I don't care what your aunt says. Humarya can threaten all she wants but I won't let them come between us because you are mine okay."

Greg nodded. "okay." She rested her head on his chest and he hugged her tight.

"I'm going to stop Humarya," she said through her tears. "But you need to work with me on this not shut me out."

"Your right, you don't need me to protect you. We will be a team on this." He brushed her hair from her face. "And just for the record, you are also mine, right?"

She went up on her tiptoes and pressed her lips to his. Her kisses tasted of her salty tears. As she pulled away, she glared at him. "I hate you so much sometimes."

He took her hand and kissed the back of it. "I love you too."

They left city hall and walked back to the house. He made sure to talk to the guards about his aunt Josephine on the way out. His original plan to be in and out without being noticed had been ruined but maybe that had been for the best. He did need to stop this. It wasn't good for him or their relationship. What Mellissa didn't realise was the whole reason he was doing all this was because he was paranoid and possessive. Paranoid about his mother's actions. Possessive over Mellissa. He had been so focused on trying to protect Mellissa and help her with her pain that he hadn't noticed he had begun to spiral. She didn't need him to protect her, she just needed him to be there, and he needed her, much more than she realised.

Council Meeting

Gregory

"Mellissa, wake up," Greg said gently shaking her shoulder. She slapped his hand away and rolled over. He climbed over her and on his hands and knees bounced on the bed.

She shoved him over. "Fine, I'm awake. What do you want?" she snapped glaring at him.

Greg sat up on the bed. "A council meeting has been called to discuss the attack on Perluves."

"I would rather you left me to sleep."

"You don't have to come. Your two-week compassionate leave isn't up yet but I've learnt my lesson and I'm telling you where I'm going."

She sat up and stretched her arms out to the side. "I'm surprised it took them so long to call this meeting."

"It's only been a day."

"They have called meetings over less important stuff in a few hours before." Greg couldn't disagree. She tumbled out of bed and pulled a towel out of the cupboard. "I'll be ready in twenty minutes."

She walked into the ensuite bathroom and Greg followed. "You don't need to worry; I have already called Luke and Tom. They will be coming with me."

"Oh wow, your assistant and one guard." She hopped in the shower pulling the curtain shut. He was hit in the head by her pyjamas as he heard the squeak of the tap turning.

"There is plenty of security around the council building." He yelled over the sound of running water. "You stay here and spend the day with Laxus."

"You're the one that said there was nowhere safer than by my side. Laxus will just have to come with." He sighed. That also meant Victoria would be coming. She still hated him. Mellissa's head popped around the shower curtain. "Are you getting in or are you just going to stand there?"

He looked down at his shirt and tie. He had showered and dressed ready for the day hours ago. Her long curls clung to her cheeks. A second shower wouldn't hurt.

They arrived at the council building just in time. Greg tried to hurry them along, but Mellissa was in no rush. She casually strolled along chatting to Tom. Greg stopped at a cupboard pulling two senior council robes out. He draped one over Mellissa's shoulders and put his own robe on as they walked down the final corridor. Neatening his robe, he walked into the meeting room.

"Ah Gregory, now that you're here we can begin," said Lady Gabrielle. "Oh, and Queen Mellissa I wasn't expecting you." Mellissa and Greg took their seats on opposite sides of the table.

"Why may I ask was the Queen not expected?" asked Lee with a sour look on his face.

Lady Gabrielle looked at Lee her lips forming a small line. "She still has a few days of compassionate leave left." She turned to Mellissa giving her a small smile. "But it is good of you to come in anyway. It is my understanding that you arrived on the scene after the attack began."

Mellissa nodded. "I did."

"Good. We will hear from Yuko first, and then you can tell us about your encounter with Humarya." Lady Gabrielle sat in her seat at the head of the table and nodded to Yuko.

Yuko cleared her throat. "Humarya was first spotted over the ocean. I led a group of soldiers to apprehend her. She appeared to be searching for something and didn't notice us at first. However, we were quickly overpowered. She then went from the coast into the city and began attacking our people. I sent word to Kai, and he deployed every available guard to protect them. I was still by the sea when I saw Queen Mellissa fly over, but it is my understanding that she fought Humarya off, protecting our city."

Lee grunted. "But you didn't see her do this."

Yuko frowned. "No, but a large number of our citizens and soldiers did."

Lee thrust his hand in my direction. "But she didn't capture the fugitive."

"I would have liked to see you do a better job." Yuko's brows drew together as her top lip curled. "Oh, but you are too busy sitting in your ivory tower to come help the water nymphs.

Lee's nostrils flared. He was about to say something when Lady Gabrielle raised her hand. "Enough," She said, "this is no time for bickering. These are dangerous times. Humarya is ruthless and unpredictable." Lady Gabrielle interlaced her fingers as she rested her elbows on the table. "Mellissa, did Humarya reveal anything to you during your fight that may give us a hint as to what she is planning."

Mellissa shook her head. "She seemed more interested in trying to get in my head. She mostly taunted me and admitted to having ordered my dad's death." She paused looking Greg in the eye. She lowered her head. "She didn't reveal anything useful to me."

Greg scratched the back of his neck. She hadn't mentioned his mother. It was already known by everyone here that Gwendolyn had faked her death and had betrayed them along with Emerson. Greg sat up straight. "Maybe I should talk to Emerson again. Being imprisoned seems to have changed him. He may be able to shed some light on Humarya's way of thinking."

Lady Gabrielle rubbed her chin. "Maybe he might know why she attacked Perluves. She never seemed interested in the water nymphs before."

"It's because she wasn't looking for the sea stone before." Said Mellissa. Greg's forehead creased as he looked at her. Mellissa interlaced her fingers as she leaned on the table. "Humarya knows Laxus is under my protection so has turned her attention to the third and final dark stone instead."

"Of course, there is a dark stone in the ocean." Lady Gabrielle said. "It would be the stone to balance the moon crystal. Perhaps contact with King Radius should be made."

"Agreed," Yuko said, "but what about the pixie boy? Humarya may not be after him right now but surely she will still want the land stone."

"You're right, we need to hide him away securely. Where is he now?" asked Lady Gabrielle.

"He is currently eating cake in the tea rooms with Victoria and Greg's assistant Tom," replied Mellissa.

"He has been staying with us in Novosvillas," said Greg.

Lady Gabrielle interlaced her fingers. Leaning forward she looked at Greg. "I think being with you and the queen is too obvious."

"May I make a suggestion," said Hogan, "The boy should come with me to the caves. They are mighty hard to navigate for anyone who isn't a dwarf. Also, Humarya won't be able to spread her wings down in our tunnels."

Everyone was silent for a moment. Greg smiled. "That's a really good idea, Hogan."

"Are we seriously going to trust the safety of that boy to the dwarfs?" Lee thrust his finger in Hogan's direction. "Especially as their leaders are hardly ever sober."

Hogan thumped his fist on the table. "I will have you know I do some of my best thinking after a few whiskeys, but I also know when to get serious. My tunnels are the last place that bird woman will think to look for the pixie for the very reasons you stated Lee."

"I am inclined to agree with Hogan." Said Lady Gabrielle, "The tunnels will be the perfect hiding place. All in favour of sending Laxus to the caves raise your hand." Everyone put their hand up except for the two witches at the table. Lady Gabrielle turned back to Mellissa. "Will you make contact with King Radius to see what he knows about the sea stone?"

Yuko raised her hand. "May I also request that Queen Mellissa, inform the King she will be sending me to the sea kingdom."

"Why do you want to go into the ocean Yuko?" asked Lady Gabrielle.

"I highly doubt that King Radius will have much knowledge of the sea stones' whereabouts. So, I will volunteer to go look for it. If we find it first hopefully, we can keep it from Humarya."

"I wouldn't feel right sending you alone."

Greg tilted his head. Yuko was right. King Radius wouldn't know much about the sea stone. The only reason they knew where the land stone was, was because Laxus had sought out Mellissa. They would have to find its protector themselves and Yuko couldn't do it alone. "I'll go with her," Greg said.

"Are you sure Gregory?" asked Lady Gabrielle.

"Yes. I'm good at research. I'll be able to help Yuko."

"No," Shouted Mellissa, "This is insane."

"Why? You know it makes sense," Said Greg.

"How does it? Radius has his own people that can deal with this."

"I thought you would be happy that we are all being more proactive this time."

Mellissa snorted. "What you call proactive, I call unnecessarily putting your life at risk."

"Isn't that what you are always doing?"

Lady Gabrielle stood. "I think we are getting sidetracked. Maybe we should vote on it."

"No, because he's not going," snapped Mellissa.

Greg gritted his teeth. "You don't get to decide that."

Lee snickered. "Maybe we should revisit my motion about the relationship between the two of you being inappropriate."

"Shut up lee," Mellissa said. "Neither of them should go. I can't protect them in the ocean. Besides, I didn't realise water nymphs could breathe underwater."

"Not many of us can," said Yuko, "it is an ability many of us lost years ago but it is a rare talent I still possess."

Mellissa shook her head. "I still don't like it."

Greg looked her straight in the eye. He could see the anger flaring in them, but he could also see she was worried. "King Radius is the keeper of the Moon crystal. His power equals yours; we will be perfectly safe."

"What about when you are between the land and sea kingdom?"

"Mellissa you are being crazy."

"And you're being an idiot." Greg heard Hogan chuckle beside him. This wasn't the place for this argument.

"Well as Lady Gabrielle said. We should vote. Who is in favour of Yuko and I going into the ocean?"

Lee swiftly raised his hand, followed by Greg and all three water nymphs. Lady Gabrielle reluctantly raised her hand, followed by three others. The only ones that didn't were Mellissa and the two dwarfs.

"It looks like we are going," Greg said.

Mellissa rose to her feet slamming her hand on the table. "It is your life Humarya threatened not mine." Her eyes flashed green, and a crack spread along the table. She turned on her heel and stormed out slamming the door behind her.

Greg rose from his seat, but Lady Gabrielle placed her hand on his arm. "If there isn't anything else, this meeting is adjourned." Everyone slowly trickled out. Greg remained in his seat. Once everyone was gone, Lady Gabrielle grasped his hand. "What did Mellissa mean about Humarya threatening your life?"

"It's nothing. Humarya was just messing with her."

"Humarya already killed Mellissa's father, you shouldn't take this threat so lightly. There is no one else closer to her now than you."

Greg pushed his fringe to the side. "It was Gwendolyn who killed Mellissa's father."

Lady Gabrielle's eyes widened. "She what? How long have you known this?"

"Humarya told Mellissa. I don't know why she didn't

mention it in the meeting."

"Because she loves you." She tugged at his hands making sure he was looking at her. "Are you sure this is the best course of action?"

"You can't change your mind now, we already voted."

"That was before I knew about the threat to your life." Lady Gabrielle sighed, her shoulders sagging. "I couldn't live with myself if something happened to you and poor Mellissa. Gregory, she has just lost her father are you really going to put her through this?"

Greg gently took her hand. "You don't need to worry about me. I fully believe Mellissa will stop Humarya, so nothing will happen to me. I will talk to her and smooth everything over."

"Oh Gregory, I don't think it will be that simple."

Greg's stomach twisted. It felt like his guilt had just stabbed him in the gut. "I know but this feels right. At first, I thought if I tracked down Gwendolyn that would help us to stop Humarya." Greg tapped the table vigorously. "But now my gut is telling me this is the path I need to follow."

Lady Gabrielle sighed as she placed her hand on his shoulder. "Very well. I just hope you know what you're doing."

Lost Heart

Mellissa

My heart was pounding and my face warm. I had stormed out of the meeting but now I wanted to turn back around and shout at everyone in that room. Clenching my fists I marched on letting my feet guide the way. How could they vote for that? At least Hogan and Caleb had seen sense. This plan was too dangerous. The risk was unnecessary. Radius was perfectly capable of helping us without Greg and Yuko travelling there. I slammed through a door, finding myself in the courtyard where the fountain with the statue of Freya at its centre was. I sat on the edge of the fountain looking up at the sculpture. I bet Freya didn't have a council that constantly voted against her. I sighed looking at my reflection. Greg was such an idiot. He had promised we would work together on this and then he goes and volunteers to go off into the ocean with Yuko. He could never call me reckless again after this stunt of his.

"There she is." I jumped at the sound of Victoria's voice. I almost fell into the fountain as she hugged me. She held me at arm's length and scowled. "Why'd you storm off?"

"I just needed some air," I said.

Laxus sat on the edge of the fountain. "Is that council being ungrateful about you saving them again?"

"No. Greg is just trying to get himself killed."

Victoria sat on the other side of me and crossed her arms. "Good riddance to him then."

"Victoria!" I said.

Laxus placed his hand over mine and smiled at me sweetly. "What exactly is it that he is doing?"

I leaned back on my hands looking up at the clear blue sky. "Greg and Yuko have volunteered to go to the sea kingdom to search for the sea stone. Greg seems to have forgotten that Humarya may be targeting him next."

"Why is she going after him?" asked Victoria.

"To get to me of course." I pressed my fingers to the side of my forehead. "This is all so exhausting."

Victoria hung her arm around my shoulders. "How about we go to the tea rooms and get some cake? Then we can talk about what an idiot Greg is."

"Sounds good." Victoria led the way to the tea rooms. As we reached the entrance Greg walked out. "There you are. I've been looking for you." He looked from Victoria to Laxus.

He took my hand. "Can we talk?"

Victoria stepped in between us. "She won't be going anywhere alone."

I pulled her back. "Victoria it's all right. You and Laxus go order us something. I will be in, in a moment." Victoria glared at Greg. Laxus took her hand and led her into the tea rooms, leaving me with Greg. I folded my arms. "So, what do you want to talk about? Going to tell me how crazy I'm being?"

"You did call me an idiot." I narrowed my eyes at him. He pulled me to the side. "I'm sorry. That's not what I meant to say."

"Then what did you mean to say?"

"I'm sorry about surprising you like that in the meeting. I wasn't thinking."

"That much is obvious. So have you come to your senses?"

"Mellissa, I'm still going."

I threw my arms down beside me. "Then there isn't much to talk about. You know you are just full of it. You say one thing, then do another."

"I'm trying to do what's right. There wasn't time to talk

about this first."

I snickered as I folded my arms jutting my hips out to the left. "You didn't need to volunteer then and there like that. Others could go. It doesn't need to be you."

His jaw tensed. "Would you send someone else in your place?"

"My role in this is completely different to yours."

He pointed at the crystal hung around my neck. "You have that and think it makes you invincible. Why are the risks I take any different from you?"

I clasped the crystal tightly resisting the urge to throw it at his head. "That is not what I think. You know the Heart comes with responsibilities I can't escape. You have a choice. I don't."

He clenched his fists walking away and then coming straight back. "You won't be happy until I'm hidden away at home while you do everything."

I slapped the finger he wagged in my face away. "Isn't that what you've had me doing while you've been secretly investigating Gwendolyn? I don't expect you to sit around at home waiting for me but I do expect you not to throw yourself into danger on a whim. This mission isn't necessary."

"I have thought about the danger." Greg sighed as he rubbed the bridge of his nose. He gently grasped my shoulders looking me in the eye. "Think of it like this, Humarya is a creature of the sky. Her abilities are not compatible with the sea. If I'm in the ocean she can't come after me." I shut my eyes. It didn't matter what reasoning he came up with, this just didn't sit right with me. Greg pulled me into a hug, and I breathed in his scent. His warm embrace almost had me crumbling into his arms. He stroked the back of my head. "It wasn't my intention to upset you."

I pushed him away. "But you did anyway. Humarya may not be able to follow you under the sea but Gwendolyn can."

"I can handle my mother." I shook my head. He placed his finger under my chin tilting my face upwards. "Just trust me."

My heart fluttered at the glimmer in his eyes as he looked at me. I gritted my teeth pushing my feelings down. I wouldn't let him sway me like this. Victoria called my name. I turned to see her leaning against the door frame into the tea rooms. She nodded behind her. "We got you some cake."

"I'm coming." I walked towards her, but Greg grabbed my wrist.

"Wait. Are you still coming back to Novosvillas with me?"

I shrugged. "I don't know. Is there any point in me being around when you never listen to anything I say?"

He stroked my cheek. "Don't be like this."

I shook his touch off. "I need to think." I put my hand between us. "Away from you."

I followed Victoria into the tea rooms. Laxus sat at a table with two pots of tea and slices of strawberry cake. I sat in between Victoria and Laxus. He poured me a cup of tea. Looking down at my cup, I felt split. I didn't know whether I should just go home or not. It didn't feel right to leave things like this between the two of us. However, all Greg did at the moment was infuriate me. He didn't listen. I might achieve more back home. It would all depend on how mad I still was by the time we needed to get the train.

Understanding

Victoria

Victoria stirred her tea while watching Greg try and smooth things over with Mellissa. They had found the perfect table tucked away in a corner but still with a view out into the corridor where she could keep an eye on her little queen. She gritted her teeth resisting the urge to go and shout at him on Mellissa's behalf. This was something the two of them had to resolve themselves, she shouldn't intervene. Laxus sighed beside her. She raised an eyebrow as she took in the boy's glum face. If he hung his head anymore his face would be in his drink. "What's up with you?" Victoria asked.

"Hogan has just informed me I am to go stay in the caves," Laxus replied.

"As in without us?" she asked.

Laxus nodded while frowning. "It seems the council have decided it is safer for me not to be by Mellissa's side any longer."

"Oh cos the Hogan will do a better job protecting you than Mellissa."

"Mellissa's job is far bigger than just protecting me. So if I am to be separated from her, hiding underground would be safer than staying above ground."

"I guess that makes sense. It'll be weird not having you around." He smiled at her, picked up his fork and dug into one of the slices of strawberry cream cake. The other slice was for Mellissa. Victoria glanced back out at the corridor. Greg had his finger under Mellissa's chin and she was staring up into his eyes. "Argh." She groaned. He was doing that thing that turned that girl into jelly. Victoria really didn't understand the appeal. Objectively, she knew Greg was good looking, but the way Mellissa could just get lost in his eyes was nauseating. It was like he had this hypnotic effect on her. "I can't take this anymore." Victoria rose from her seat. Laxus glanced up at her eyebrow raised. She pointed at the two teapots on the table. "Her tea is getting cold." Victoria strode over to the entrance of the tea rooms and leant her shoulder on the door frame. "Mellissa." She nodded towards their table in the tearoom. "We got you some cake."

"I'm coming," Mellissa said. She smoothed her dress down with her hands and stepped towards Victoria. Greg grabbed her wrist and muttered something Victoria couldn't hear. Victoria's jaw tensed resisting the temptation to just drag Mellissa away.

She wasn't sure what Mellissa said to Greg, but she turned away from him and walked towards the tea rooms. Victoria led the way over to their table. The two of them sat down. Mellissa sat nibbling at her thumb nail. Victoria pushed the plate with the strawberry cake on towards her. "Here I know it's one of your favs."

Mellissa looked at the cake and grinned. "Thanks."

Laxus picked up one of the two teapots and poured a cup handing it to Mellissa. "So what did he have to say for himself?"

Mellissa mouth was stuffed full of cake. She held up a finger to 'gesture one moment please'. Victoria rolled her eyes at the mess the girl had made in the minute she had been sat at the table. Mellissa wiped her mouth on a napkin. "He apologised for catching me off guard but says he is still going, evening knowing the danger." She looked down at her hands as she twisted the dirty napkin between her fingers. "He just wants to feel like he is doing something to help with the situation we are in."

"You know he feels a lot of guilt about his mother," said Laxus, "This may be his way of making up for what has happened."

"but he shouldn't feel guilty. He didn't commit her crimes." She looked at Victoria, "He didn't even know about them until after the fact."

Victoria tapped her fingers on the table, holding back the snide comment she had wanted to make about Greg and his murderous mother. Looking at Mellissa's wide pleading eyes made her heart soften. Victoria took a sip of her tea. "Did you forgive him?" she asked.

"Not really, I told him I needed time to think."

"But you're going to?"

Mellissa wrapped her hands around her cup of tea but didn't take a sip. "Forgivingness isn't the issue, acceptance is. I don't think this is something we will agree on but I'm gonna have to accept this is his choice."

Victoria bit her lip and scrunched her nose. "I kind of get where he is coming from."

"You do?" said Mellissa and Laxus in unison.

Victoria shrugged. "Yeah. I mean he has been brought up being told he is meant to be someone important and well that happens," She waves her hand around in the air. "But then he falls in love with a girl who turns out to be this wicked badass of a queen. You also find out that your mother is actually one of the bad guys among other stuff. It can make you question your role in things."

Mellissa stared at her mouth a jar, just blinking. Victoria looked down at her drink watching what remained swirl as she stirred it. "I understand that feeling because sometimes I question my role as a guardian. I mean you are so powerful, what exactly am I protecting you from?" Victoria smirks. "But then you do something stupid, like falling out a tree of your own creation and I remember why I'm needed."

Mellissa reached across the table and gently squeezed Victoria's hand. "I didn't realise you felt like that."

Victoria looked up at her friend and sighed. "The thing is you shine so bright that those around you can sometimes feel inadequate."

"I'm sorry. I never meant to."

Victoria held tight as Mellissa went to pull her hand

away. "I know you don't do it on purpose. You literally can't help being the keeper of the heart." Victoria released Mellissa's hand and leaned back in her chair. "All I'm saying is that I may have been too harsh on Greg and I actually can understand what he is feeling."

"And everything with his mum" Mellissa started to say but trailed off.

"Will have just amplified that feeling of uselessness."

Mellissa chewed on her bottom lip. "So what should I do?"

Victoria shrugged. "I can't tell you what to do but Greg has always been a good researcher. I mean he found you when so many others had failed."

Mellissa stood so suddenly that her chair rattled behind her. "I need to talk to Greg." She walked around the table and wrapped her arms around Victoria's neck hugging her. "Thank you." She pulled away and locked eyes with her ice guardian. "If you ever find yourself questioning your role again, just know I will always need you as my best friend." Mellissa hurried out of the room and down the corridor towards the council members' offices.

Laxus cleared his throat. "Are you feeling okay?"

"Oh shut up." Victoria gulped down the rest of her drink and held the empty cup out to Laxus. "Pour us another."

He folded his arms. "Manners young lady."

"Please," She said extending the second half of the word.

Laxus smiled picking up the teapot and pouring her a drink. Victoria sighed. That talk left her feeling so exposed. But hopefully what she had said helped sort things in Mellissa's head. If it had, the icky feeling she felt right now, was worth it.

Confusion

Mellissa

I ran through a grey mist. The wind was blowing hard, I couldn't hear anything over it. My vision was blurred by the fog. But through the dank greyness shone a bright light. I ran towards the light and skidded to a halt coming face to face with a wall of water. My heart felt like it might stop beating. I screamed as the water came at me. Flames blasted through the water turning it to vapour. Matt grabbed my wrist. "Mellissa you can't freeze at the sight of the water."

"But water shouldn't move like that," I said.

"No, it shouldn't," Matt said, "Which is why you have to overcome it."

"How?"

A strong gust slammed into us, blowing me and Matt apart. I landed with a thud. The mist returned shrouding everything in grey. "The darkness is back," Matt shouted. The water rose again. I threw my arms up creating a barrier of light. The water sizzled away.

I lay awake unable to sleep after my weird dream. Greg was fast asleep beside me. He looked so peaceful as I listened to his shallow breaths. It wasn't fair that he could sleep so soundly, while I was here wide awake. My mind wouldn't shut up. That dream was a sign that something bad was going to happen. What Victoria had said in the tea rooms had made me see things from a different view, but I still felt conflicted. I had contacted King Radius as the council had wanted. As Yuko had theorised, he hadn't known anything about the sea stones' location but was happy to help. He had been very enthusiastic about me sending two of my most trusted council members to assist him. They were going in two days and it filled me with dread. I sighed, why couldn't I be a leader like Radius? He knew what he was doing and seemed so sure of himself, whereas I was anything but. I pressed my palms over my eyes. I just wanted to protect everyone. If something happened to Greg, I wouldn't be able to bare it. I slammed my hands down on the mattress and pushed up out of bed, giving up on sleep.

"Hey, where you going?" asked Greg leaning on his elbows. I was sure he had been asleep.

"Downstairs," I said, "I can't sleep."

"What's wrong?" he asked.

"Nothing."

"Mellissa." He said my name in that I know you're lying tone of his.

"Everything is wrong Greg. This whole situation we are in. The fact that you're leaving in two days."
Greg pulled me back into bed. I laid my head on his chest and he wrapped his arms around me. "I'm sorry," he said.

"It doesn't matter how many times you say that it doesn't make this better."

"I know but this is something I have to do."

"Why is it? Why do you have to go? There are plenty of other changelings that could accompany Yuko."

He ran his fingers through my hair. "I have to do something to help because I'm partly to blame for all this."

I sat up and frowned. "No, you're not. None of this is our fault. This is all completely out of control."

Greg sat up and rested his elbows on his knees. "After I let my mother go. She went looking for Humarya. I know this because she asked me to help her. She wanted me to leave you. I knew what she was planning, and I didn't stop her. I allowed her to help Humarya with her plans.”

“Greg, do you remember just after we first met?” He nodded as I interlaced my fingers with his. “You told me all I had to do was go reinforce a seal on a tree.”

“Don’t remind me. That all went terribly wrong.”

“Exactly. You didn’t know things weren’t going to be that simple, the same way you couldn’t foresee any of this happening.”

“I still can’t help feeling responsible.”

I turned his hand over in mine and traced a circle on his palm with my thumb. “The ones who are responsible are Humarya and Gwendolyn. You don’t have to do this.”

“If this mission is so dangerous, why aren’t you trying to stop Yuko from going? You can’t let our relationship cloud your judgment.”

“You know that’s not fair.” I poked him in the chest and pouted. “The situation with you and Yuko is completely different. Yuko doesn’t have a target on her back. Besides if it was up to me this whole mission wouldn’t be going ahead.”

“I told you I will be perfectly safe in the ocean.”

I rolled my eyes. “And Humarya’s powers don’t work underwater. I know but that doesn’t make me any less worried.”

Greg scooped me up in his arms pulling me close. “It’ll be fine. We’ll find the sea stone and we will be back in no time.”

“You know things are never that simple.”

“Okay so it might be a bit more complicated than that but I’m sure while I’m gone you will be getting into all sorts of trouble on land.” He shrugged and flashed a cheeky grin at me. “For all we know by the time I return, you may have already captured Humarya.”

I pushed his fringe out of his eyes. Those green eyes of his always melted my heart. “I don’t want to lose you.”

He cupped my face in his hand. “You will not lose me.”

“You can’t promise that.”

Wrapping his arm around my waist he tugged me close. Resting his forehead on mine, his lips gently brushed mine. “I will always find my way back to you no matter what." He stroked my cheek softly with his thumb. I bit my bottom lip as I placed my hand on his chest. I could feel his heart hammering rapidly. With his hand cupping the back of my head, he leaned in and kissed me. I laced my arms round his neck pressing my body against his as I kissed him back, loosing myself in the moment.

To the Sea

Gregory

The train whooshed along quietly. They had spent the journey mostly in silence. Mellissa stared blankly out the window. Victoria was sat next to her glaring at Greg. Tension clung to the air. Greg wished he hadn't booked them table seats so that they weren't looking at each other. Greg stood. "Does anyone what anything from the refreshments carriage?"

Mellissa looked up at him. "I'll have a drink."

"Anything else?" She shook her head looking back out the window. Greg walked down the aisle. The refreshment trolley would be by again at some point, but he was fed up with the dirty looks Victoria kept giving him. He already felt bad enough and didn't need her reminding him how awful she thought he was with her eyes. Mellissa claimed she was okay with him going to the sea kingdom, but she still seemed troubled. She hadn't slept much the last few nights and he was sure her nightmares had returned. His heart was in turmoil, and he was sure hers was too. He didn't like the idea of his actions upsetting Mellissa but at the same time he felt deep down in his gut that this was what he was meant to be doing. Whenever Mellissa ran off into battle, he always felt so useless, but he knew it what she was meant to be doing. He couldn't sit around doing nothing. Going to the sea kingdom meant he would be doing something to help fix things. Call it fate or destiny, but this was the path he was meant to follow.

Greg reached the refreshment carriage and bought two drinks and a pack of white chocolate and raspberry cakes, they would be something Mellissa liked. With his items in hand, he turned around and almost walked into Victoria. "What are you doing?" he asked. "Did you want something?"

"Yes," said Victoria.

"Well, I'll give you some money and you can get what you want."

She crossed her arms and sneered at him. "I don't want a snack. I want to talk to you." Her eyes narrowed. "Alone."

A part of Greg wanted to tell her to go away but instead, he followed her to a quieter carriage on the train. Before he could say anything, Victoria whirled round jabbing a finger in his face. "Do you know what you're doing?"

Greg looked at the items in his hand. "Getting snacks."

"Don't act dumb," she said, "You know I mean with this whole mission to find the sea stone."

Greg sighed leaning on the side of an empty seat. "I'll be honest not really, but I have previously done well at finding things that others have struggled to."

"No." She threw her arms down beside her. "Maybe I wasn't clear. Do you know what you're doing to Mellissa by going on this mission?"

Greg's heart sank as he looked at the floor. "She says she has come round to the idea."

Victoria rolled her eyes. "That's because you seduced her into submission."

"No, I haven't"

"You really think I haven't noticed? Every time she starts to worry you resolve it by having sex. You realize that doesn't solve the problem."

Greg suddenly felt warm. That hadn't been what he was doing, at least not consciously. "Everything will work out. I have to do this, so I can help fix the mess I made."

Victoria waved her hand at him dismissively. "Yeah, yeah I know how you feel responsible about all the bad stuff your mum has done. If you ask me, I think you are being stupid."

"Maybe I am but I need to do something."

Victoria sat in an empty seat and looked up at the luggage rack. "You know Mellissa doesn't blame you for any of this."

"That's just because she is too kind."

"Yeah she is but in this instance she is right." Greg's jaw dropped. She pointed at him. "Don't look so surprised. I know I went off at you when I found out what your mum did but Gwendolyn's actions are not yours. The guilt is not yours to bear. Don't let these negative feelings affect the one good thing you have in your life."

Greg rubbed the back of his neck. "You're right I don't completely know what I'm doing but I do believe Mellissa will be okay. You will be by her side. When she's home she will also have Harkura, Samson and everyone else."

"Didn't she tell you?"

Greg frowned. "Tell me what?"

"She is making me stay in Perluves with her until you return."

"That isn't necessary."

"She won't be persuaded otherwise." Greg's shoulders sagged and his heart felt heavy. Victoria jumped to her feet and grabbed the front of his shirt causing him to stumble backwards. She glared at him her eyes glowing ice blue. "But let's get one thing straight." The temperature in the train cart lowered and ice formed on his shirt where she gripped it. "I swear if you get yourself killed, I will bring you back just to kill you again. Mellissa won't be able to handle another loss."
She let go of him and walked away. Greg ran his hands down his shirt shards of ice falling to the carriage floor. He glared in the direction she had gone. He was sick of her attitude towards him. If it had been anyone else, they would have been arrested for assaulting an elder. Mellissa's guardians constantly got away with overstepping. His heart ached; deep down he knew Victoria was right. She had actually been really insightful, and he had no idea what he was doing.

Yuko led the three of them down to the beach. She had met them at the train station with a carriage. The journey through the rocky path down to the coast had been awkwardly quiet. Greg heard the waves roaring against the shore before he saw them. There was little snow here, but the air was still icy cold. The wind whipped through his hair causing him to shiver. Mellissa and Victoria walked in silence as Yuko skipped along beside them chattering away. Yuko had changed her navy blue priestess robes for a dark wet suit. It was much more suitable for swimming than what Greg was wearing but what he wore didn't matter as he would be shifting before entering the water.

"Gregory, what sea creature will you shift into?" Yuko asked.

Greg shrugged his shoulders. "I haven't thought about it."

"I suggest something large that won't attract predators." She tapped a finger to her chin. "A shark maybe, or an octopus."

Greg looked up and down the beach. There was hardly anyone about making the guards scattered along the beach stand out. As they approached the water Mellissa gripped his arm tightly. He could hear her taking slow steady breaths. Greg stopped and looked at Victoria hoping she understood what he wanted. She sighed, rolling her eyes. "Yuko," said Victoria, "I would like to talk to you about where Mellissa and I will be staying in the city."

"Oh, you will stay in the temple. Kai will see to you both." Yuko pointed at two guards near the road above. "Those guards will escort you into the city."

"That sounds great, but I have other concerns." Victoria linked arms with Yuko walking away with her.

Greg took Mellissa's hands in his, turning to face her. "I'm sorry, I've been an idiot. If you don't want me to go, I won't."

"What?" Mellissa looked at him her brown eyes confused.

"Victoria kindly pointed out on the train that I didn't

fully understand what I was doing, and she was right."

"That's why she followed you." Greg nodded. Mellissa pulled closer to him, placing her hands on his chest. "A big part of me wants to make you stay." She looked out to the ocean. The wind blew loose strands of hair onto her face. "The water still makes me uneasy but it's too late to turn back now. Yuko can't go alone, and it would take a while to find someone else to accompany her. Even I have to admit it wouldn't be good to delay too long."

Greg looked up at the clear blue sky trying to think of alternatives. He still felt he should go but Mellissa was more important to him. If he hadn't been so stubborn, he would have realised this sooner and would have had time to come up with another plan. "Samson can go in my place," he suggested.

Mellissa tilted her head sideways. "You can't send my chief of staff."

"I know I can't."

"I also don't think you want to stay."

Greg cupped her face in his hands. "I also don't want to upset you. I tricked myself into believing you would be okay because I thought this was what I should be doing. I now realise what I should have been doing was supporting you. I may feel useless standing on the sidelines but ultimately it will be you who stops Humarya."

Mellissa shook her head forcing him to let go. "You have never been useless. I wouldn't be where I am now without you." She threw her arms down turning away from him. "A part of me wants to call this mission off. If I even could, after all, I was, outvoted. However, I don't think Yuko would listen and you still feel like you have to make up for what your mother did." Greg went tense. Mellissa spun round her eyes wide. "I didn't mean to make you feel bad. It's just-" She took hold of his hands holding them close to her heart. "I am scared of losing you because you feel bad about something I don't blame you for."

"I mean it when I say I'll stay for you."

She pushed his fringe to the side, giving him a small smile. "Why couldn't you have come to this realisation while I was still willing to be selfish and keep you here." She ran her fingers along his jawline. "Staying is not what you want. What you want is for me to be okay." She shook her head as her bottom lip quivered. "But that is something I can't do. I don't know how to be fine anymore, but I can respect your decision to go."

Greg stroked her cheek pushing the curls that had escaped her braid from her face. Her smile was sad, and her eyes didn't sparkle in their usual way, but he could see she meant what she said. Pulling her into his arms, gently he leaned in and kissed her. The sound of someone clearing their throat caused them both to jump. Greg turned to see Yuko and Victoria watching them. "Gregory, we really must get going," said Yuko.

He nodded. "Right, of course." He walked towards the water with Yuko.

"Have you decided what you are to shift into?" asked Yuko.

Greg pulled his jacket off. "I was thinking a dolphin."

Yuko nodded while giving him a big grin. "Yes, that sounds like you." She stepped out into the water until her knees were covered.

"Just give me a moment." Greg ran back across the beach to Mellissa and scooped her up in his arms kissing her fiercely. Her hands cupped his face as her lips parted against his. Warmth radiated from her and he never wanted to let her go. "I love you," he said.

"I love you too." She replied breathlessly, her face flushed.

He kissed her again, breathing in her sweet scent of cherry blossoms. He rested his forehead on hers. "Will you keep hold of this for me?" She nodded as he handed her his jacket. She squeezed his hand. He kissed her softly as he slipped his hand from hers. "I'll be back before you know it." Greg ran back into the water joining Yuko. Once they were far enough out, they dove under the water. Greg shifted into a blue dolphin and the two of them swam deep into the ocean.

23

Cottage

Mellissa

The air puffed in front of my face as I panted. The cold breeze was a welcome comfort against my face as sweat dripped down my forehead. Victoria slapped me on the back. "Come on slow poke, we still have a mile of beach to run along."

I clutched my side as I pushed a stray piece of hair from my face. "How is it going for a morning run with you is worse than with Harkura?"

She shrugged. A smirk crept onto her face. "Longer legs."

I chuckled. Her yoga pants and sports hoodie exaggerated the length of her already long legs. "I guess every step you take is like two for me."

She draped her arm over my shoulders. "You have a point. For your little legs, you have probably taken twice the number of steps as me. I will allow you a break."

She handed me a bottle of water out of her backpack and took one out for herself. I sat on the wall that separated the path we were on and the sandy beach. We had run from the city of Perluves along a path that followed the coastal line. I looked out at the sea as I gulped down my drink. While my dry throat had cherished the hydration, my stomach now churned. Victoria placed her hand on my shoulder. "Why so glum?"

"I'm not."

She raised an eyebrow. "You are looking out at the ocean pouting with those sad eyes of yours." She stuck her bottom lip out, crinkling her eyes.

I pushed her away by her shoulder. "I do not look like that."

"Greg is fine," she said, "and there have been no more sightings of Humarya since your fight."

I interlaced my fingers and wriggled my nose. "That's part of what worries me. She was so relentless before, so why hasn't she tried again?"

"I don't know, all we can do is hope that Greg and Yuko manage to find the sea stone first."

I looked down at my feet dangling just off the ground and dug my nails into my thighs. My heart felt heavy, there was a panic that made me want to run out to the ocean and forcefully pull Greg and Yuko back to land, not that I was sure that was something even my powers could achieve. But there was also this feeling of dread that had me frozen, sat on this wall. I shook my head and grunted. "I'm such a mess."

Victoria tugged my arm. "Come on princess, lets go back to the city and get some breakfast in you."

I hopped down off the wall. "I will have you know that it's queen."

She clasped her hand to her chest in fake shock. "I'm so sorry your majesty." She dropped into an exaggerated bow. "Come on queen, get your but moving so we can eat."

I laughed and we ran back towards Perluves.

Rain plummeted down from the dark grey clouds. Thunder roared above. My green dress clung to my skin, and I shivered. My vision was blurred due to the force of the downpour. I called out for Harkura and Victoria, but no one responded. I wrapped my arms around myself and pushed forward. My legs were stiff, and I had no idea where I was going. I yelped when a hand grasped my shoulder. "Mellissa," said Matt. He was completely dry despite the rain.

"What's happening?" I asked.

"You're dreaming." He looked around. "It's not the best dream, fate is trying to keep me out."

"I don't understand."

"The tree's knowledge was never meant to be shared but I had to warn you."

"Warn me of what?"

Thunder roared above us. Matt clasped my shoulders and bent down to my height. "All you need to know is that the darkness's return is almost upon us." His face was tight, and his brows furrowed. He clasped my shoulders. "This is going to be like no other battle you have fought, but I believe in you."

I shook my head. "But the darkness is already back. I've already fought Humarya."

"Mellissa, she's not" Matt's words were cut off by lightning flashing and thunder crashing. The rain turned to hail plummeting me. I yelled covering my head with my hands. I shouted for Matt, but he was gone.

I woke gasping for breath. Throwing my covers off I sat up and looked around the room. It was still dark and I could just make out the other bed across from me. Victoria's snore quietly vibrated through the room. I let out a long breath and rubbed my forehead, it was just a dream. I swung my legs over the edge of the bed slipping on my slippers. The priestesses had put us up in a large room in the temple. We both had a double bed, on opposite sides of the room. Pulling on my dressing gown I walked over to the double doors that led to the balcony. I placed my hand on the glass, looking out at the ocean. My heart felt hollow.

I jumped at the sound of my communis ringing. I grabbed the device wondering who would be calling me this early. I activated my communis. "Hello," I croaked.

"Queen Mellissa, sorry to ring you this early," said Mary.

My pulse raced at the sound of Greg's chief of staff's voice. "Is everything all right?"

"Yes, there is no danger, but I have some information," she replied, "Before Gregory left he tasked me to track down his mother."

"He did?" I frowned rubbing my chin. "Wait yeah, he mentioned something about that."

Her voice sounded eager as she spoke quickly. "Since Gregory isn't here, I thought you were the best person to report my findings to."

"You found her?"

"I have tracked Gwendolyn to a cottage. It is a secluded area, near the coast. You're actually not that far from it."

"That's great." My heart jumped for joy. "Can you send the location to my tabular."

"Of course. What are you going to do?" asked Mary.

"Storm that cottage and hopefully capture a criminal."

"Good luck, your majesty."

"Thanks." My communis deactivated.

I ran over to Victoria's bed shaking her awake. She sat up yelling, chucking ice blasts. I ducked narrowly dodging her magic. I held my hands up in surrender. "Victoria it's just me."

Her eyes went wide and she leapt from her bed grabbing my arms. "What's wrong? Why are you up so early?"

"Mary has found Gwendolyn." My tabular pinged. "and that's her forwarding the location."

Victoria smirked. "I guess we better suit up."

Victoria and I quietly zig-zagged our way down the path between the sandy dunes. The cold wind whistled as snowflakes scattered down from above. We both had our coat hoods pulled up and scarfs tightly wrapped around our faces to try to protect ourselves from the sand lashing around us on the gust. Priestess Kai had wanted to accompany us along with a squad of water nymphs soldiers. We had persuaded him that the two of us were enough. Smaller numbers meant we could sneak up on Gwendolyn more easily. We had taken a carriage part of the way and walked the rest. We were only about 30 minutes away from Perluves. Mary hadn't been exaggerating when she said the location wasn't far.

Victoria held her hand up to me, signalling me to stop. I halted my steps. She placed her finger over her lips and ushered me closer. I tiptoed to her side. She pointed out just beyond the dunes. The sandy hills opened up into a small clearing of rocks and sand. At the centre was a beige cottage with a thatched roof. It looked like something out of a fairy tale, where an evil witch lay in wait for her prey.

Victoria pointed up towards the roof. Dark grey smoke puffed out of the chimney. "Looks like someone is in," she whispered. "I'll go in through the front. You fly up and over to the back." I nodded and shot up into the air. Victoria ran to the cottage and kicked the front door in. I quickly dropped down at the back of the house, landing in a small rocky garden. Quickly scanning the area, I saw nothing but stones, sand and the ocean in the distance. Frowning, it was too quiet. As I went to open the backdoor it swung open. A loud blaring siren assaulted my ears. I jumped back swirling light energy into my hand as glass creature lunged at me its sharp claws drawn. Pushing my hands forward I blasted light, shattering it. I flinched as another creature flew out the door. Before I could react it burst sending glass scattering around my feet.

Victoria stood in the doorway, her brows drawn together and her jaw tight. She nodded towards the inside of the house, gesturing me to follow her. I stepped inside and clasped my hands over my ears. The wailing siren was worse in here. Victoria wooshed over to a device on the wall and slammed her fist into it. As she pulled her fist back ice spread across the broken machine. The awful screech stopped. "Stupid alarm system," she muttered.

We walked through a small kitchen into a cosy living room. A fire kindled in the hearth. "Someone was here, but we seemed to have just missed them," Victoria said.

I gritted my teeth as I grumbled in frustration. I scanned the area. There wasn't much in the room, only a wooden table and two chairs. A basket of wool and pile of logs next to the fire. "There has to be something in here to help us. This trip can't be for nothing."

Victoria placed her hand on my shoulders. "Lets look upstairs." I nodded. She led the way up the narrow staircase. The ceilings upstairs were so low Victoria had to crouch. "I'll check that room and you look in the other." She headed into the first door on the right. I headed a few more steps down the corridor through another door. It was a bedroom. In the middle of the room was a double bed covered in flowery bedding. On either side of it were a chest of drawers and a vanity. I went to the chest of drawers pulling each draw out. Rummaging through, clothes and trinkets. I sighed as I found nothing significant. I went to the vanity and again found nothing. I punched the wall, as I let out a growl.

"Mellissa," Victoria shouted from the other room. I swiftly ambled out of the room I was in and into the one where she was. This room looked to be some sort of office, with a desk and multiple filing cabinets against the walls. Victoria was knelt on the floor with papers and scrolls scattered all over the floor. She was gripping one sheet of paper tightly in her hand. My pulse quickened as I took in the distressed look on her face. "What is it? What have you found?" I asked.

"Mellissa." Her voice was shaky, her eyes full of worry as she looked up at me. "I think Gwendolyn has located the sea stone."

Under the sea

Gregory

Greg, in the form of an octopus, flipped the pages of yet another book. The sea king's library was one of the grandest he had seen. From the outside it looked like a small coral-like building, but inside was a vast space. Shelves of books lined the wall and there were rows upon rows of bookcases full. This place made the library in Novosvillas look tiny.

King Radius had greeted them enthusiastically. They had been given a tour of the underwater city. Yuko had been gasping and squealing all the way around. The king had planned other activities, but Greg had kindly refused as the journey had tired the two of them. Once Greg and Yuko had rested, they had got straight to work. Yuko had gone with King Radius to visit a group of scholars. She wanted to learn about any legends they knew of long-life beings. After all, all legends had an origin. One may hold a clue to the stone's location.

Greg had been shown to this library by Queen Harmony. She had shown him to a quiet area in the back with a table. He had shifted into an octopus so he could carry more books and easily flip pages.

Greg sighed as he shut yet another book and added it to the pile of unhelpful texts. So far he had found nothing with any insight into the stones protector.

"Not found anything useful yet?" asked Queen

Harmony.

Greg looked up to see the mer-queen on the other side of the table holding a pile of books close to her chest. Greg shook his head. "No, I don't know what I was expecting to find. We had this same issue on the land. We too have very few references in our history books to the dark stones."

"It makes sense if what you told us is true. The gods wanted to keep their existence hidden, there wouldn't be much written of them." Harmony placed the books on the table. "But I thought these may be of use to you." Greg picked up the first book with his tentacles. It looked a lot older than the others. Its seaweed bindings were decaying and its waxy pages thin. "They are from my late father's personal collection," explained Harmony, "After dropping you here, I remembered that he had some ancient texts. They are very rare." She stroked the cover of one of the books, with a small smile on her face.

"Thank you," said Greg, "I will take great care of them."

"I know you will," she nodded and left him to his research.

Greg spent the next three hours reading the books the sea queen had given him. His heart raced as he reread, a passage for the third time. This was it. The information he needed. The Kraken. This was one of the legends Yuko had mentioned. One she had gone to get more information on. He stumbled over his many legs, tangled amongst them. He needed to find Yuko and the king. This Kraken was the long-life being they were looking for.

Greg swam behind King Radius and his guardians, El the pink scaled, oarfish and Torq the orange skinned stargazer. Greg had shifted into a swordfish, so his movements were sleeker and faster through the water. His stomach was in knots but he was sure he was on the right track. Greg had shot out the library to find King Radius, Yuko and the scholars they were visiting. He had shown them the drawings of the caves in the book queen

Harmony had given him. One of the scholars had recognised it, explaining it was one of the areas theorised that the story of the Kraken originated from. The cave of the Kraken was a well-known fable, but the mer-folk never thought it real, making King Radius dismiss the possibility. However, Greg with assistance from Yuko had managed to persuade Radius to at least visit these caves. They had followed the King through a portal and now they were descending into dark, depths.

"These caves are well, beyond the Kingdom's borders," said King Radius, "Us merfolk don't travel out here often."

The water temperature suddenly dropped and Greg shivered. Yuko swam closer to him. "Are we sure this is a good idea?" she whispered.

Greg frowned. "Of course. We need to know if this *Kraken* is the protector of the sea stone."

She shook her head. "That's not what I mean. Maybe the King should have brought more people with us. We have no idea what sort of greeting we will get."

"I'm sure it will be fine," replied Greg, "We want to appear peaceful."

Radius halted and held his trident out to the side. "We are here. I will go with Torq and scout out the cave."

"Shouldn't we stick together?" asked Yuko.

"If this really is where the Kraken lives, we do not want to overwhelm it with too many visitors."

Yuko clenched her fists but nodded. "We will keep watch from here." Greg swam to her side and she placed a hand on his back. Radius and Torq swam to the cave, leaving them with El.

El's eyes bulged as the king and Torq entered the cave. She placed an arm over her chest. "Everything will be all right." She seemed to be speaking more to herself than to them. They waited in awkward silence. The longer they stayed there the tighter Yuko's grip got on his back.

A high-pitched scream echoed through the water. El shot forward and Greg followed her closely. Radius darted out of the cave, dragging Torq's limp body with him. His tail flipped rapidly as he bounded towards them. A roar boomed out of the cave as a shock wave rippled through the water knocking them sideways. A large mercreature emerged from the cave. It was built like a merman, with a long tail, and muscular human-like torso. However, it was covered with grey scales from head to tail. The Kraken snarled showing off its fangs. El screeched sending a shockwave into the beast.

Greg swam to Radius' side. "What happened?"

The king's eyes were wide as he shook his head. "I don't know. We were talking to him nicely, he seemed cooperative when suddenly his eyes went black and he started attacking." Radius looked down at his guardian he was carrying. "Torq protected me." His eyes landed on Greg. "Take him to safety." Radius placed Torq over Greg's back. He gripped his trident tight and the crystal in the centre of the fork glowed brightly. Radius charged forward light cascading around him.

Greg swiftly glided through the water away from the fight. He found a spot behind some sea rocks and coral and placed Torq down. Greg's jaw tensed. He was useless in this like this. He couldn't use his healing magic while he was in the form of a swordfish. He couldn't even evaluate Torq's condition.

A squid shot by Greg's hiding spot. He narrowed his eyes at it. A blue stone glistened in its grip. Greg gasped. "The sea stone."

Greg hurled himself forward. As the gap between him and the squid closed, he shifted into an octopus slapping the squid with four of his eight legs. The squid shuddered ejecting ink and dropping the stone. Greg launched forward grabbing the sea stone. The squid flipped over and shifted into a sailfish. It jabbed its long nose at him, but he swatted it away with his many legs. He pushed backwards away from it. "Mother," Greg shouted. "Stop this now."

"No Gregory," She yelled snapping her sharp teeth at him. "You are the one that must stop. Give me the stone and together we can create a better world with Queen Humarya."

"You're delusional."

"Give me that stone," She yelled. "I am your mother you will do as I say."

"Never," Shouted Greg.

Gwendolyn's body shuddered as she shifted into a grey shark. Greg curled two of his octopus legs around the sea stone. Magic pulsed through him as he focused on a location. He may not be able to access his healing magic while shifted but he could do this. Summoning magic was like breathing for him. He didn't need to say the spells anymore. White light shimmered in his grip and the stone disappeared.

"What have you done?" screamed Gwendolyn. Greg cried out as teeth sunk into his side. His body tensed as pain seared through him. Yuko shouted his name. The water around him swirled. He saw stars as the pressure on his side was yanked away. Yuko was beside him pulling her arms back and forth affecting the current of the water. Gwendolyn in shark form tried to swim back towards him but Yuko kept her away. She looked like she was swimming away when suddenly she spun around slapping Yuko in the face with her tail. She swung her body back slapping the high priestess again. Yuko slammed into some coral. Gwendolyn dove towards Greg and headbutted him on his injured side. He tried to call on his magic to form a shield but she sunk her teeth into him again. She ragged her head to the side throwing her son down. He yelled in agony. The water around him turned red. Greg's heart felt heavy as his body went limp and slowly sunk down into the cavernous ocean.

Distraction

Mellissa

Seagulls circled above squawking. The breeze tickled my cheeks bringing with it the scent of sea salt. The waves crashed against the shore sweeping across the sand making me flinch. Taking a deep breath, I wrapped Greg's jacket tighter around myself and continued walking along the beach. Not so long ago I wouldn't have been able to bare being so close to the ocean. I had come a long way since then. But if it had taken me this long to get over the scars Kadon had caused; how long would it take me to recover from my recent trauma? I wasn't consumed with my grief anymore, but I still felt like I had a hole in my heart. There were these feelings of anxiety and dread, that I couldn't explain bubbling beneath the service, that if I let loose, I would be lost to my rage. So I pushed my emotions down, wishing I could speak with my dad, to hear his advice. He would know just what to say to help me sort through what I was feeling.

I shut my eyes, savouring the feel of the cold air on my face. My heart ached. It had been a long week without Greg. Our jobs often meant we didn't see each other for weeks at a time but I still missed him. And ever since we had found Gwendolyn's cottage, I hadn't been sleeping. The danger of this mission had become all so real, and it made me feel sick to my stomach. I shouldn't have been so reasonable that day on the beach when they left. I should have been selfish, keeping Greg here by my side.

"Mellissa," shouted Victoria. Her long blond hair blew elegantly in the wind as she walked toward me. "You can't keep doing this."

"Doing what?" I asked.

She looked down at me with pity in her eyes. "Spending all your time walking along the beach waiting for him to return."

"But we haven't heard anything yet." I looked out at the ocean. The waves rolled onto shore dissolving into sea foam. "We haven't been able to tell them what we found amongst Gwendolyn's things. They don't know that she has located the stone."

"I'm sure everything is fine. You know the term no news is good news? I think it applies here."

I glared at her. My hand cradled the crystal around my neck. It was smooth beneath my fingers, and I turned it back and forth. "I should be able to make contact with King Radius. This silence isn't right."

She placed her hand on my shoulder, giving me a small smile. "That's just because you're anxious. If something was wrong we would have heard about it."

My shoulders sagged. Was this what Greg had meant when he said he felt useless when I left him behind? If so, I now understood why he hated it so much. The need to do more was starting to overwhelm me. I just didn't know what the next right move to make was.

Victoria's gaze lingered on the horizon. "There isn't a lot we can do. The ocean isn't your domain. So technically this is King Radius' problem, not yours."

My jaw dropped as my eyes went wide in shock. "How can you say that?"

Victoria rolled her eyes and shrugged. "I'm sorry but until someone gets a lead on Humarya we are stuck."

I turned as I felt the sand shifting behind us. Three guards ran towards us. "Your majesty," one said panting, "We have just received word that Humarya has been spotted by Urbem Folium."

"What?" Victoria and I said in unison.

"Humarya is in your city," he repeated. "The priestess' have offered assistance from the guard."

Victoria gripped my arm tight. "How long do you think the barrier will hold?"

"I don't know."

"You have to fly ahead but I won't be able to come with you."

My heart was pounding, and my feet itched to run. I shook my arms out to the side and slowed my breathing in an attempt to calm myself. I needed to think. Victoria was right I had to fly ahead, there wasn't time for reinforcements.

"Victoria send word to Harkura that I'm on my way." I said, "Tell him only to engage in a fight if the barrier falls before I arrive."

She folded her arms, jutting her hip out to the side and raised an eyebrow. "This is Harkura we're talking about." My body tensed. She was right. Harkura wasn't going to hide behind the barrier while Humarya attacked the city. He was tough but he couldn't beat her alone. I needed to be quick. Taking a running start across the sand I leapt into the air flying towards home.

The cold air bristled down my face and my long braid whipped around behind me. All I could see for miles was the green of treetops. I would be upon Urbem Folium soon, but I had no idea what to expect. If the water stone was Humarya's target it didn't make sense for her to attack my city. Unless she was just trying to get at me. This could just be another way of her exacting revenge. My body tensed as I slowed my flying speed. If I came in too fast, I would just crash land in the city. *Everything would be all right, and the barrier would hold.* At least that was what I kept telling myself. The barrier had been put up six months ago when Humarya had first become a threat and I hadn't removed it after. Something I was glad of now. Anyone could leave the barrier, but it would repel dark magic from entering.

I stopped mid-air when I spotted her. My pulse quickened as I took in what she was doing. Shadows wrapped around her as she blasted the barrier on the city. A dark smog covered the area she had attacked but as it cleared a smile spread across my face. Her attack hadn't even made a scratch and the barrier was still standing. I lunged forward letting my magic flow. Static cracked through the air as I let lightning ripple through my body, striking Humarya. She shrieked as she fell. Stretching her wings out she stopped herself from tumbling into the trees. I flew towards her firing more lightning but this time she was ready. A flurry of shadows flew at me fizzling out my attack and engulfing me. I pushed my arms out transforming the Heart into its staff form and releasing a pulse of light dispersing the shadows. Humarya flew towards me drawing back her talons. I spun around holding my staff up to protect me. Her talons clanged as they caught on my staff. Her yellow eyes narrowed on me. "So, the rumours were true, you did abandon your people."

"I haven't abandoned anyone," I yelled pushing her back with my staff. Sweeping it round I fired rays of light at her.

She batted my attack away with a swipe of her arm. Lifting her wings up and then sharply down, she smacked me hard in the chest knocking the breath out of me. A gust of icy wind slammed into me, sending me hurtling towards the forest. I called out to the trees and they reached for me. Before I could take hold of the branches another gust crashed into me. I fell straight through the barrier and crash-landed in the city with a thud.

"Mellissa," shouted Samson. He pulled me to my feet.

"What are you doing out here?" I asked.

"We ordered everyone into the castle in case the barrier fell," he said, "Harkura then had the few soldiers we have to surround the building. He then bolted when he sensed you arrive, and I may have followed." There was a grim look on his face. His brow dripped with sweat, and dirt was smudged across his cheek.

I tugged at his arm. "Why would you follow Harkura?"

His breathing was hard and ragged. "I thought he might need help."

My mouth hung open in disbelief. I knew Harkura wouldn't stay put but I thought Samson would have. We both jumped as shadows slammed into the barrier above. Cracks splinted across it. Flames exploded behind Humarya. She batted at her wing as fire sizzled along her feathers. A whip of fire wrapped around her yanking her away from the barrier.

"Go back to the castle Samson." I pointed in the direction he needed to go. "Have healers ready just in case." He nodded and ran in the direction of the castle. My heart pounded. Harkura was out there fighting alone, and I wasn't sure how many more hits the barrier could take. I flew straight up above the city. I circled around until I spotted them on the ground amongst the trees. Humarya had Harkura wrapped in shadows. I charged toward them firing balls of light. I landed with a thud and skidded along the earth. Swiping my staff across the ground I cracked it. As I spun my staff around clumps of dirt flew at Humarya. She released reels of shadows slashing threw the soil, but it wasn't enough. She was plummeted with earth. With a quick flick of my wrist, I surrounded Harkura in light freeing him from the shadows. He was on his feet in a flash, charging at Humarya ablaze with flames. He jumped up, kicking her in the chest causing her to tumble back. As he landed in a crouch, he swept his leg round blasting her with a wave of fire. Humarya's legs were taken out from under her by the flames. As her body hit the ground, I slammed my staff down and the tree roots reached up out of the earth, wrapping around her. Harkura ran up close reaching for the air stone around her neck.

Humarya screeched. Shadows flew from her body slamming into Harkura and me. I braced myself holding tight to my staff. Light illuminated from me as I pushed back against the shadows. Humarya screeched again and a whirlwind caught me and Harkura, throwing us up. I quickly waved my hands forming a flower bed to catch us but before we hit the ground another gust slammed into us. We smacked into the trees hard. I groaned as I fell to the floor.

"I forgot what pests you and your guardian were," growled Humarya. She lifted her hand, snaking shadows towards Harkura. "I should have killed you when I had you in my dungeon."

I dug my fingers into the earth sending tremors through the ground. She stumbled, then the earth below her shot up sending her flying. She opened her wings to steady herself. As I stood, I commanded the trees. They wrapped their branches around her wings. She thrashed her arms and legs about randomly firing shadow balls. I protected Harkura and myself with a barrier. A jolt shot threw me as two trees were sliced by shadows. A wall of darkness encased us. Holding my staff high, I swiped it down splitting the shadows with light.

I blinked a dozen times, my eyes readjusting to the brightness. As my sight cleared, I saw Humarya fly away lopsided, her wings were singed, and one was bent inwards. As she flew up through the trees, I lost sight of her. I clenched my fists taking a wide stance. Pushing off the ground with force, I launched myself into the air but when I emerged from the trees, she was gone.

Samson and Harkura trailed me as I walked up to my room in the castle. Everything inside the city was unharmed, except for the spot where I had crashed. The land was cracked, and the crops crushed but that was easily fixed with elf magic. All the cottages still stood, so did the market and all the herb gardens. The barrier had taken damage, but it had done its job in protecting the city. I should be relieved that we had come out of this with no one harmed. We had won the fight, but it felt too easy. She had up and run without bothering to deploy her glass creatures. They would have helped her in the fight so why hadn't she used them? I threw my room door open, and it slammed into the wall behind it. My boots flew across the room as I kicked them off. I slumped down on the sofa resting my head on the back of it. Once again, my dress was ruined. I was covered in dirt and my skirt was a tattered mess. When I had dressed that morning, it was to walk along the beach not to fight.

Harkura sat across from me in the armchair, his indigo eyes checking me over. Samson hovered around the edge of the room. He seemed unable to stay still. "Are you sure you don't need a healer?" Samson asked.

"I'm fine," I said, "but Harkura took a few hard hits."

Harkura sat up straight pushing his shoulders back. "I am also fine."

"I don't like this." Samson's face twitched as he walked back and forth. "What was she doing attacking the city?"

"Samson come sit." I tapped the cushion next to me. He sat beside me putting his hands in his lap holding them tight as if to force himself to stop moving. "Look," I said pushing my hair behind my ear. "I don't know what this was all about, but it has become clear that I need to come home,"

The side of Samson's mouth twitched. It was like he was trying to look calm and collected but panic was breaking through. "Are you not happy with how we dealt with things?"

I put my hand out to him in what I hoped was a reassuring way. "You have all done well in my absence, but I can't keep hiding away. For some reason, Humarya thought I had abandoned the city."

Harkura leaned forward placing his elbows on his knees. "I believe she may have been just trying to unsettle you."

I looked down at my hands. Harkura may be right but that didn't get rid of the pang of guilt I felt in the pit of my stomach. I had run away to Novosvillas as I couldn't handle my grief and then run to Perluves because my dad's death had left me paranoid about losing someone else. I had abandoned my people because I had let myself fall apart but not anymore. The barrier popped into my mind. It was damaged but it still held. I may be hurting inside but I would stand strong.

"That may have been her aim but I'm not going to let her get to me." I stood. "I'm going back to Perluves to get Victoria and my things, then we are getting proactive. Rather than waiting for her next attack, we are going to find her."

Harkura smirked. "Now we're talking."

"Perhaps you could just send word to Victoria to come back with your stuff," said Samson, "It would be a better use of your time to begin working on finding Humarya than travelling."

The suggestion made me cringe. Victoria wouldn't like being ordered back to Urbem Folium like that, but he was right. I turned to Samson. "Please, contact her for me and let her know what's happening?" He nodded. "Harkura, can you talk to Tamara for me? I'm going to need some more suitable outfits for fighting. She should have already been working on some stuff for me."

"Of course. Then what?" Harkura asked. "Do you have a plan to find Humarya?"

"Come on Harkura when do I ever have a plan?" I rubbed my chin. "Let's just meet in my office in half an hour and brainstorm ideas."

"And what are you going to do in the meantime," Harkura asked.

I swept my arms up and down my body. "Get a shower. I may not be injured but I'm filthy." Samson and Harkura left my room to complete their tasks. I headed into the bathroom and turned the shower on. The sound of the water hitting the shower floor made me think of my dream about Matt. His warning in the dream had been about overcoming water and the darkness returning. I had thought the darkness was Humarya but that didn't make sense, she didn't have water powers unless he was warning me about what would happen if she got the sea stone. That was pure darkness, and its power was water-based. I grabbed the side of the shower as a pain shot through me. My heart felt like it had just split. Greg was in danger. I needed to go talk to Harkura about this. I turned the shower off and headed back into my room.

Before I got to the exit Samson burst in. My heart raced. Samson didn't let himself in like my guardians did. He was always respectful and knocked. "Samson, what's wrong?" I asked.

He clasped his tabular in his hand so tight it looked like he may break it. The colour had drained from his face. "It's a message from Victoria, she says she has been calling you nonstop."

I put my hand to my head. "I think I left my communis in the temple at Perluves. What does she want?"

"Yuko has returned."

My heart skipped a beat. "What about Greg?"

His gaze lowered as his features tensed. "It says that Yuko returned alone."

26

Spinning

Mellissa

My head was spinning. The room I was in, was too small and too hot. I paced back and forth. After hearing Victoria's message, I got Samson to call her. She didn't know much except that Yuko was in the infirmary. Hearing her words felt like being stabbed in the chest. Yuko had returned hurt and alone. The word *alone* echoed in my mind. Where was Greg? As soon as I had finished talking with Victoria, I had flown back to Perluves and headed straight to the temple. The priestess' had placed me in a sitting room, with a sofa, two chairs and a table. No one had told me anything so far and it made me want to blast through the building. I took a deep breath shaking my arms out beside me.

The door creaked open. "Mellissa, there you are." Victoria walked in. "They told me you had arrived, but this place is like a maze."

I was by her side in a flash. "Victoria what is going on? Why won't they tell me anything?"

She put her hands on my shoulders. Her brows drew together. "They don't know anything. Yuko was badly hurt when she turned up. She was taken straight to be healed. No one has spoken to her yet, so we don't know what happened."

"Something bad obviously. Greg is gone."

"We don't know that yet."

"Greg wouldn't let Yuko return alone." I felt physically

sick. My body shook as my breathing became rapid. "If he was okay, he would have healed her himself."

"You should sit down." She gently put her arm around me and guided me over to the small table, making me sit in one of the wooden chairs. She gave me a weak smile. "Your journey back and forth must have been tiring. I can see if someone can get us some tea."

The gentle tone of her voice and the forced smile made my heart ache. She knew I was right but didn't want to say it. I shook my head. "I don't want tea. I need to know what happened out there."

The corner of her eyes creased as her lips pressed together. "I don't know what to say."

"There isn't anything you can say." My nails dug into the palm of my hands, as I felt my eyes filling with tears. "I knew something bad was going to happen."

"You couldn't have known. Not really. You are not an oracle."

I looked at the floor. "I dreamed of Matt. He warned me the darkness was returning."

"Mellissa, it was probably just the stress making you dream of Matt. We already knew Humarya had returned."

"No, he told me I had to overcome the water." I looked her in the eye. "I didn't understand it at the time, but this is what he was warning me about. Something bad is happening in the ocean."

Victoria sat at the table opposite me putting her head in her hands. "How can Matt be warning you in dreams? He is trapped in the tree of time."

"He said something about the tree showing him stuff." I reached across the table placing my hand on her arm. "I don't know the how, but the Matt in my dream was real."

"Even so if there is a problem in the sea it is up to King Radius to sort it."

I stood stamping my feet. "Not when it's taken Greg from me." I clenched my fists. "And Radius has helped me on land before."

She looked at me her mouth a jar. "That was different

you actually asked for his help." How could she wipe her hands of this so easily? I'm sure she would go into a rage if Radius' guardians spoke of the problems of the land in the same way. I stomped to the door. Victoria was on her feet in the blink of an eye. "Where are you going?"

"To the sea kingdom."

She slammed her hand on the door as I reached for the handle. "You can't," she said.

"Why not?" I shouted.

"Because even with the Heart crystal you can't breathe underwater."

I flung my arms down, clenching my fists. My body shook in frustration. "But I need to find Greg." My shoulders sagged as all the fight left me. Tears rolled down my cheeks. "He can't be gone. He just can't."

Victoria pulled me into a hug and stroked my hair. She made gentle cooing noises as I cried on her shoulder. My heart was a shattered mess.

Victoria sat beside me at a table in a large room. Priestess Kai had brought us up here and provided us with tea and scones. Victoria nibbled at a scone, while my share on the plate remained untouched. My gaze wandered around the room. There was a large open fire, surrounded by blue and green mosaic tiles. Two large tapestries depicting water magic movements. This room had high ceilings and a balcony overlooking the ocean. It was much finer than the small overheated one they'd had us in before.

"Queen Mellissa," said Kai, "The High Priestess is ready to speak with you." I stood as I saw Yuko and Kai walking to the table. Yuko gave me a weary smile. Her blue skin looked paler than usual and dark circles surround her eyes. Her usually glossy black hair, lay limply on her shoulders. She looked like she should be in bed.

"Yuko are you okay?" I asked.

Kai helped Yuko sit at the table. Sitting beside her Kai poured two cups of tea, putting one in Yuko's hand. "I am healed enough." Said Yuko. Her hands were shaking so much she was forced to put her cup down.

My stomach churned as I sat back down. For Yuko to still look this bad after being healed something truly terrible must have happened. I gulped, dislodging the lump in my throat. "Yuko, where's Greg?"

She looked out towards the balcony. "I don't know."

"What- how-" I shook my head digging my fingers into my palms. "I mean-"

Victoria placed her hand over mine. I lowered my gaze. "What happened?" Victoria asked.

"I don't really know." Yuko's brow creased and her eyes glazed over. "It all happened so fast."

Kai gently patted Yuko's back. "It is okay, just start at the beginning." He sat solidly beside her letting her use him for support.

Yuko straightened her back placing her hands on the table. "Well, we were in the old castle library. It was magnificent really. I'm not much of a book person but Gregory was right in his element. He shifted into an octopus so he could hold more books." The side of my mouth twitched as I imagined Greg being shown this new library full of books he would have never seen before. How excited he must have been thinking about all the new things he could learn.

Yuko continued talking. "We split up. He scoured the shelves of books and I went with King Radius to speak with some scholars. Our research led to the same discovery. The scholars spoke of a legend and in some old books Gregory found information of an extraordinary sea monster. We concluded that this legend of the sea Kraken and this sea monster where one in the same. The descriptions of it sounded like, this being had a very long life span, like the pixies and Valkyries. Gregory theorised it had become seen as a monster due to its attempts to keep people away from the dark stone it protected."

"We told King Radius about this Kraken and luck would have it he knew of the creature's cave. We set out with the king and his guardians but when we reached the cave the Kraken attacked us." Yuko lowered her head and dug her nails into the backs of her hands. "It was truly monstrous. There was no reasoning with it. The creature was pure rage. Even the King struggled against this creature's wrath." Yuko's voice wavered. "But it wasn't the creature that injured me. It was a shark."

"A shark? I don't understand," I said.

"Neither did I at first but Gregory did. There was another changeling in the ocean. While the king and his guardians dealt with the Kraken. Gregory and I fought this changeling."

I gritted my teeth. "Gwendolyn."

"Gregory's mother?" asked Kai.

I nodded. It had to be her. "What did she do to him?" I looked straight at Yuko, but she wouldn't meet my gaze.

"She was there to get the sea stone, but Gregory got to it first. I'm not sure what he did with it, but he cast a spell and it disappeared. He was hurt when she took him, but I was too injured to stop her." Her gaze finally met mine. Her blue eyes were taught with dark circles underneath. "I'm so sorry Queen Mellissa. I should have done more and, fought harder. I made my way back here as fast as I could to find you, but I collapsed before I could."

I reached across the table gently placing my hand over Yuko's. "It's okay you did what you could. You should go get some rest; you've been through a lot."

Yuko nodded. Kai helped her up and supported her as they walked out the room. I strode over to the balcony staring at the ocean. The waves splashed onto the shore. The sun glistened on the surface of the sea making it look so beautiful, but I knew the dangers of the water. Victoria squeezed my shoulder. "Are you okay?"

"No," I said, "but I will be. Greg is alive and he will remain that way until they get the stone's location out of him."

"So, we just have to rescue him before that happens."

"Exactly." I turned to face her. "Send for Harkura. Tell him to bring whatever I have of Greg's in my room." I bit my thumb. "And Samson too, he is probably the closest blood relative Greg has."

"What are you going to do?"

"I'm going to drag the sea king to land. He has a lot of explaining to do."

Tied Up

Gregory

G reg drifted in and out of consciousness. His head was pounding. Cold air drifted over him making him shiver uncontrollably. When had he resurfaced? At some point, he must have unconsciously shifted back to normal. His wrists were tied behind his back and his legs bound together. He was laid on his side, on hardwood that was causing his leg to go numb. Trying to focus his eyes he looked around. It was too dark to see anything but from the way the floor under him rattled and bumped about he knew he was moving. Probably in some sort of trailer. Wriggling his arms and legs he tugged at his bindings. He winced as pain shot through him. His side was bleeding. The wound burned as he tried to bend round, but he was unable to reach it to heal himself. If it wasn't healed soon, it could mean the end of him. His mother in the form of a shark had bitten into his side. He knew he was missing a big chunk of flesh. The last thing he remembered was his blood spreading out in the ocean. The sea salt had stung his wound and he had been sinking. Something hard had hit him in the head. Fog clouded his mind again as he drifted off.

Greg wasn't sure how much time had passed when he snapped awake. His body seared in agony. It felt like he was on fire as sweat dripped down his brow. Voices chattered nearby. Light burst through the darkness causing him to squint. Someone was looking down at him. His head was swimming.

He couldn't think clearly. "Heal him, now," a female voice shouted.

Greg groaned as fingers prodded at his side. He yelled as they rolled him onto his front. Pain seared through him and he gritted his teeth. A terrified woman looked down at him. Her hands were shaking as she placed them over his wounds. He heard her recite the familiar spell of healing. One he had cast many times himself. The pain began to recede, and the burning ceased. He sighed with relief as he felt his skin knot back together.

The woman screamed as she was yanked away from him. Green eyes looked down at him. They were the same green eyes he had. His mother frowned as she patted him down. "He will be all right?" she asked.

He couldn't make out the low whisper of a reply the woman who had healed him gave. Gwendolyn stroked his cheek, then disappeared from his view.

Greg wriggled in his restraints. The pain was gone. He sat up and dust was chucked in his face. He sneezed as the powder was inhaled. It smelled like lemon grass. *Sleeping powder*! Greg shook his head trying to dislodge the powder, but it was too late. His eyelids felt heavy, and his mind couldn't focus. Small lights danced around the wooden wagon. He fell back with a thud, as his limbs went numb and slowly drifted off.

Greg tugged at his restraints again. He awoke about an hour ago to find himself tied up in a cave. His first thought was to shift into a small creature and escape. However, his shackles had shrunk in size with him. Next, he had transformed into an elephant hoping to break the chains. This time his shackles grew in size. That's when he realised, the chains were enchanted, designed specifically to detain a changeling.

Greg gritted his teeth resisting the urge to scream out in frustration. He leant against the hard rocky wall. Water dripped from the ceiling and a cold breeze whistled through the cave. Outside he could hear waves crashing against the shore, meaning he was still near the ocean. Greg wriggled his wrists trying to loosen the binds with no luck. Mellissa had been right. He never should have gone into the ocean. Just as she had predicted, Humarya had sent her minion in. So many people had warned him against this course of action but he hadn't listened. He thought he could handle Gwendolyn, but she had somehow overpowered him and now he was her hostage. He was an arrogant fool.

Footsteps splashed in the puddles of water scattered around the cave. His mother grasped his shoulders, pressing his back into the cold, jagged wall of rock. "Your awake thank the gods," She said, "You must tell me what you did with the stone."

Anger flared inside him just at the sight of her. "I will never tell you where to find it." He lunged forwards and she scuttled backwards, out of his reach. The chains clanged against the wall as they yanked him back.

"Please Gregory." She clasped her hands in front of her. "Everything I have done is to keep you alive. My queen will not be happy when she realises, I failed to bring her the sea stone."

"That's not my problem," he snapped.

"She wanted you killed before just to upset the elf queen; what do you think she will do now you have actively got in her way?"

"I'd rather die than help you destroy the world."

"You don't mean that." She stroked his cheek. "Let mother protect you."

He jerked away tugging at his restraints. "You broke my father and now you're destroying my life. You're a monster."

Gwendolyn stood holding her hands close to her chest. Her eyes filled with tears. "You're just upset. I will leave you to think for now, but Queen Humarya will be here soon, and she won't be as gentle as me."

She walked away with her head held high. Greg gritted his teeth, thrashing against his binds. He shifted into different animals over and over with no result. Letting out a frustrated shout, he slumped to the floor. His hair absorbed moisture from the cold ground and his wrists burned from the struggle. That woman was delusional. How could she still be claiming to be doing this for him? She was completely insane. This wasn't the way a mother was meant to treat their child. His stomach twisted in turmoil. He had no mother. His mother really had died when he was seven, this woman walking around now was nothing to him. He thrashed against his restraints again. There had to be a way out of this. He wouldn't stop trying to find a way out, but he had meant what he had said, he would die before he helped Humarya get her hands on the sea stone.

Rage

Mellissa

The wind whipped through my hair and the cold crisp air stung my cheeks. My heart thumped loudly in my ears and my stomach twisted with rage. Victoria stood silently her hands behind her back, a few paces behind me. I wasn't sure if she liked my plan, but she hadn't tried to stop me. I held my staff out in front of me. The water brushed over my feet. Light burned brightly from the Heart crystal a top of my staff. I stood legs apart, my body tense and with an iron grip on my staff. Closing my eyes, I took a deep breath, focusing my energy. "Bring me the sea king," I whispered to the Heart crystal. Lights shot out of the crystal hovering over the water. They circled around. "Bring me Radius," I shouted. The lights dived down into the ocean. I felt my power travelling in and out. Lower and lower into the depths of the ocean. I willed the lights to find him. A shock wave bristled through me as my power clashed with the moon crystal. I held strong pushing my will against it. My power surged as I forced the Moon crystal to yield. I opened my eyes to the water swirling in front of me. It rose to form a funnel. I stepped back, staff in hand ready to strike. The water dissipated and there stood King Radius.

His shimmering, turquoise tail held him up and his fins flipped in the shallow water. His broad chest was bare and he clasped his trident tightly. The moon crystal glimmering at the centre of the fork. A golden crown sat atop his head. His jaw was tense and the muscles in his arms taut. His gaze wandered along the beach. "What is the meaning of this?" His voice boomed with authority.

I lowered my staff and stood tall. "I summoned you here to answer my questions."

His eyes settled on me, as if only just realising who brought him here. "Queen Mellissa? How did you overpower me, to summon me like this?"

"My will was stronger than yours," I said through gritted teeth, "Now, I have some questions about the Kraken attack."

His brows drew together as he sucked in his cheeks. "How do you know about that?"

"Did you not notice the two people I sent to your kingdom were missing?"

He stood tall, shoulders back puffing out his chest. "It had been noted. A search party has already been sent out and my people were coming up with a plan of action."

My hand tightened around my staff. "Did that plan include informing me?"

"I had hoped to rectify the mistake before that became necessary."

"You what?" I yelled. Victoria placed her hand on my shoulder. I rolled my shoulders taking a deep breath.

"I am not used to being spoken to in such a manner," Radius said.

I glared at him and my nostrils flared. "I trusted you to look after them and you failed."

Radius stomped his trident down splashing water up. "I am a king; I will not be spoken to in this way."

"And I am the Queen!" I shouted, "and you thought it was okay not to tell me the danger I was sending my people into." My jaw tensed as I held his stare.

I- I-" He stammered as he lowered his gaze. The tension in his posture seemed to fizzle away. "Sorry Queen Mellissa. I let my pride get in the way, but I ensure you I am doing everything I can to find your people." His shoulders sagged. The look of regret on his face softened my anger.

"Luckily, I already know where they are. Sort of."

"What do you mean?" he asked.

"Yuko found her way back here. She was hurt but the healers saw to her."

The king smiled and looked like he might jump for joy. "And Greg?"

My body tensed. "Humarya has him."

The smile on Radius' face dropped. "This is my fault. You are right I should have told you the dangers my kingdom has been facing. I was selfishly excited when you said you were sending Greg to us. He was the one that first identified the spirit creature we were dealing with. I hoped his knowledge would help."

"But that was months ago. That spirit creature is still causing you problems?" I rubbed my chin. It was also the same creature we had theorised had come to land and helped Humarya steal the air stone. Had it been searching for the sea stone for all those months on her behalf?

"The spirit has continued to plague us on and off for months." Radius paled as a shadow came over his features. "It took over the Kraken making it attack us and while we fought, the dark stone he protected was stolen."

I tugged at my hair. This spirit truly was working for Humarya. Its ability to go anywhere and everywhere unseen gave her a massive advantage. "The spirit creature is working for Humarya. It took over the Kraken, so Gwendolyn could steal the stone."

"Who is Gwendolyn?"

"A changeling traitor. She was the one who attacked Yuko and took Greg."

"I am sorry I didn't tell you about this sooner." Radius's mouth twitched at the corners and his forehead creased. "All this time the spirit was searching for the sea stone. I should have done more." He sighed looking defeated. "I should have asked you for help, but I was too prideful."

My heart felt heavy. This was all too much but I couldn't be mad at Radius. He was just a man, and I was finally seeing him for the flawed king he was. He and I were more alike than I'd realised. He may have been raised to rule but we still both had our insecurities. Neither of us was perfect and had made mistakes. What was important was what we did next.

He held his hand out, his eyes pleading with me. I placed my hand in his and he grasped it tight. "I will do whatever it takes to help find Greg. You must be hurting, and I am to blame for it."

"This isn't your fault. Yes, some things could have been done differently but Humarya would have found a way no matter what we did."

"I must learn to put my pride aside. This problem is bigger than either of us. We must work as a team."

"I will track Greg from the land. You work any leads you have in the ocean."

"I will share anything I find with you." We looked each other in the eye and nodded. "We will get him back." Radius turned toward the ocean. Placing his finger in the water he circled it round. The water swirled forming a portal. He looked back at me one last time, his eyes full of worry, and dived into the swirling water, disappearing.

Samson rolled back and forth on the balls of his feet as he nibbled at his fingernails. "I don't know how much help I will be. Greg and I are only cousins the family tie might not be strong enough."

I placed my hand on his shoulder. "That's why I had Harkura bring me some of Greg's possessions. Your blood should give us a general area then his jacket should take us the rest of the way."

We were back at the temple. Harkura and Samson had arrived not long after I had spoken to King Radius. Harkura was a nymph on a mission, itching for a fight. Dressed all in black looking like a ninja. Whereas Samson was a nervous wreck, who couldn't stop fidgeting. Kai had let us back into the large room upstairs, so we could discuss things amongst ourselves. The priestess had also been kind enough to provide us with a map for our spell. It detailed the whole magic world. Victoria had laid it out on the table, and it was what we were all currently standing around.

Harkura pulled a small glass bottle of what looked like sand out of his pocket. It was the tracking dust we needed to perform any sort of tracking spell. "We should just get on with this. I know what it is like to be captured by that woman." His eyes darkened. "We do not have time to waste."

With a pop, Harkura removed the cork on the bottle and sprinkled a small amount of tracking dust over the map. In a swift movement, he flicked his wrist producing a blade and sliced open Samson's hand. Samson winced as blood oozed from his palm. It all happened so quickly, that if I'd blinked, I would have missed it. "Say the spell," Snapped Harkura.

Samson cringed but did as he was told. Dripping his blood onto the map he recited the tracking spell. "Blood to blood, heart to heart. Find my missing loved one so we can be reunited."

The blood that had pooled in the middle of the map shot towards the coastal region. The four of us peered over the map. It went straight out to sea and began to circle a bunch of islands and then it stopped. With the magic gone the blood just sat there soaking into the paper of the map.

I pulled out a pen and circled the islands. There were about four of them in the circle formed by Samson's blood. "I guess that's where I will start. Four small islands shouldn't be too hard to search," I said.

Victoria yanked at my sleeve turning me towards her and held one hand up in front of me. "Wait a minute you are not going alone."

"The fastest way out there is to fly. You heard Harkura we don't have time to waste."

"We also need to be smart about this." Victoria flattened out the map on the table and pointed at the area that had been circled. "Look how remote those islands are. It's a trap. Humarya knew we would track Greg. She wants you to act rash and come alone."

I clenched my fists as my face heated. "I can't just leave

him there."

"I never said we would. Just that we are coming with you." Victoria pointed at me then to herself and Harkura. "Humarya will expect you to arrive from the sky. That's why the three of us will take a boat."

I groaned as I tugged at my hair. "But a boat will be too slow."

Someone coughed in the corner. "Not if I come with you." Kai stepped out from behind the drapes. He stood with his hands clasped in front of him and a stoic look on his face. "I can manipulate the currents to make the boat sail quicker." I pressed my forefingers to the sides of my head. I should have known the water nymphs would have been spying on us.

Shaking my head I grabbed the map off the table. "No, I'm not risking anyone else unnecessarily. I'll go myself."

Harkura grasped my wrists. He looked me straight in the eye. His blue eyes burned with determination. "We will not risk you, Mellissa. Victoria is right, this very well may be a trap. Your judgment is skewed when it comes to Gregory."

I opened my mouth to object, but I couldn't think of a retort. He was right. They all were. My emotions were heavily affecting my decision making. "Fine," I said pulling my arms from his grip. "What do you suggest?"

"We work together." He took the map off me spreading it back on the table. "Bringing Kai will be our best bet. His ability to manipulate the water will get us across the sea faster." Harkura pointed at the circle I had drawn on the map. "If we sail here, we can then use Greg's jacket to perform a tracking spell. If it doesn't work, I am pretty sure your strong emotional attachment will help you and the crystal locate him anyway."

"What do you mean you're pretty sure? I would like to be more certain than that."

"Your ability to search the land with the light from the Heart is a unique technique, only used by you, so I can't be too certain. However, I believe when you get close enough to the islands you will be able to locate Gregory." He pointed at the islands on the map. "These may be in the middle of the ocean but are still land, and you have done amazing things before when the right emotion motivates you."

I rubbed my chin. Harkura sort of made sense. My strong emotions had allowed me to bring the sea king to me. Why couldn't I do the same with Greg? Radius had been in the ocean out of my domain, and I had still managed to summon him. This could work and Humarya wouldn't see it coming. I stepped away from everyone so that I had space. Shutting my eyes I focussed on my magic pulling it to the surface. The Heart radiated around my neck. It hummed to me. 'Please find Greg' I thought, 'and bring him back.' The crystal shot out a light.

"What are you doing?" asked Victoria. I felt hands grasp my shoulders, but I ignored them. The crystals light warmed my soul. I could feel it travelling over the ocean. It skimmed the top of the water and bounced on to land again, flying into a cave.

"Mellissa," whispered a voice. I gasped as darkness obliterated my light. My heart pounded so hard in my chest that I was scared the whole room could hear it. If Victoria hadn't been holding on to me, I would have fallen to the floor. Her forehead was creased and her eye's full of worry. "What was that?"

"I just thought what Harkura said about the light of the crystal was a good idea." Holding tight to Victoria's arms, I looked up at her. "I felt him. Greg's in a cave somewhere but I also felt a darkness. Humarya is there." I bit my lip.

Victoria glowered. "What is it?"

My heart felt like it was cracking as tears threatened to fall. "He said my name. He sounded so weak."

She cupped my cheek with her hand. "It's all right we are going to get him." She turned to Kai. "Can you get us a boat ready?"

Kai nodded and marched out of the room his priestess robes billowing behind him. Victoria pointed at Samson. "You are staying here. You're no good in a fight."

Samson fidgeted with his shirt collar. "I would probably just get in the way, but I am worried about my cousin. Please make sure he is all right?"

"I'm not coming back without him," I said.

Harkura held a black bag out to me. "I suggest you suit up. It's a little something from Tamara." I smirked taking the bag from him and opening it. Inside was a new training outfit. "Much easier to move in than your dress," said Harkura.

I pulled out a black tunic, similar to the one Harkura was already wearing. "That it is."

He chucked another bag a Victoria. "There is also one for you."

I gripped my new outfit tight. In the end, it didn't matter what I wore. Humarya had made this fight personal, and she was going to regret it. She had ordered my dad's murder and now she had taken Greg. I was being fuelled by rage. Humarya was in for the shock of her life, with the fight I was about to bring to her.

Taken

Gregory

A cold wind whistled through the cave. Greg shivered as he lay curled up on the cold, damp floor. His wrists burned were his ties rubbed but the pain was nothing compared to the deep scratch down his back. Humarya had returned and just like Gwendolyn had warned she hadn't been happy. She had busted his lip and his eye throbbed with pain. Humarya had left him lying on the floor and stormed out of the cave when her interrogation had yielded no results. His mother had fluttered after her. It didn't matter what she did to him, he would not give in. He had been full of rage but now his heart had a sparkle of hope. He had felt Mellissa's light moments ago. She was looking for him. Which meant she would be coming. All he had to do was buy time.

Greg flinched as someone grabbed his arm. Gwendolyn pulled him up into a seated position. She held a cup to his mouth. He tried to push her away. She clasped the back of his head. "Drink, son." She tipped the cup. Water spilt out the side of his mouth as he gulped down the drink. His chapped lips and dry throat were soothed by the liquid.

Gwendolyn placed the empty cup on the floor. She pulled a cloth out of her pocket and dabbed it along his forehead. "Please Gregory, tell Queen Humarya where the stone is. I do not like seeing you get hurt."

Greg snickered. "Then why did you bring me here? You had to know what she would do to me."

She placed her hands in her lap and frowned. "You didn't give me a choice. If you hadn't gotten in my way."

"You have always had a choice," shouted Greg causing him to cough. His lungs burned and his ribs ached. He hung his head losing the strength to fight. "You chose to leave me as a child. You chose to join Humarya. You have chosen to keep me captive and stand idly by while she tortures me."

Gwendolyn stood clenching her fists. She looked down at him. "Well, you made a choice too. You chose that girl over your family."

"You are not my family," Greg screamed.

Gwendolyn picked up the cup and marched away. Greg closed his eyes resting against the cave wall. Its coldness soothed his injuries.

Greg stirred to the sound of his mother's voice. She stood at the opening of the cave. Light shone brightly at the opening causing him to squint. He could just make out her silhouette as she rubbed her chin. "Do you think that it will work?"

"Yes, I have done it before," said a deep voice. Greg pushed himself as far forward as the chains would allow him but could not see another person. Gwendolyn stepped into the cave. Her forehead was creased and her red hair was sticking out of the bun on top of her head. She turned towards him and Greg shut his eyes lowering his head. "And you can get the information without hurting him," she said.

"Everything he knows I will," said the voice. It was a male voice. "But it will hurt especially if he fights me."

Greg opened one eye slightly. He still couldn't see anyone with Gwendolyn, but he could hear them. What was going on? Gwendolyn clutched her hands to her chest. "I don't know."

"He will live. Are you sure your queen will not just kill him if he doesn't do what she wants?"

"You are right my lord."

Greg shut his eyes tight resisting the urge to scream.

Once again, his mother was placing his fate in the hands of another. Who was she talking to? The voice seemed so familiar, but he couldn't place it. He couldn't wait around for Mellissa he needed to get himself out. Unfortunately, his chains were designed to perfectly trap someone with his abilities. Greg slowed his breathing. He could figure this out he just needed to think.

His body tensed as he felt darkness surround him. Talons scratched his scalp as he was grabbed by his hair and his head tilted back. He opened his eyes to a pair of yellow eagle eyes staring at him. "You have had time to ponder whether you wish to live or not," said Humarya, "Now tell me what you did with the sea stone."

"I sent it away." He tried to pull himself out of her grip, but she held on tight.

She waved her other talon below his face shadows dancing along it. "Sent it where?"

He shrugged staring straight back at her. "I do not know where." His face twanged as she backhanded him. He hissed as shadows wrapped around his arms slicing his skin. He would not give her the satisfaction of hearing him scream. Glaring at her, he steeled himself ready for her next strike.

"My Queen wait." Gwendolyn pulled at Humarya's arm.

Humarya shoved her to the floor. Lifting her talon, she formed a shadow ball. "What do you think you are doing?"

Gwendolyn held her arms up over her head. "I mean no disrespect. I just thought there may be an easier way to get information out of him."

"And what is that?"

"Use the spirit. He can slip into Gregory's mind and find out what he knows."

Humarya narrowed her eyes on Gwendolyn. "Was this your idea or it's?"

Gwendolyn sat on her knees and held her hands up to Humarya pleading. "I swear it was mine. I only live to serve you. You should use the spirit creature to your advantage."

"A spirit?" Greg muttered. His head crashed into the

wall as Humarya slammed a gust of wind into his chest. His lungs felt like they were about to burst as the air was sucked away from him.

"My queen we need him," Gwendolyn said. Greg slumped to the side as the force holding him ceased.

Humarya stood in the middle of the cave. "Spirit," she said.

Greg shivered as another dark presence entered the cave. The hairs at the back of his neck raised. "What do you need?" said the deep voice from before.

"Find out what the boy knows."

"Of course."

Greg shuffled back against the cold cave wall. The voice sounded excited at Humarya's command. He was pressed up against the wall when he felt the darkness hovering over him. His whole body went numb as a coldness washed over him. Greg shook his head as a dark voice laughed in his head. His head suddenly stopped moving. He attempted to move his body, but his limbs wouldn't respond.

"I am in control now." The voice from before was now speaking to him from inside his head. It laughed. "Oh, you know so much. This should be fun."

Greg recognized the dark presence. He gasped as he placed the voice. "No," said Greg. His words were slow. "It can't be."

"But it is and now you are going to help me destroy the elf queen you love so much." Kadon cackled inside his head. Greg screamed as Kadon's spirit burrowed deeper into his mind.

Shattered Heart

Mellissa

I held tight to Harkura's arm. We were huddled in a small rickety boat, being propelled forward by Kai's water magic. With every movement, I feared we would topple overboard. The blue sky was clear without a cloud in sight. There was a chill in the air, but the breeze was gentle. It would have been the perfect day for a leisurely day out, but this calm weather worked against us. It would have taken us hours to get anywhere in these conditions. Luckily, we had Kai. He stood at the back of the boat, swaying his arms to and throw. Every motion he made had the boat hurling to our destination. Water splashed up the edges of the boat as we jolted along making me feel queasy. I buried my head in Harkura's shoulder. I wasn't sure how much longer I could handle being at sea. Harkura gently squeezed my hand. "We are almost there."

I looked up and gasped as we approached three small islands. Victoria had hold of Greg's jacket. She poured a veil of tracking dust over it and chanted the spell and it began to glow. She held tight to it as it floated up and tugged forward. It pulled her to the right. Kai adjusted his stance. Sweeping his arms around he pulled the boat in the same direction. Water gushed up and splatted into the boat. I dug my nails into Harkura's arm as I took a sharp breath. "Just breathe," Harkura said as he pried my fingers from his arm. He held both my hands in his stroking my palms. I shut my eyes focusing on the feel of his fingers running over my skin. Slowing my breathing to match the rhythm he had made. A sudden wave of magic squeezed my heart. I opened my eyes as I gasped.

Harkura's grip tightened around my hands. "You can sense him now?" I nodded looking towards the shore in the distance. Now that we were almost on land, I could sense Greg's aura, which meant I could find him on my own.

Harkura tugged at my hands, drawing my attention back to him. "Do you remember the plan?" he asked.

I coughed clearing my dry throat. "I fly ahead to draw out Humarya, while you guys find and rescue Greg."

Harkura nodded. "I will send up a blaze once we are clear and then you get out of there."

"Remember you're just the distraction," added Victoria, "So don't overdo it."

"I know what I'm doing." My two guardians glanced at one another. I rolled my shoulders back and looked up at the clear blue sky. Without any clouds, I wouldn't have any cover. My stomach churned as I stood in the boat. I gulped down my worry. As gently as possible I took flight, rocking the boat. I flew high up into the sky and over to the island.

Closing my eyes, I let my senses take over. My heart lurched as I sensed him. I zoomed through the air following Greg's aura to a cave. Sand flew up as I landed causing me to cough. Once the dust settled I scanned the area. Something didn't feel right. Trees lined the area to the right. Sand and rocks covered the rest of the area for miles. It appeared to be a quiet beach. Shutting my eyes I focused my senses on feeling for magic. A cold shiver travelled along my spine. There was a dark presence near. I let my senses guide me. I walked across the beach to a rocky area towards a cave. A shock wave hurtled though my body as I stood at the cave entrance. Victoria had been right; this was a trap. I was being drawn into a tight space. But this could work in my favour. It may be difficult to dodge attacks inside, but I would be surrounded by rocks, my element. Also, I wasn't alone. Harkura, Victoria and Kai were not far behind me.

Pulling the heart from around my neck I transformed it

into staff form. I took a deep breath and walked into the cave keeping my eyes peeled. Water dripped from the ceiling and a cold breeze blew through the cave causing me to shudder. I held my staff out in front of me, lighting my way. I almost tumbled over my own feet as I saw someone curled up on the floor. Running to his side, I skidded onto my knees my staff clanging on the craggy ground. I gently pulled Greg onto my lap. His hair was matted and he was covered in dirt.

"Mellissa," said Greg. His voice was broken. "You came."

I carefully pressed my fingers to his face. His left eye was swollen, and his lip was split. "Of course, I did."

"I should have listened to you."

"Shh, don't worry about that now." I wrapped my hands around the chains binding him. Light burst from my hands, destroying them. Greg rubbed his wrists. They were red raw. I stood pulling him up with me. I tugged one of his arms over my shoulders and held him close supporting his weight.

"You are so predictable," said Humarya. Her dark wings blocked the entrance. "Coming here by yourself."

A flurry of shadows crashed into us. I lost my grip on Greg and was slammed into the rocky wall of the cave and slummed to the ground. Gritting my teeth I pushed up off the floor. Victoria would hold this over me for ages. She had been completely right in how Humarya had expected me to act. Humarya lifted her arm up and slashed downwards releasing more shadows. Magic bubbled up inside me. I held my hand out and my staff flew into my hand. Light burst from the heart crystal illuminating the cave. Humarya hissed covering herself with a wing. Greg also yelled as he pulled away from me. I turned towards him. He was on the ground with his hands clasped over his face. I pulled my light back and Greg lowered his arms. He was too weak to withstand my power. I had to draw her away from him. My heart tightened. I was going to have to leave him behind.

Humarya cackled. "Poor little queen, all alone, unsure what to do."

My heart warmed as I felt them. I smirked looking her

straight in the eye. "But I'm not alone."

Flames burst behind her. She staggered as one of her wings caught fire. Ice spread across the other wing. Humarya spun on her heels her eyes looking as if they were about to pop out of her head. Shadows pulsated around her. She ran at what I assumed was Victoria and Harkura.

I ran to Greg's side. I slung his arm over my shoulders again and wrapped my arms around his middle. "Come on. While they keep her distracted, we'll get out of here."

Greg's head hung low almost as if he had lost control of his neck muscles. He was on his feet but was moving so slow. Our height difference made it hard to support him. "You brought your guardians," He said in a low voice, "She was so sure you would come after me alone in a panic."

The way he was talking was off. What had she done to him? I dragged him towards the exit. "Now isn't the time to talk about this."

"I told her you were full of surprises." He stumbled as we neared the mouth of the cave. I caught him before he could fall wrapping my arms around him. He clung tightly to me.

"We just need to get you to the boat and" My words were cut short as Greg lurched forward pressing his lips to mine. My body went stiff and my eyes widened. His kiss felt wrong. I went to push him away when a sharpness shot through my stomach. I looked down at the knife sticking out of my abdomen, Greg's hand holding the handle.

I tried to cry out but my voice got stuck in my throat. He leaned in whispering in my ear, "You have no idea how long I've wanted to do that." I stuck my palm in his face trying to get away from him, but he slapped my hand away. He gripped the back of my head, pulling at my hair and pushed the blade in deeper. Pain soared through my body. As I went to scream, he clamped his hand around my mouth. My eyes met his and my heart plummeted. The emerald green of his irises were jet black.

Greg smirked bringing his face so close I could feel the warmth of his breath on my skin. "Oh, I wish you could see the look on your face. It is delightful."

He pulled the knife from my stomach, an agonising

shock wave rolled through me. My legs gave out as I cried out in agony. This didn't make sense. Greg would never do this to me. I could still sense his aura but there was something else with him, something dark. I had mistaken the darkness in the cave for Humarya, but this thing holding Greg captive was pure evil.

I wrapped my arm around my wound and clutched my staff in the other. "What have you done to him?"

Greg stood tall neatening his collar. He swept his arms over himself. "Do you not like my new look? I knew it would get you to lower your guard." He leapt towards me grabbing my hair and placing his knife under my neck. "I'm going to enjoy slicing you open elf-ling."

My eyes widened. It couldn't be but I could feel the truth of it in the pit of my stomach. He growled staring at his hand holding the knife. His grip on me loosened and I scrambled away. "I am in control," He said.

The knife tumbled to the floor and he dropped to his knees. "Mellissa." Greg looked up at me his eyes green again. His face was tight and sweat dripped down his forehead.

I gasped. "Greg." As I went to move toward him, I doubled over. I clutched my stomach, it felt like it was on fire. Blood seeped onto my hand.

Greg grabbed his right hand with his left as it went to reach for the knife. "Mellissa, run. I can't hold him for long."

"But Greg, I can't leave you."

"You have to. Kadon is too strong."

My blood ran cold. Even though I had known that was who was controlling him, the words uttered by Greg almost made my heart stop. "Run," Greg shouted. His head dropped and he was grasping the knife again running at me. I swung my staff releasing a wave of light. Blasting him away. He cried out and thrashed about on the floor. Shadow surged from him and then leapt back into his body.

My head was spinning, and my limbs were numb, but I forced myself up. Steading myself with my staff, I ran the best I could out of the cave. Running in no particular direction, I shouted for Harkura and Victoria. A loud boom sounded nearby. There was a crash and shrill cry. My vision was blurring, and I fell face-first into the sand. I rolled over and screamed as Kadon in Greg's body stood over me knife in hand. He lunged towards me, but a blast of fire sent him flying. Harkura scooped me up in his arms. I winced as he clutched me tight to his chest and ran towards the water.

I wrapped my arms around his neck. "That wasn't Greg," I said my voice barely a whisper.

"I guessed that," said Harkura, "I assume some sort of glamour charm to catch you off guard."

"It is so much worse than that." My head toppled back and Harkura adjusted his hold to support me better.

Victoria appeared beside Harkura, running out from behind a cluster of rocks. "We need to be quick," she said, "My ice won't hold her long." A bird swooped down at us. Victoria didn't even look at it as she blasted it with ice. The bird shifted into an unconscious Gwendolyn as she hit the ground.

"What happened?" shouted Kai as we reached the boat.

"Our plan went to crap in seconds," said Victoria, "We need to get out of here."

Harkura placed me in the boat and gently stroked my head. Victoria and Kai pushed the boat off the beach and jumped in. Kai pushed his arms out, then pulled back propelling us forward at a high speed. It felt like the waves he made would rise over the sides.

Victoria knelt beside me. I knew my vision was off as she was surrounded by stars, but it was still daytime. She placed her hand over my stomach. I gasped; coldness swept over my body as she froze the wound. "That should hopefully hold until we get you to a healer." Victoria frowned. "What happened to Greg?"

"It was Kadon," I said.

I heard them all let out shocked gasps. "What?" said Victoria.

"The spirit. He has hold of Greg."

She shook her head. Her golden hair looked like rays of light. I reached up to grasp a strand and clasped air. My hand flopped back on my body. Everything ached and my mind was jumbled. Victoria took my hand. "You're not making sense."

I felt a tear silently rolling down my face. "The spirit creature is Kadon and he has taken over Greg's mind." It was the last thing I managed to say before everything went white.

Rescue

Victoria

"Mellissa," shouted Victoria. A lump caught in her throat as her chest tightened. She gently shook Mellissa's shoulders but there was no response. Mellissa's dark lashes had fluttered shut as she lay sprawled out on the boat floor and the colour had drained from her features. Victoria pressed her fingers to Mellissa's neck and let out a sigh of relief as she felt her pulse still strong.

"She has just passed out," said Harkura. He had hold of Mellissa's wrist and his other hand on her forehead.

"What happened?" yelled Victoria.

"I found her on the ground bleeding with what looked like Greg about to attack her." He ran his fingers through his black hair his forehead creased. "I thought Humarya had a minion use a glamour charm."

"That's not what Mellissa said."

Harkura shook his head. "We just need to get her to a healer then we can figure this out." He turned to Kai. "Can you move any quicker?"

Sweat dripped down Kai's forehead and his robes billowed it the wind. "I'm going as fast as I can."

Victoria looked down at Mellissa. Her usual warm brown skin was pale. Her black tunic was soaked in blood. Ice stuck out of her midriff. Victoria clenched her fists, she wasn't sure if freezing the wound had been a good idea but the bleeding had stopped. Her heart hammered in her chest, felling like it was about to explode. This wasn't meant to happen. They had had a plan, yet they had still walked straight into Humarya's trap. '*Mellissa is going to be okay*' she thought over and over. Victoria hung her head fighting back tears. Yet again she had failed to protect her. She took a deep breath rubbing her face with her palms.

The boat jerked to the left. "Kai, what are you doing?" shouted Victoria whipping her head round to glare at him.

"It's not me." Kai's eyes were wide with panic as he pointed up at the sky.

Victoria's chest tightened as she looked up to see Humarya flying. The wind swirled around them. Victoria's hair whipped around in the air. She threw herself over Mellissa as the boat rocked to the left again. Water sloshed up the sides. Kai swiftly circled his arms and pushed the current out steadying the boat.

"Victoria," shouted Harkura. Before she could respond he had jumped up and thrust himself into the air with flames. Victoria's magic surged from within. Pushing her hands out she froze the surface of the sea and created ice steps. Harkura landed on them and ran up. When he got to the end he leapt off them grabbing onto Humarya's wing and setting her ablaze. The two of them spun in the air. Harkura lost his grip on the wing and was hurtling down. Victoria swished her arms catching Harkura with her ice. She created a slide and he slid back towards the boat. Before he reached them her ice burst. Victoria screamed as shadows whipped her, burning her skin. Her body sizzled with pain. Closing her eyes she focused her powers and magic spilled out from the pores of her skin. The shadows around her froze. She pushed her arms out with force and shattered the ice, freeing herself.

Victoria frantically scanned the area. "Where's Harkura?"

"He fell in and hasn't resurfaced," replied Kai.

"Can't your water magic save him?" Victoria asked.

"I'm doing everything I can to keep us steady and moving in this gust Humarya has created." Victoria looked over at Kai properly. Kai stood propelling his arms around. His features were creased and sweat dripped down his forehead. Panic bubbled up inside her. Mellissa was already hurt she couldn't lose Harkura too.

Humarya cackled above them, drawing her attention back to her. Shadows danced around her. She pulled her arm up gathering the dark swirls into her hand. Victoria stood pressing her hands together mustering as much magic as she could spare. Humarya slashed her arm down firing a gigantic ball of shadow. At the same time Victoria threw her arms forward her magic flowing and created an ice barrier. It shattered on impact. The dark ball hit the surface of the water creating a tidal wave. The boat was hurtled up and capsized. Victoria dove towards Mellissa hooking her arms round the unconscious girl. She braced herself, ready to be submerged, but it never happened. She looked around to see the water funnelling around her. It was like they were in a ball of water. "Kai how did you do this?" she asked.

"This is beyond my power." He said.

"Then how?" Kai shrugged. He looked in awe at the water swirling around them.

A dark figure appeared outside the ball. Victoria used one arm to pull Mellissa closer to her chest, while drawing a magic into the other. Harkura stumbled through the wall of water. His eyes locked on to Victoria. He placed a hand over his heart and smiled wearily. "Thank the gods you are okay," he said.

"I was about to say the same to you," said Victoria.

Another shadow appeared outside. In strode the sea king. He had legs instead of a tail. He ran over to Victoria and knelt in front of her. "Is the queen aright?"

Victoria narrowed her eyes at him. "She has been better."

"We need to get her back to land. We have to be quick, I'm not sure how long Humarya will stay subdued." He stood and held his arm out. Light seeped from his fingertips. The water around them shifted, gathering in front of his hand. The sphere they were in got small as a circle appeared in front of the King's hand. "Can you all swim?" he asked. They all responded affirmatively. He knelt back in front of Victoria. She instinctively held Mellissa tighter. Radius held his arms out. "Let me take her. I have opened the portal as close to land as I could, but we will still be under water. It will be easiest for me to swim while carrying her."

Victoria gritted her teeth. "Okay." She reluctantly let Radius take Mellissa from her.

He cradled Mellissa in his arms. "Take a deep breath and follow me." He walked through the portal. Victoria sucked in as much air as she could and followed closely. With Harkura and Kai right behind her. The portal closed once they were all through. Radius shot upwards like a torpedo, swimming at inhuman speed and had Mellissa out of the ocean in a flash. Victoria kicked and propelled her arms, swimming as fast as she could. Her lungs burned for air. A hand grasped her wrist. Startled she turned to see Kai holding onto her, with Harkura's wrist in his other hand. He tugged at them both and then pushed them forward. They both shot upwards and surfaced on the beach.

Victoria coughed and spluttered while trying to take in as much air as possible. Harkura crawled along the sand doing the same. "Mellissa," he said.

Victoria's heart felt like it had stopped. Her body ached all over and it protested as she pushed herself up onto her feet. King Radius still had Mellissa in his arms. Victoria ran over to them, Harkura closely behind her. "Her condition is unchanged," Radius said.

Victoria brushed her fingers along Mellissa's cheek. Her skin was ice cold. "We need to get her to a healer." She looked around frantically for Kai.

A wave crashed on the sandy beach and Kai walked out of the water hand placed together in front of him. "Follow me," he said, "I have called on the best healers for the Queen."

They didn't have to go far. The healers found them before they even got back to the city. King Radius set Mellissa down on the stretcher they had with them and the healers began their work. Victoria stood by helpless as she watched. The Healers recited spells and their hands glowed. The ice melted away as her skin knit back together. Mellissa gasped and opened her eyes briefly. Her eyes quickly fluttered shut again but her skin was back to its normal warm brown. She looked more like she was sleeping. One of the healers approached Victoria and Harkura. "Her wounds are all healed. This was a difficult one so there will be a scar."

"But she is okay?" Victoria interrupted.

The healer nodded. "Yes. Physically the queen is fine. She is just resting. We will get her in our carriage and get her back to the temple."

"Thank you," said Harkura, "We will follow."

Victoria's legs turned to jelly as she burst into tears. It was like all the adrenaline that had kept her going drained from her body in that instant. She dropped to her knees unable to remain standing. Tears streamed down her face. Harkura enveloped her in his arms. "She's okay."

"I know- it's just- I really thought we might of- and then when you disappeared during the fight." Victoria choked on her tears.

"shhh just let it all out." Harkura hugged her tight, stroking her wet hair. Victoria nestled her face in the crook of his neck, letting the tears fall freely. She would get this all out her system now, so when Mellissa woke up she would be back to her normal self. She wouldn't let her queen see her like this. Victoria curled into Harkura's arms, letting all her feelings flow.

Injured

Mellissa

aves raged against the shore. Dark clouds thundered above and a cold gust pierced my skin. My hair whipped around my face. I put my hand on my forehead and squinted trying to see through the grey mist. I screamed as Matt lurched forward grabbing my shoulders.

His eyes were wide and sweat dripped from his forehead. "I don't have much time. We were never meant to have a voice." He looked from side to side as if we were being watched. "There's a prophecy and it's been unwinding around us for thousands of years."

I tried to push him away, but he held on tight. "Matt you're hurting me. I don't understand."

"The darkness has come for you, but the light can stop it."

Thunder roared as hailstone pelted us. Waves surged towards us. I screamed as water crashed down on us sweeping us out to sea. Matt shouted my name. I reached out to him, but the current pulled me under. My heart raced and my limbs went numb. I shut my eyes as I sank deeper and deeper.

I shot up in bed and screamed in agony. Pain surged through my midriff like it was burning. I pulled the sheets away looking over my body for the source of pain. Bandages were wrapped around my centre. Apart from that the rest of me seemed okay.

My heart ached as I recalled how I was injured. I had failed. Greg was still with Humarya and she had done far worse to him than I could have ever imagined. My hand shot to the Heart crystal around my neck. I let out a slow breath. It was still there. Swinging my legs over the edge of the bed I looked around my surroundings. I was in a large four-poster bed with blue drapes hanging from the posts. The room was grand with glass double doors leading to a balcony looking over the ocean. There wasn't much else in the room apart from a simple wardrobe, set of drawers and the table next to the bed. I was back in Perluves. Most likely the temple living quarters. They loved their sea view here. I ran my hand over my head. My hair had been pulled from its braid and it was a ratty mess. I didn't understand how any of this had happened and the one person I knew I could count on to help me find the answers, was currently having his mind tortured by Kadon. I gripped the edge of the bed. Kadon was back. My pulse raced as I jumped out of bed. I needed to do something but I didn't know what. I needed to find the others. We had to alert everyone to Kadon's return. My head swam, making me dizzy. Kadon had never really been gone. All this time he had been roaming around as a spirit doing god knows what. And now he possessed Greg. Humarya was ten times more dangerous with him by her side.

Victoria walked into the room and almost dropped the drink she was holding as she looked at me. She placed her cup on the set of drawers and marched over to me. "What do you think you are doing?" She grasped my shoulders turning me back towards the bed and gently but forcefully made me get back into it.

I folded my arms as she draped a blanket over me. "I'm just trying to figure out what's going on," I said.

Victoria sat on the edge of the bed. Her lips pressed together in a tight line. "We are back at the temple in Perluves. You were too injured to take anywhere else." She looked up at me. Her blue eyes had dark circles under them. She leaned forward and pulled me into a hug. "I was so worried."

"I'm sorry, I didn't mean to," I returned her hug and patted her back. "I'm fine. Just a bit sore."

Victoria pulled away quickly. "I'm sorry. I didn't mean to irritate your wound."

"No you didn't, and I like it when you hug me." I placed my hand over hers. "It's just if I've been healed why do I still feel so rubbish?"

Her forehead creased as she looked away from me. "Somehow you were stabbed in the exact same place as when Kadon stabbed you before. It made it harder for them to heal. You will have a scar and your body will ache. The healers ordered for you to rest."

I ran my fingers through my hair shaking my head. Stabbing me in the same spot would have taken precision and extensive knowledge of my past wound. Even Kadon shouldn't have known the exact spot he had struck me before. Back then he had just lashed out in anger. I couldn't believe it had just been luck but how had he done it? I looked up at Victoria scrunching my face. "How did we get away? Did your ice hold long enough for Kai to get us back?"

Victoria frowned shaking her head. "No, it was King Radius."

"What?"

"He appeared out of nowhere protecting us. Then he created a portal in the water bringing us to shore."

I felt hollow inside. I was a failure as a crystal keeper. Once again Radius had come to my rescue, even after I had shouted at him. Greg was still captured. The two big enemies I thought I had defeated were now working together.

"Mellissa look at me." Victoria hooked her finger under my chin turning my head. "Whatever you are thinking, stop, now. We were caught off guard, but this isn't over."

"Of course, it isn't." I may be a failure but that didn't mean I was going to give up. Greg needed me. The whole world did. It didn't matter how much I messed up; I would never stop trying. I might eventually get things right but that would never happen if I just stopped. I stood rolling my shoulders back. My body still ached but I had too much to do to sit around in bed. "Take me to the others."

Victoria placed her hand on my shoulder. "You need to be checked by a healer."

I jerked her hand away and looked her straight in the eye. "Take me to the others." She nodded and I followed her out of the room.

As Victoria and I entered the room everyone went silent. It was a large room that looked to be some sort of dining room. A large table was at the centre of the room, where Yuko, Kai and Radius sat. They appeared to have been in deep conversation before we walked in. Harkura was stood in the corner by a grand sideboard encasing pretty plates. He was talking to a petite girl with pink skin. She had short dark hair and bright silver eyes.

Harkura smiled at me as a wave of relief washed over his face. He strode over and hugged me, squeezing the breath out of me. "You're awake, thank the gods. I was worried you might be out for days like before."

My chest tightened at his words. "How long has it been?"

"Only a couple of hours," he said. I looked over his shoulder at the girl he had been talking to. Her pink scales shimmered in the light and she had webbed fingers. She must be with Radius. Thinking about it she looked slightly familiar. Harkura followed my gaze. "That is El," he said, "one of the King's guardians." Some of the tension in my shoulders eased. For some reason it made me feel better that Radius had one of his guardians with him this time.

I walked over to the table where the others sat. Radius stood. He now had legs and was wearing turquoise trousers with a gold top, which matched the golden crown atop his head. His short brown hair was flecked with grey, but he still looked young. His bold choice of colours suited him well. The wide stance he took and the way he held his head high, oozed authority. He bowed his head to me. It was a small gesture, but it was one of respect. "It is good to see you are all healed. Your wound looked awful."

I forced myself to smile trying to mirror his authoritative stance. "Thank you for assisting us in getting back."

"You are welcome, I wish I could have arrived sooner to help in the fight."

"You can help me fight now." I stood tall and tried to look as in control as possible. "I'm going back after Humarya and Kadon."

"You can't," said Yuko. She stood bracing herself on the table. Her usual blue colour still hadn't returned, and she looked peaky. "You have only just woken up and we need to consult with the council."

The urge to scream overwhelmed me but I clenched my fists taking a deep breath. There was no way I was wasting my time consulting the council. I had made that mistake before. "There isn't time for that," I said.

"If this spirit creature is Kadon the others must be informed," Yuko said.

My jaw tensed. "The spirit *is* Kadon. Trust me."

"Of course, I trust you." She walked around the table. Taking my hand, she gently stroked the back of it. "It's just with the amount of blood you lost, you may have been hallucinating."

I yanked my hand from hers but before I could speak, Kai stood grasping Yuko's shoulder. "I do not believe the queen was hallucinating. I was there when she was healed. The healers had difficulties due to it opening up an old wound." Kai's brows scrunched together as his blue face turned pale. "I do not think it was a coincidence that she was stabbed in the same place again. This was Kadon's work. Trying to seriously wound her, in the hope she wouldn't make it to a healer in time."

Yuko frowned as her eyes turned downwards. Harkura came to stand beside me, his arms behind his back and his shoulders stiff. His dark blue eyes were a glow with power. "That darkness I felt on the island was one I have felt before. I know it isn't something we want to believe but Kadon is this spirit. With Kadon by her side, Humarya is too dangerous to give any more time to achieve her goals."

"I agree," said Radius. He nodded towards me. "I will fight by your side again. This mad woman must be stopped, and Gregory freed of this evil spirit".

Yuko gasped, her hands shaking in front of her mouth. "You are right you must go quickly."

Radius looked down at her. "Why the sudden change of attitude?"

Her blue skin looked almost white as she grabbed the back of a chair bracing herself. "Gregory did something with the sea stone. If Kadon is in his head, he will lead them straight to it."

I almost rolled my eyes but managed to stop myself. "I'm glad you have come around Yuko. Time is against us. You and Kai go to the council and tell them what is happening. The rest of us will go after Humarya."

Yuko nodded. She almost tripped as she shuffled toward me. Grasping my hand, she bowed. "May the gods bless you and guide you in this upcoming battle." She stood and looked up at me. "Kai and I will deal with the council on your behalf. I have faith in you, Queen Mellissa." She gestured for Kai to come and the two of them left the room. I had never been blessed by the high priestess before, maybe that was what had been missing in my previous fights.

Victoria stood beside me. "I hate to throw shade on that blessing, but do we know how to get Kadon out of Greg's body?"

The fragile pieces of my heart felt close to disintegrating. I rubbed my bandaged stomach. "When Kadon stabbed me, Greg was able to take back control but only for a minute or two."

Harkura shook his head. "We are not letting him hurt you again, in hope of that letting Gregory take control." Harkura looked to Radius. "With all your dealings with the spirit under the sea, have you found anything that can harm it?"

Radius rubbed the stubble on his chin. "Everyone that was possessed was left with no memory and it was only for short amounts of time. What is happening to Gregory is completely different."

I wrapped my hand around the heart crystal. "He was repulsed by the light of the Heart. Maybe enough of it will force him out of Greg."

Harkura wrapped an arm around my shoulders. He looked at me, his eyes full of pity. "I don't like the sound of maybe but if it's all we have." I gulped down the lump in my throat. Harkura would do anything to protect me. Including hurting Greg. This had to work.

King Radius coughed. He nodded to the other side of the room. "Do you mind if I talk to you alone for a moment?"

I bit my bottom lip trying to not let my uncertainty show. "Sure." He lead us over to the corner away from the others. I folded my arms. "What's wrong?"

"Nothing is wrong." He glanced back at the others. His eyebrows furrowed as he looked down at me. "I realise you must be hurting. I don't know how I would cope if I was in your shoes right now."

"What's your point?"

"I think I should be the one to deal with Kadon."

My jaw tensed as I shook my head. "No, it has to be me."

He tilted his head as he frowned. "Does it? Kadon is currently inside Gregory's body are you sure you will be able to fight him in that form?" He held his hand out and light danced around it. "We can both produce light energy. You should focus on Humarya and I will free Gregory."

I pulled at my loose curls. As much as I hated to admit it, he was right. I wanted Greg back more than anything, which left me emotionally vulnerable. When I came face to face with Kadon in Greg's body again, there was no guarantee I could fight him to my full ability. "Okay," I said, "but don't make me regret trusting you again."

Radius placed a hand on my shoulder. His stare bore into me. "I will not fail again." He clapped his hands together, making me jump. "Good, we have a plan of action but how do we find them."

I smiled at him for real this time. "That's the easy part. Greg may be under Kadons control, but he is still Greg and easy for me to track. Once we find their location, you portal us to the closest pool of water and then the fight begins."

I winced as I pulled on my top. Victoria had insisted I see a healer before leaving. Bed rest had been recommended but that suggestion was going to be ignored. My heart sank as I looked down at my stomach. The bandage had been removed. I brushed my fingers over the slightly raised area of my skin. It still felt sore, but it was healed as much as they could manage. The healer had said it would likely scar. Since being introduced to magical healing the idea of being left with a scar didn't seem possible. Kai had been right. Kadon had done this hoping I wouldn't survive. He had known it would be hard to heal. The room swayed around me and I grabbed onto the closest solid object, which happened to be the dresser. Kadon had known this thanks to Greg's extensive knowledge of healing. He had known where to strike because Greg had been the one to heal me before. I dug my nails into the dresser. My blood boiled as I thought of what Greg must be going through. I couldn't even begin to imagine how awful it must be to have my memories riffled through like that.

I was brought back to reality as Victoria marched into the room. She dropped a bag at my feet. "Take that off."

"Why?" I asked. I narrowed my eyes at her. She was wearing what looked like blue leather armour. It was very form-fitting.

She smirked at me, her eyes sparkling icy blue. "Kai has provided us with some lightweight armour. It is something new they have been working on. They had planned to unveil it later this year and put it up for sale, but after what happened to you, Kai thought he would gift us a few sets."

I pulled a top similar to the one she was wearing out of the bag and stroked the fabric. It was smooth and light. "What sort of leather is this?"

"It's not leather. It's a specially engineered fabric that is super strong and lightweight. Way better than leather. If it works the way Kai said, you won't be getting stabbed again. At least not by a normal blade."

I nodded turning the outfit over in my hands. It didn't seem possible that the flimsy jacket could stop a knife, but I would take any help given. I slipped into the outfit. It was more comfortable than it looked. It felt extremely light, almost as if I weren't wearing anything. Matching boots were in the bag with two sets of silver gauntlets. I picked up one of the gauntlets and squealed as a blade popped out of it. Victoria grabbed it off me. "Careful."

"Why would I need something like that?" I asked.

She slipped the gauntlet onto her arm. With a flick of her wrist, the blade retracted. "These are mine. Pretty cool right? Another gift from Kai. Who knew the priestess was hiding such beauties?" She picked the matching one out of the bag and put it on. "Those are yours. No blades. Just for defending with."

I tugged at a loose curl. "I suppose Harkura has a set like yours."

"He does, along with a surprising amount of other hidden weapons. I don't know where he hides it all."

"Why do we need so many weapons? Aren't our powers enough?"

Victoria placed her hand on my forearm and crouched so we were at eye level. "In a normal fight, yes, but Mellissa, this needs to end. This time we need to make sure Humarya can't return."

"I can't do that. It's wrong."

"We know you can't. That's why Harkura and I are the ones carrying the weapons."

"But-"

She placed her hand up. "No buts Mellissa. I will do what I have to." She walked over to the door and looked back over her shoulder. "You do realise Harkura is always armed. He is just very good at concealing it."

Her blond hair shone in the light as she left. I hadn't

known that, but it made sense. The way Harkura had produced that blade out of nowhere when we were doing the tracking spell. He always had that knife on him. I had just never paid close enough attention before. My stomach twisted. Humarya had done so much wrong. She was the reason both my parents were dead. She was a monster, but could I stand by while they killed her?

Possessed

Gregory

The sun shone brightly in the sky. Robins chirped in the trees as a gentle breeze rustled the leaves. There was a light dusting of snow on the ground but there were no signs of any more falling anytime soon. It was a beautiful winter's evening, if Greg hadn't been here against his will, it would have been a perfect walk in the woods. But instead, he was a puppet being made to walk through the northern forest. Everything felt wrong. It was as if his body was covered in pins and needles. Greg's legs moved of their own accord. Humarya and Gwendolyn followed him in the sky. Their shadows loomed over him. This darkness lurking inside him had rooted its way in and taken control. Greg tried to stand still, to just stop moving. He tried to put his arms out, to grab on to anything nearby, a tree, a branch, or a rock but his body wouldn't respond to his demands.

"Stop that," hissed Kadons voice in his head. "You are getting on my nerves."

"I will never stop fighting you." Greg tried to shout but his voice wasn't his to control.

Kadon laughed using Greg's voice. "I am the one in control so you may as well give up."

Greg bristled at the words coming out of his mouth that were not his. "I'd rather die than let you use my body to hurt anyone else."

"I believe you would, but I have become fond of this

body of yours," Kadon said in Greg's voice. "There are benefits of looking like an elder and the turmoil it must be causing that girlfriend of yours."

"Shut up, don't talk about her." Greg tried to shut his eyes. He tried to tune Kadon out. Images of stabbing Mellissa ran through his mind. Her blood on his hands and the pure joy Kadon had felt. The same way Kadon could hear Greg's thoughts and see his memories, Greg could also see Kadon's thoughts. They were sharing a mind, but Kadon was the one in charge.

Kadon laughed again. "Do you think she survived? Thanks to you being the one who healed her after my final battle with the elf queen, I was able to strike her in the same spot." Greg wanted to scream. To claw at his own face. He would throw himself off a cliff if it meant taking Kadon down with him. Kadon's laughter grew darker. "Oh, your memories of her are good. Who knew how sensual the little elf-ling could be? I should have pretended to be you for longer and had my fun with her first before stabbing her to death." Images of Mellissa in different compromising positions reeled around his mind. Every thought Kadon had of her ended with her death.

"Get out of my head." Greg pushed these thoughts at Kadon, trying to force his will on him. They stopped moving. Kadon growled at him. It was working. Greg pushed harder.

Gwendolyn swooped down in bird form shifting back as she landed. "What are you doing?" She looked to the sky. "My queen won't be happy about the delay."

She scowled when he didn't respond. Greg's body didn't move but, on the inside, he was full of turmoil as he fought Kadon for control. Inside his head the two shared blows, attempting to force their will on the other. Greg dropped to his knees panting. He flicked his wrist putting up a barrier between him and Gwendolyn. Her eyes widened. "She will kill you."

"I don't care." Greg turned to run but then he froze.

"I won't be pushed out so easily." Kadon's voice growled in his head.

Humarya landed with a thud. Her yellow eyes bore into Greg. She lifted her hand wrapping him in shadows. "Kadon if you can't control the boy, I better dispose of him."

"No," said Kadon back in control. "I need this body. His insider knowledge is useful, and I like his powers. Shape shifting is such fun".

Her nostrils flared. "This isn't a game."

He bowed, giving her a sweet smile. "I'm sorry my queen. It won't happen again." Greg could feel how much Kadon had hated saying those words to her. Kadon knelt before Humarya, taking her hand in his and gently brushing his lips across it. "If you would continue to follow me, I will take you to where the boy hid the stone."

Humarya pulled her hand away and snarled. "If you cease to be useful, I will dispose of you." Humarya flew back into the sky. With a flick of his wrist, Kadon freed Gwendolyn. She bowed before shifting into a bird and following Humarya into the sky.

Kadon and Greg both glared at Humarya's figure above the trees. Greg was full of hate towards her, but that hate wasn't just his. "You are up to something." Greg thought.

"Of course, I am," replied Kadon, "And you are going to help me destroy this world." Greg tried to clench his fist. To shout, kick, to just do anything. "I won't let you take control again. Your body is mine now," said Kadon.

Greg felt the venom in Kadon's words but, that didn't faze Greg's resolve. He would keep fighting. Before he had avoided looking into Kadons memories out of fear of what he would find. The glimpses Kadon had pushed at him had been bad enough but those had been what Kadon had wanted him to see. They had been Kadon's way of torturing him. If Greg delved deeper, he may be able to find a way to stop him. Greg would do whatever it took to stop Kadon, even if it meant sacrificing his sanity. What Humarya had planned was bad enough, but Greg was sure whatever Kadon had in mind was a lot worse.

Greg's mind was ringing. His head felt like it was about to

explode. Kadon's mind was stronger than anything he had felt before. He was ancient and full of hate. His darkness seeped into every crevasse. His claws firmly dug in. Greg's mind was wavering, but he couldn't give up. If he stopped fighting, Kadon would win. He would lose control of himself forever. They were still walking through the forest getting closer to their destination. Greg had no control over his body's movements.

"Are you finally realising you can't beat me," Said Kadon.

"You know Humarya is just using you," Greg said.

"Come on now, you have seen enough of my thoughts to know I am the one using her."

"She is the one with all the power. You can't win. If Humarya doesn't dispose of you first, Mellissa will stop you."

Kadon cackled. "That is if the elf-ling is still alive." He swept his arm over the whole of Greg's body. "Besides Mellissa wouldn't want to hurt what I'm wearing."

Kadon said Mellissa's name in a sing-song tone. Greg's head throbbed as he pushed his will at Kadon. Nothing happened. He was weakening while Kadon grew stronger. Mellissa was alive, he told himself. That he was sure of. If she hadn't survived, he would have been able to feel it.

Kadon groaned in disgust. "Your hope is nauseating. Would you just give in already and stop annoying me?"

Greg would have clenched his fists if he could. "Is this not how it always is when you take over someone?"

"Usually, their mind goes to sleep, and I go about my tasks in peace. However, you are just so… so stubborn."

Why was the effect on Greg different? Thinking back Greg didn't have any recollection of how much time had passed from Kadon entering his mind, to when he stabbed Mellissa. Greg's mind had gone to sleep but he hadn't realised. It was Mellissa being hurt that had snapped him awake. The reason Kadon was having so much trouble controlling him was because he had hurt the person Greg loved more than anyone else. If it wasn't for that Greg may not have woken up.

The sound of gushing water caught Greg's attention. They were nearly at the lake. Greg hadn't been thinking when he sent the sea stone away. He had sent it to the first place that popped into his head. He wasn't sure why this lake was what he thought of, but it seemed far enough away to make the stone hard to retrieve. Unfortunately, that also meant it would be hard for Mellissa to get here to stop them. Pain seared through Greg's mind. He was weakening, maybe he should just go to sleep. He tried to shake his head but of course, he couldn't.

"That's right just go to sleep," Kadon whispered. The ground shook and they stumbled forward. Greg's mind snapped back into action. That was no normal tremor. Kadon growled. Mellissa was here.

34

Burning Light

Mellissa

The tracking spell worked perfectly. It had pinpointed Greg's location to somewhere in the northern forest. There was a lake on the edge of the forest so that was our target. Hopefully, it wouldn't take long to find them once we arrived. The five of us walked down to the beach dressed in matching blue armour provided by Kai. It didn't feel like I was wearing armour due to it being so light and flexible. Radius and his guardian El walked ahead talking amongst themselves. My stomach felt uneasy. The plan was to leave Kadon to them and let Radius free Greg. I rolled my shoulders loosening my tense muscles. I had to have faith in the two of them. Radius' light would be enough. I wasn't sure what El's abilities were but if she was anything like my guardians, she would be deadly.

Radius walked out into the ocean to where it was deeper. Placing his hand in the water, he swirled his hand around forming a portal. He turned to me. "After you, Queen Mellissa."

I took a deep breath, hoping my hands weren't shaking as bad as I thought. Harkura took my hand and nodded. I gave him a weak smile. Together we walked through the portal. We were pulled down and water swallowed us up. I sunk deeper, my limbs locking up. Darkness swept through the water. My body jolted upwards. Harkura hooked his arm under me and kicked upwards pulling us to the surface. I gasped for air.

Dazzling sunlight blinded me, causing me to almost sink back down. Harkura held me tight keeping me afloat as we swam to land.

Whatever this suit was made of was impressive. We had been fully submerged in the lake, but it had absorbed hardly any water. My hair however was dripping wet. Harkura covered himself in flames drying himself. His suit didn't have a scorch mark on it. "Is my suit also fireproof?" I asked.

"They all are." He said. "It's an annoying feature, I don't need our enemies to possess." He smirked. "Luckily, the outfit doesn't cover the head."

I looked back towards the lake. The sun glistened on the surface and the light breeze created gentle waves. The same darkness I had felt while submerged was calling me back to the lake. "Do you feel that?" I asked.

"Feel what?" Harkura asked.

"That darkness. Something evil is here." A squawk echoed above. I looked up to see a bird circling above the lake. Harkura pulled me into the trees as he scanned the area. "I think the darkness you are feeling is Humarya approaching."

I looked back at the lake to see the others pop up. They swam towards shore. Radius' face was tight as he looked down at the lake. He felt it too. "No," I said, "It's the dark stone. It's in the lake." I stepped out towards the water but Harkura pulled me back as glass shards fell at our feet. The shards grew into sparkling glass creatures. The ones closest slashed their sharp arms at us. I ducked narrowly dodging the attack. Flames erupted in front of me shattering them in one go but more appeared. I slammed my hand on the ground shaking the terrain. The earth opened up swallowing the creatures. As I stood, I rolled my hand into a fist, closing the hole.

Humarya landed in the clearing by the lake, black wings held high. Her eagle eyes narrowed on me. As she went to flap her wings down, a loud boom rang through the forest. Humarya toppled onto the ground. El stood behind her arms wide. She clapped her hands together. Another loud boom and an invisible force slammed into Humarya.

A squawking bird swooped down scratching at El's face.

She fell to the ground while trying to swat it away. Radius blasted the bird with water, sending it hurtling into the forest. As the bird hit a tree it shifted into Gwendolyn. Harkura growled beside me. "I will deal with her." Heat radiated from him. I heard the clink of a blade being released as he ran at Gwendolyn.

Humarya screeched throwing her arms out wide. Glass creatures popped up all around us. With Victoria and El by his side, Radius began smashing the creatures. The creatures were not hard to defeat but Humarya had an endless supply of them. I sent a wave of light out, shattering a bunch of creatures in my way. Greg was nowhere in sight, but I could feel him nearby somewhere. I shook my head. I had to trust Radius would free Greg. My gaze fell on Humarya. She was my target. Holding my hand out, the Heart crystal shot to my hand in staff form. I twirled it round firing light at Humarya. She blasted shadows at me. Our attacks collided causing an almighty bang. We both hit the floor hard, but I was up in an instant. I ran at her. A spark of electricity ran through my body. I pulled my hand back ready to strike when something crashed into me. My feet were taken out from under me, and my lightning shot into the sky. Greg was on top of me pinning me down. He smirked at me. "Hello, elf-ling."

Water wrapped around Greg, and he was yanked off of me. Radius was at my side pulling me to my feet. I quickly glanced at the others. Victoria and El were dealing with the glass creatures, that kept forming. Harkura was locked in a fight with a bear.

Greg snarled baring his teeth at us. My chest tightened as he looked at me with black eyes. That wasn't Greg, I reminded myself, but Kadon. Radius pulled his hand back and hit Kadon with a hydro blast. Water whips in hand Radius ran at Kadon. Kadon shifted into a bird and flew up into the sky. He circled round and slashed at Radius. My stomach churned as I watched Kadon using Greg's powers. I shook myself, snapping myself back to the current fight. My opponent was the deranged bird woman. I turned to her to find her surrounded by shadows. As she lifted her arms. I threw up a barrier prepared to take the hit. She smirked as she changed direction at the last minute. She fired a flurry of shadows at Radius. I yelled his name but I wasn't quick enough. He cried out as he was hit head-on. Humarya flapped her wings hard creating a whirlwind around Radius. As I clenched my fists the ground began to shake knocking her off balance. Her attack on Radius weakened. I spun my staff ready to bring lightning down on her when talons dug into my raised arm. I yelped as bird Kadon scratched at me. I whirled around ready to blast him, but he shifted swiftly into a snake wrapping himself around my neck. The feeling of his scaly skin made my blood run cold. As he tightened his snake body around my neck, I fell backwards struggling to breathe. I dug my nails into his skin as I clawed and scratched but he just tightened his grip. Stars filled my vision. I clamped my hands on him releasing light. He slithered away hissing. I coughed as I took in deep breaths, my neck burning. I jumped up and turned round just in time to see a tiger pouncing at me. I dove to the side. Spinning round I released more light at Kadon. He roared as he fell to the floor shifting back to human form. He thrashed around on the ground. Seeing him look like Greg again made me freeze. Kadon flipped up onto his feet. With two daggers in his hand, he slashed at me. I thrust my arms up in front of me. His blades clanged against my gauntlets. I blocked as he thrust both daggers at me. His nostrils flared. He kicked me hard in the shin causing me to buckle. As he slashed his daggers down, I crossed my wrists over catching his blades with my gauntlets. As I twisted my wrists his daggers were yanked from his hand. I caught them, swiftly throwing them behind me. His black eyes widened as I grabbed his arms. Kicking his legs out from under him, I yanked him over flipping him on his back. He kicked up hitting me in the chest. As he rose from the ground, he threw a punch at me. I dodged to the right, catching his arm as I did. My power burst from within surrounding me in light. He yelled, scratching at me with his free hand. A black shadow hovered around Greg as one of his eyes turned green. It was working. Kadon bit down on the hand that was holding him. We both stumbled backwards. I grasped my hand. The shadow was gone, and both his eyes were back to being black, but he looked at me eyes wide. The colour had drained from his skin. As I stepped forward, he jumped back. He turned to run but I was quicker. Grabbing him, I twisted his arm around and pinned the other to his side. Holding him close I surrounded us in light. The dark shadow began to withdraw from Greg but then it was sucked back in.

"No," yelled Kadon. He thrust his head forward, smacking me in the face. My eyesight blurred as a stinging sensation spread across my jaw, but I didn't let up. Gritting my teeth I pushed more light outwards, illuminating the area. As he went to bite me again, I grabbed the side of his face. I pulled his body close with one hand, while pushing his head back with the other. The shadow began to shudder out of Greg again. We both dropped to our knees. With one hand locked around his arms and the other holding his head in place. I channelled everything I had into repulsing Kadon out. He let out an ear-piercing scream, as the shadow flinched away from the light. Greg flopped into my arms.

"Greg," I cried. I pushed his fringe back. "Greg."

"Mellissa," he whispered. He looked at me with his emerald eyes before closing them and passing out. I laid him on the grass and felt for a pulse. Tears filled my eyes as I felt his pulse beat under my touch. My relief was short lived. I had been so focused on my fight that I had forgotten about the others. I stumbled as I rose from the ground. My body was exhausted, but I still had to fight. I gasped as I spotted Harkura lying on the grass a massive slash across his face. El was passed out beside the lake. Victoria and Radius were holding back Humarya with a combination of water and ice. I had to help them. As I ran forward a fish flipped up out of the water transforming into a bird, a blue stone glimmering in its talons. "No" I whispered to myself. As I went to fire a bolt of lightning at the bird a darkness crashed into me. Kadons voice hissed at me. "You are always getting in my way but if I take your body-"

"I don't think so." My body was illuminated in light again, causing Kadon's spirit to shudder away. I dropped to my knees panting.

The sound of Humarya's mad laugh sent shivers down my spine. I looked up to see Victoria blasted across the clearing by water. Shadows wrapped around her.

Humarya cackled. "It's finally mine."

Radius snapped a water whip at her, which she counted with her own. In her hand shone a blue stone. She thrust it out towards Radius sending water gushing at him. He crossed his arms in front of his face deflecting it. My blood ran cold. She had both stones. Forcing myself to my feet, I sent tremors through the earth, opening the ground beneath Humarya. Roots sprung up dragging her down and I swiftly closed the ground back up over her. I knew it wouldn't hold her long, as I could already feel her shadow seeping back to the surface. "We need to escape now," I yelled.

Radius nodded his muscles tense. With a flick of my wrist light encased Victoria, freeing her from her shadow binds. I didn't need to tell her what to do, it was as if she had read my mind. She ran to Harkura and hurled him over her shoulders, fireman style. Radius heaved Greg up and over one of his shoulders and then El over the other. He jogged over to the edge of the lake and dipped his foot in the water. "Where should we go?"

"The lake outside the capital," I said. The ground shuddered as Humarya burst out of it. She threw shadows at us. I put up a barrier, but it shattered on impact. "Go quick," I shouted. Victoria jumped into the portal, followed closely by Radius. Humarya hurled shadows at me. I pushed a wall of light at her as I fell backwards into the portal.

35

Prophecy

Mellissa

The portal closed as I fell through. My body felt like lead as I sank. My lungs burned craving air but my limbs didn't respond to the need. Harkura wasn't here to pull me along this time. I needed my legs to move, to kick me up to the surface. My heart was heavy weighing me down. My eyes fluttered shut accepting my fate. A strong hand grabbed mine and yanked me to the surface. I gasped as my lungs filled with air. "Queen Mellissa are you all right?" Radius asked.

"Yes, thanks to you." He pulled us onto land. Greg, Harkura and El lay on the grass unconscious. Victoria sat beside them panting. I crawled over to them too weak to stand. "Are you alright?" I asked.

"Yes," she said.

"What about them?" I nodded at the others laid out.

"We need to call for help. I don't think we can get them all back in our current state."

"Your right." The sun was low and the sky darkening. The day was becoming night and I had no idea who was in the capital. Even if they hadn't managed to gather everyone yet, Yuko and Kai should be here by now. I pulled my communis from my jacket pocket, but I dropped it. My fingers were too numb to work it.

Victoria picked it up. "Don't worry I got this." She

activated my communis without issue. "I don't feel the cold like you do."

Radius slumped down next to us. "This is a disaster. I am sorry to have failed you."

I looked at Radius sat there. His shoulders sagged and the light was gone from his eyes. I gulped down a lump in my throat. "If you failed. Then so did I."

My body ached all over I was completely drained. I crawled along the wet grass, dragging myself over to kneel beside Greg. From the rise and fall of his chest, I knew he was breathing. I pushed his fringe to the side. My eyes filled with tears at the sight of the red raw, twisted flesh on the side of his face. Those burns I had inflicted upon him. I laid my head on his chest. As I listened to his heart beating, I closed my eyes.

I sat dangling my legs off the side of a hospital bed, itching to escape. A healer was examining me, checking I was all right but all I wanted to do was be by Greg's side. My injuries were nothing in comparison to his. Whatever fabric the armour from the water nymphs was made out of was amazing. I needed to order a hundred rolls of it. This was the least amount of injuries I had ever come out of a fight with. The only one who had received a significant injury out of the five of us was Harkura but he had been seen too swiftly. According to the woman who had healed him, his outfit absorbed most of the attack and the scratches on his face were superficial. It had been a blow to the back of his head that had knocked him out. They had kept Harkura and Victoria in the same room as me, so I knew they were okay, but the others had been swept away separately. It was driving me crazy not knowing how they were but at least I knew Greg wasn't alone. When we had called for help, Lady Gabrielle had come for us herself. She hadn't left Greg's side from the moment she saw him. Her face a washed with worry.

"Okay, you are all clear," said the healer, "Just take it easy for a bit."

I nodded, with no intention of taking the advice. I

hopped down off the bed. "Where was Greg taken?"

She pointed down the hall. "Lord Ainsworth is in room 12, down there to the right."

I thanked her and was out of the room as fast as my legs could carry me. I walked into Greg's room and gasped. My heart felt like it had been ripped apart all over again. He was covered in bandages, but I could still see the red blotchy skin they covered. His burns had begun to blister before we made it to the capital. He had looked awful when they wheeled him off on a hospital bed, but I had expected them to work some spell and get him back to normal.

"Mellissa." I jumped at the sound of my name. I hadn't noticed Lady Gabrielle sitting in a chair beside his bed. She looked pale and her usually neat bun was a mess. She stood straightening her blazer. "You are all healed then?"

I nodded slowly. The room was warm and stuffy. My head spun as I took in how bad Greg's wounds looked. "How is he?" I asked.

"He is stable." She said, "However he remains in a coma."

"What?" Tears threatened to fall as my bottom lip quivered. I swallowed the lump in my throat. Tensing my jaw to stop myself from crying. "Why haven't they healed his burns?"

She stroked the top of his head giving him a sad smile. "They are not ordinary burns. They are laced in dark magic."

I looked down at my hands, turning them over, disgusted at what they did. "But I'm the one that burned him," I whispered.

Her eyes snapped to mine. There was so much pain in her stare. "If this was purely your magic at work the healers wouldn't have had so much trouble. Your power is pure light. Kadon must have tried to fight to stay, burning Gregory in the process."

My heart was in pieces. I wanted to believe that this was all Kadons fault, but it was also mine. My dream of Matt had warned me something bad was going to happen, but I'd ignored it. I never should have left him back on that island. I should have found another way. A warm hand rubbed my back. "Mellissa this isn't your fault," said Lady Gabrielle, "It was Gregory's choice to go to the sea kingdom."

"I should have protected him." I clenched my fists. "I should have defeated Kadon properly the first time."

"No one could have seen this coming." She sighed pinching the bridge of her nose. "But Mellissa why didn't you inform me this was happening? I had to hear from Yuko. You almost got yourself killed and then you went straight back out to fight."

"There wasn't time. It all happened so quickly. I couldn't risk wasting time in a council meeting."

"I understand that Gregory's life was in danger, screw the council." She placed her hand on my cheek. "I would have been right by your side fighting to get him back."

My stomach was in knots. Of course, she would have helped me. Greg was like a son to her. She loved him too. "I'm sorry." My voice broke on the last word as the tears broke through. "I was just so scared that I would lose him but I" my words cut off unable to finish what I was saying. I didn't know how to put what I was feeling into words. Lady Gabrielle wrapped her arms around me hugging me gently. I cried on her shoulder until I had no more tears left.

Lady Gabrielle stepped back placing one hand on my shoulder, with the other she hand me a handkerchief. "It's okay you freed him on Kadon's control and he will recover." She gave me a gentle smile, but it didn't reach her eyes. "You should sit with him. I will get us both something hot to drink." She patted my back and left, leaving me standing at the end of Greg's hospital bed.

I dried my eyes with the handkerchief and tucked it away in my jacket pocket. I pulled the chair closer to the bed and sat side him, holding his hand. Greg didn't look himself. He looked almost grey with angry red flesh sticking out of the sides of his bandages. The only recognisable feature was his red hair. I pushed his fringe to the side. I felt empty inside. Like a piece of me was missing. "You have to wake up," I said, "You said you would always find your way back to me." Tears rolled down my cheeks again. "I need you to come back to me." I held his hand close to my heart, wishing I could magic him awake. That I could make everything better but even the Heart crystal didn't have that sort of power.

High winds whip at my long braid. The armour I wear is of the royal green of the elves. It is much heavier than anything I'm used to. The clear sky has turned pink as the sun sets. I stand on a mountainside staring into a cave my heart racing. I take a wide stance as I look into the cave. Red eyes glow in the darkness.

"Queen Freya," says a deep voice from within the cave. "What is it that you seek in the mountains."

"You know why I have come." I say, "Kadon has become a much bigger problem than anticipated."

"Kadon is a problem for the land dwellers. The land is not my domain."

"How can you say that?" My anger flares. I step forward clenching my fists. "Kadon murdered the sea king and stole the moon crystal. The world will fall into chaos. This is a problem to us all."

Smoke puffed out of the cave. "I will not risk my people by starting an unnecessary war."

"The war is already here," I shout, "The question is whether you will do something before Kadon turns his attention to the skies. Do you think he will be satisfied with just ruling the seas and land?"

"That will not pass."

"How can you be so sure?" I ask.

"I have foreseen it. It is the keeper of the heart that will stop him."

Rage bubbled up inside me. "If you have the power to see the future. Why didn't you warn the sea king? Why did you not stop Kadon before he murdered hundreds of people."

"The leprechauns are land folk and as I said that is not my domain."

"What sort of answer is that" I say through gritted teeth, "You had the power to prevent so many deaths and just sat up here in your cave doing nothing." I felt my power sizzling to the surface. Taking a

deep breath, I pushed it back down.

"You miss understand. I only knew of the leprechaun's movements after they first attacked. I do not simply see the future as I wish but what I have foreseen tells me that Kadon will be defeated."

I crossed my arms my hip jutting out to the side. "Then what is it that you have seen?"

"I have seen the rise of darkness like never before. The world will be on the brink of chaos but there is a light of hope. The keeper of the Heart will defeat the darkness and bring balance to the world. Kadon is the darkness."

"Why does that mean I have to face him alone?" I ask.

"It is how I foresaw it. The keeper of the heart standing alone against the darkness."

"So, what if you saw me alone." I swipe my arm to the side, clutching the heart crystal in my other hand. "Fight by my side. Kadon won't stand a chance against the two of us together."

The red eyes flashed in the darkness. "I never said it was you I saw."

My heart sank a dark pit opened up inside me. "If I am not the Keeper of the Heart you saw, then how long is the war going to last? How long are you willing to stand by while innocents die?"

"I do not know how long the war will last. The keeper I saw, may or may not have been you. That part of the vision was unclear. What I do know is that it is not time for the skies to get involved."

"But why?" I ask almost pleading with him. "Just because some vision you had. We could change things, prevent what you saw from happening."

"We cannot. This is the way of prophecy. What is seen cannot be undone. Fate will ensure what has been prophesied will come to pass."

Rage swept through me. My hands burned with power. "You should be ashamed of yourself. You have all this power, and you do nothing with it."

"Calm yourself, Queen Freya." Another puff of smoke sweeps out the cave. "It would be wrong of me to fly down to the land throwing my power around."

"Your heartless. A coward too scared to even try." I narrow my eyes at the figure in the cave. "You should be ashamed to call yourself a

crystal keeper." I throw my arms down to my side and run off the edge of the mountain.

I awoke in a nice plush bed. Once again, my body ached all over but I was safe, back in my rooms at the council. I ran my hand through my hair, thinking about my dream. It had been months since I had dreamed of Freya. The last time it happened was just after I defeated Kadon. My heart sank. Kadon was back and now I was dreaming of Freya again. It couldn't be a coincidence. Last time my dreams had been trying to tell me about Freya and Kadon's relationship. This time the dream had been different, but it held a message. Freya had been speaking to someone in a cave, about a prophecy. *The prophecy.* I sat up in bed and pressed my fingers to the sides of my head. Matt had also said something about a prophecy. I had ignored that last message because so much had been happening. But now with this second dream. Humarya had also mentioned back in the summer during our last battle about a lizard and a prophecy.

I was out of bed in a flash and in Victoria's room shaking her awake. "What is it?" She groaned as she sat up swatting me away.

"I had a dream about Freya," I said.

"Okay, and what is so important about this dream?" She yawned as she stretched her arms out.

"It wasn't a normal dream. It was a memory of Freya's. It was about a prophecy, the one Humarya spoke of."

She leaned forward, more awake than before. "You mean the one that led to her hunting down all the elves?"

I nodded as I sat on the edge of her bed. "But she got it wrong Victoria. The prophecy wasn't about her, but she helped it come true. It was always about Kadon." I placed my palm on my forehead pushing my hair back. "This is what Matt meant, about us all being wound up in it for thousands of years."

Victoria rubbed her forehead. "I don't understand. What has Matt got to do with this."

"He also came to me in a dream a few days ago,

warning me about a prophecy and how we are all caught up in it." I tugged at my hair. "And now this dream. It's like we are all trapped in this fight of light and darkness."

Victoria put her hands up in front of me, causing me to stop talking. She pushed her long blond hair from her face and looked at me with her piercing blue eyes. "Okay, just tell me about the Freya dream first."

"All those years ago when Kadon stole the moon crystal, Freya went to the keeper of the sun crystal and he told her that he had foreseen a prophecy. The keeper of the Heart will defeat the darkness and bring balance to the world."

"Okay," She rubbed her chin. "If Kadon was this darkness why didn't Freya bring balance to the world? She was the keeper at the time."

I thought back to my dream. The voice in the cave had said that part was unclear. I clasped Victoria's hand. "But she did. At least for a while. Freya defeated Kadon. The world was at peace for thousands of years but then Kadon began to break free." I stood and paced the length of the room. "When the lizard told Humarya the prophecy he inadvertently set things in motion for the darkness to return. That's where I come in. Now I have to step in and be the light of hope. It's why that part of the vision wasn't clear, because it was going to take more than one Keeper of the Heart to do it."

Victoria grasped my shoulders forcing me to stand still. "Stop, you're talking too fast."

I looked up at her my eyes wide. "Victoria, I don't think the Keeper of the Sun crystal is a person like us or a merman like Radius. I think he is a powerful sky creature. The keeper of the sun crystal is a giant lizard."

Victoria shook her head rubbing her forehead with her fingers. "Okay, now I'm really lost."

"The keeper of the sun crystal is a magic lizard. He told Freya the prophecy." I waved my arms about hoping my hand gestures would help illustrate what I said.
"Then his successor, the current owner of the sun crystal, told the prophecy to Humarya. Neither thought they needed to get involved because what has been prophesied will always come

to be."

Victoria sighed. Her forehead was creased, and her brows drawn together. "What I'm getting from all your crazy rambling is that the keeper of the sun crystal lives in some cave and has the power of foresight."

"Yes, but more than that." I groaned in frustration. Pacing again, I thought over the prophecy trying to find the words to convey to Victoria what I meant.

"How do we know this prophecy is real?" She put her arms out as she sat on the edge of her bed. "You said Kadon was the darkness in this prophecy but it's Humarya that's the threat. She is the one with two dark stones. Kadon is just a spirit."

I stopped pacing and stared at the wall in front of me. She was right, at the moment Kadon was powerless without a host. What if the lizard had misinterpreted his vision? I rubbed my chin recalling my dream again. Kadon was the part he had been sure of. It was the identity of the keeper of the Heart that had been unclear. "It just means Kadon is planning something bigger and far more dangerous than we realise. There is no way someone like him would settle being someone else's minion." I spun around to look at her. "He's going to betray Humarya and take the stones for himself. It's like Humarya is just a tool thrown into this mess by fate to make the prophecy come true." I walked to the door. "I have to tell Greg."

Victoria grabbed my wrist. "Mellissa he is still unconscious."

I tightened my grip on the door handle. "I know but he can hear me when I talk to him. I know he can. This is the sort of thing he would want to know."

I didn't dare turn to look at her. The look of pity on her face would break me and I had told myself I would be strong, I had shed enough tears already. The more I spoke to him the easier it would be for him to find his way back. Greg would wake. I knew it in the pit of my stomach. We had been through too much for him not to come back to me.

Regroup

Mellissa

I sat in a council meeting staring blankly ahead. My ears were buzzing as they all droned on around me. Everyone had something to say about what had happened. They were scared. Which was understandable but as usual no one could agree on what to do next. Everyone's reaction toward me was one of two. They either pitied me or blamed me. I didn't need either response. Neither would help solve our current problem. Humarya was now armed with two dark stones, and we had no idea what she had planned next. Then, there was Kadon and whatever he had planned. I held my head in my hands as I leaned on the table. Everything was all such a mess. I let them argue amongst themselves not listening to a word said. This wasn't where I wanted to be. I should be in the infirmary, by Greg's side. Victoria had gone to sit with him while I was here, but it wasn't the same. I needed to be there if he woke up.

"Queen Mellissa." I snapped back to reality as Lee shouted my name. He flashed his hand in my direction while turning to look at Lady Gabrielle. "She isn't even listening. Miss high and mighty, thinks she can do as she wishes. We should have been consulted before she ran off after Humarya."

I clenched my fists under the table. Lady Gabrielle put her hand up to quiet everyone. "These are unique circumstances. There wasn't time to call a council meeting. If Mellissa hadn't acted, Humarya would have retrieved the sea stone and we wouldn't even know about it. In addition, Gregory would still be captured, and Kadon's return would still be unknown."

Lee crossed his arms and scowled as he sat back down. "If you ask me Gregory and Yuko were reckless. They never should have been put in charge of finding the sea stone."

I gritted my teeth as anger rolled through me. As I pushed my chair back, Lady Gabrielle placed her hand on my arm and shook her head. Kai glared at Lee. "You should be ashamed of yourself," snapped Kia, "No one saw you volunteering at the time. They were taken by surprise. They both have received serious injuries. Gregory is still in the infirmary."

Lee crossed his arms as he pouted, making him look like a sulking child. "Well, if I had gone, it's not like Her Royal Highness would have been so quick to come to rescue me."

"None of us would." Kai looked at Lee as if he had smelt something rotten.

Lady Gabrielle stood, she glared at Lee. "That is enough. If you haven't got anything constructive to say, then be quiet. Our world is in a state of emergency, as the leaders of our people we need to agree on a course of action that keeps everyone safe."

Lee sucked his teeth, and his lips became a thin line. "If you want to keep everyone safe, I suggest we hand her over." He pointed at me aggressively. "Both Humarya and Kadon want her dead. Surely, we can trade her for our safety."

"Are you serious?" asked Lady Gabrielle. Lee nodded. Her jaw went tense. "Mellissa and King Radius are our best defence against Humarya. We also do not make bargains with mass murderers."

"I don't hear anyone else coming up with ideas," said Lee.

"We can open up the caves to more people," Said Hogan, "Send our most vulnerable underground. We also have many escape routes that only a dwarf could navigate."

"But you are already hiding Laxus," Lady Gabrielle said, "Humarya may target the stone he has next."

Hogan leaned forward his arms resting on the table. His brow furrowed. "I think we should send Laxus to the human world. Send him as far away from this as possible."

Lady Gabrielle frowned. "I don't like the idea of potentially endangering the humans, but you might be right. The further away he is the harder it will be for her to find him."

"You never know she may not even go after the boy," said Hogan, "With the sea and air stones in her possession she is stronger than any being in existence. This may satisfy her thirst for power."

"She still won't be able to raise the dead," I said, "Her goal has always been to bring back her dead husband. Even with two dark stones, she won't be able to do this. Humarya will seek more power."

"Are we just meant to run and hide?" snapped Lee. The vein on his forehead was bulging. "We should be preparing our armies and sending them after her. Enlist both the crystal keepers and fire them at her."

"When you send our soldiers into battle will you march with them?" I asked.

He pursed his lips together as he tilted his head upwards. "Of course not. I will co-ordinate from here."

I slammed my hands on the table. "You were so quick to criticize Greg and Yuko, but you are not willing to make the same sacrifice. How many lives are you willing to offer up to Humarya's wrath?"

"This is war. It is what they are trained for."

Lady Gabrielle placed her hand gently on my arm and glared at Lee. "Our armies should be deployed to protect the people. Where exactly would you send our soldiers anyway? We do not know where Humarya is."

Lee opened his mouth to speak but I was done listening. My temper was about to break. I stood as my powers longed to be set loose. "I've had enough of this. I will not be your weapon." I turned on my heels and marched out of the room. Lee shouted something after me. I assumed it was something rude, but I didn't hear. I was done listening to him.

Harkura fell in line beside me as I stormed down the

corridor. He didn't bother asking what happened in the meeting, I supposed my face said it all. I couldn't sit around that table discussing how to deploy soldiers like this was a game. These were people's lives. I knew Lady Gabrielle understood this, but Lee was heartless. I shook my head. They were not the ones I needed to be co-ordinating with. Hogan was right. Humarya was now the strongest person on the planet. Even with Radius' help, it would be a struggle to fight her. Someone grabbed my wrist. I whirled around ready to strike, stopping myself quickly.

"Where are you going?" asked Lady Gabrielle.

"To the infirmary," I said.

Her shoulders drooped. "I know you are worried about Gregory, but we need you. Don't let Lee get to you. He is an idiot. You know I would never be so flippant about people's lives like him."

"I know," I said, "I need to see Greg before I leave. It is also where Radius is."

Her forehead creased as her lips turned down not quite frowning. "I don't understand."

I bit my bottom lip. "Humarya is too strong. I'm going to find the keeper of the sun crystal. If the three keepers unite, we can nullify the darkness."

"But no one knows where this keeper is."

"The hawklings do." I clasped her hand. "Promise me you will look after Greg while I'm gone."

She squeezed my hand. "Of course, I will. Mellissa, please keep in contact. We still need to coordinate our movements with one another, and I like to know you are safe."

"Don't worry about me, just focus on keeping all our people protected." Her eyebrow rose as she tilted her head. "I will stay in contact," I said.

She nodded, giving me a sad smile. Harkura and I made our way over to the infirmary. Greg's condition was unchanged. I tried to take comfort in the fact he hadn't gotten any worse, but it didn't help the turmoil I felt in the pit of my stomach. It didn't feel right to leave him like this, but I had to go. I just needed to get Radius on board with my plan. I was sure he would be easier to convince than the lizard, but it was time for the keeper of the sun crystal to come down from his cave.

Radius stared blankly out the window. We were in the visitor's area in the hospital. I was sitting in the corner by the window. When the king and I approached the area, everyone stared and cleared the space. No one came within two meters of us. Some people occasionally glanced our way, but they left us alone. They must have known things were serious if the two of us were here together. I had explained my plan to find the keeper of the sun crystal to him and about my dream of Freya meeting with the lizard. He had since been silently looking out the window. He was a hard man to read. He was usually very bubbly and enthusiastic but his whole aura seemed to have changed. He was stoic and quiet. Throughout the whole conversation, his facial expression hadn't changed. He had just nodded occasionally. I needed to know what he was thinking. We didn't have much time and I wanted to get moving as soon as possible. He turned round after what felt like hours of silence. "I cannot go with you."

"Why not?" I asked.

"I think you are right about the three crystal keepers uniting but I think you must make the journey alone. I will stay here in case of an attack."

"Radius you won't be able to stand against her alone."

"And neither will these people."

"I understand what you're saying which is why I want us to go now. We only have until Humarya realises she still can't raise the dead. Then she will be on the attack again. I will be able to travel a lot quicker with your help. I can't open portals as you do."

His eyes turned down as sadness swept over his features. "I suppose your right. This lizard may be more willing to listen if we both go. If he is like his predecessor in that dream of yours, he may not be easily moved." He sighed as his shoulders dropped. "It just doesn't feel right. I have already put my people on high alert, but I should be there to lead them."

I placed my hand on his forearm. "I don't want to leave Greg, not like this. I don't want to leave my people unprotected. I feel like I have been away from home for too long, but we would all fall if I went back now. I am doing this for them all. To give us a fighting chance."

"How are you so wise, at such a young age?"

"I don't know if I'm wise, but I have lost a lot which can make you see things differently." My heart felt heavy as I pushed my hair behind my ear. "I hope that when she does attack, she will come for the two of us."

He put his hand on my shoulder, his gaze solemn. "I will get El and change back into that weird armour."

"You know our armour may not hold up against Humarya's new power."

"Yes, but it is better than going in shirtless. I will meet you back here in a moment." He walked off with his head held high. I went back to Greg's room. Victoria was sat beside him and Harkura was leaning against the wall. I was already in my armour and so were they. They both looked at me.

"We leave soon." I said, "but I need one of you to stay here."

I locked eyes with Victoria. She stood shaking her head. "No, you are not leaving me behind."

"This isn't a dangerous mission. Maybe you should both stay. I would feel better knowing you are both here in case something goes wrong."

"That is not happening," Victoria said.

"No," said Harkura. "We are meant to protect you."

"I need you to protect my heart." I took Greg's hand and stroked his cheek. "Please Harkura."

His stance softened. "Mellissa-"

A loud bang shook the building. Another bang. An alarm shrieked from above. I put my hands over my ears. "What's going on?" I shouted over the noise. We ran out of the room and a healer bashed into us.

"Your majesty, there was an explosion over the road at

the council building," said the healer, "We need to evacuate."

My blood froze. We were already out of time. I dug my nails into my palm to shock myself into action. "Harkura with me. Victoria stay put."

Victoria grabbed my arm. "I am not your subject you cannot order me around. I will fight."

I clasped her hands between mine. "Please Victoria, I need you to stay here. I will fight better knowing you are here keeping Greg safe. There is no one else I trust more."

Her jaw tensed. "Fine, I'll protect the infirmary."

I hugged her tightly. "Thank you." Harkura grabbed my hand and we ran out of the infirmary. Outside the streets were in chaos. People were running all over screaming. Smoke billowed out of the council building. The high roof was on fire. Harkura and I dodged our way through the crowd, running in the opposite direction to them. While everyone was escaping, we were making our way back in. My heart raced. I hadn't expected her to realize her powers limitation so soon. With every step we took, dread filled me. This may be our last chance to stand against Humarya and we were massively unprepared.

The Fall

Mellissa

I choked on smoke as we ran. Sweat dripped down my head. Once we had gotten past the initial chaos everywhere was clear of people. The guards had made a quick job of evacuating the building. The fire spreading from above had probably helped get everyone out fast. We had been informed by a guard the only people unaccounted for were the council members.

Harkura and I made our way further into the building. The corridors in the council building were eerily quiet. We were heading to the meeting chambers as I assumed the meeting had continued after I left. Harkura slowed down in front of me as we reached the corridor before the meeting room. He put his finger over his lips while gesturing for me to come closer. I tiptoed over. Harkura pointed to his ear. I listened carefully. People were still inside. I could hear muffled voices. My ears twitched as I heard Humarya cackle. Why was she attacking the council? They didn't have the power she needed. I felt numb as a wave of realisation washed over me. I had hoped she would target me when she went looking for Laxus, but I wasn't the only one that knew where he was. Every person in that room had the information she wanted on Laxus' location. It would only take one of them to break. Harkura grabbed my wrist as I went to step around him. He shook his head and pointed further down the corridor. Radius and El were tiptoeing towards the doors from the opposite direction. El signalled us with her hands. I had no idea what she was trying to say but Harkura seemed to as he made his own gestures back.

"Can you track the vibrations made by those in the other room?" Harkura whispered.

I placed my hand on the floor. Closing my eyes, I sent waves of magic through the ground. Vibrations ran through the floor back to my hand. "There is a group huddled together and three figures standing separately."

"Can you tell which is Humarya?"

I nodded. Her movements stood out from the rest due to her wings. "She is standing on the right towards the corner. I think Gwendolyn is on her left but I'm not sure who the third person is apart from everyone."

"Our target is Humarya. We need to time this right. We'll get one chance to attack together." Harkura signed something to El and she nodded. "On the count of three, we strike." He held up three fingers and counted down. All at once the four of us charged in aiming our attacks at Humarya. A loud boom echoed through the building as she slammed into the wall behind her, and it crumbled on top of her.

A dagger flew past my head narrowly missing my face. A man with short silver hair smirked at me. He was tall and stocky with pale ghostly skin. His grey eyes shimmered as he smiled at me. "It can't be," I said. Although I had never seen his face before I recognized his dark aura. "Run," I shouted at the council members. They were all on their feet and running out of the room.

Shadows burst out of the rubble. Humarya shot up. She blasted the door sending Yuko flying just before she could get out. Hogan dived through the door as the entrance collapsed in on itself. Most of the council had managed to flee, except Lady Gabrielle, and Yuko. Lady Gabrielle ran to Yuko's side. I angled myself in front of them, their escape route now blocked.

Humarya's eyes narrowed on me. "It's nice of you to join us, Mellissa." The hateful way she said my name sent chills down my spine.

"I wasn't expecting to see you again so soon," I said.

She strolled casually across the room to where Kadon stood. "I have a new adviser. I believe you two are familiar with one another." My whole body tensed as Kadon grinned. "He has served me well, so I rewarded him with a new body. No longer does he need to borrow the forms of others?" She looked down at her hands, twirling them round as shadows danced around them. "How is it I can do that, but I still can't bring back my husband?"

"Kadon was a spirit." I said, "He didn't die properly the first time, but your husband is truly dead. It doesn't matter how much power you steal." Shadows slammed into me. I screamed as I smashed into the back wall and slumped to the floor.

"I didn't ask your opinion," yelled Humarya. Her nostrils flared and her eyes looked as if they were about to pop out of her head. "Where is that pixie boy? I need the land stone to complete the set. I will become invincible, and the impossible will then become possible."

"I'll never tell you," I said. Humarya pulled her hand back and slashed me with a water whip. My cheek burned where she made contact. Flames engulfed Humarya. She whirled around putting them out with her new water powers. Harkura ran at her. With a flick of her wrist water crashed into him sweeping him away. Radius brought his trident down sending out a flash of light. El opened her mouth letting out a high-pitched cry. I clasped my ears. Humarya dropped to her knees holding her ears. A dagger flew at El's face. Harkura tackled her to the ground as the dagger whirled over them. Radius yelled running at Humarya, but she hadn't been the one to throw the blade. It was Kadon. He smiled at me. I flinched as Radius flew across the room, shadows wrapped around him. Humarya was suddenly right in front of me. With my hand engulfed in light, I punched upwards. She slapped my wrist away, snuffing out the light with shadow.

She grabbed my wrist and her talons clanged off my gauntlets. I twisted free, kicking up at her as I did. Her head jolted back as I made contact. Blood gushed from her nose. Her eyes bulged as she lifted her arms. Shadows sprang at me. I tried to deflect them with light but there was too much darkness. Her shadows slashed at me. I winced as they sliced threw my outfit. She lifted her arm and the shadow pulled me off the ground. "Where is the boy with my stone? Tell me or I will kill everyone in this room."

I shook my head, looking down at her, hoping my face didn't portray the pain I felt. "You're going to kill us all anyway so I may as well keep this secret."

Humarya growled as she yanked me towards her grabbing me by the scruff of my neck. As she pulled her other hand up to strike, I engulfed myself in light causing her to flinch. I jumped up kicking her in the chest with both my feet. She tumbled back. I landed in a crouched position. The air crackled as I rose up firing lightning in her face. Humarya flipped up in the air and slammed back to the ground. I ran forward, firing more light before she could recover. She slid across the floor convulsing as the electricity hit her. Rings of light appeared around her wrists as Radius spun his trident in small circles. Harkura ran at Humarya on the ground, the blades from both his gauntlets drawn. Kadon dived at him before he could reach her. Pulling out daggers of his own, he fought back Harkura.

Humarya let out an almighty screech. Shadows erupted from her. The whole room shook as we were all smothered in darkness. Everything was black and I couldn't see any of the others. I tried to push back with my light, but it had no effect. As my light dwindled, I fell to my knees. The darkness dissipated and my vision returned. Humarya had Radius wrapped in shadows on his knees and a blade to his neck. I pushed up to my feet ready to charge.

Humarya pressed the blade harder to his neck. I froze on the spot. The armour we wore protected his neck, but I couldn't rely on that to save him. "That's right don't move little girl. Now give me what I want."

"I don't have the land stone," I said.

"But you know where it is."

"Don't tell her anything," Radius shouted.

She yanked his head back by his hair. "Nobody asked you." She sliced the dagger along his cheek. Radius gritted his teeth. Sweat dripped down his brow. "I have noticed ordinary weapons bounce off that armour of yours but what if I wrap my shadows around the knife?" She flipped the dagger over, shadows clung to the metal blade. As she caught the blade, she swiftly dug it into Radius' shoulder. It sliced through the armour like it was nothing. A smile spread across her face as she yanked the blade out. Radius bit down on a yell. She pointed the dagger at his neck again. "The next blow will be through his throat. Now you little-"

Humarya's eyes went wide and her grip on Radius loosened. He slumped forward as she staggered back. El ran to Radius pulling him away with her. Humarya clutched a wound in her stomach, blood seeping out behind her hand. She turned reaching out to Kadon. His grey eyes shimmered as he plunged his dagger into her chest.

She slumped to the ground. "Traitor." She spluttered, blood bursting from her mouth.

Kadon knelt beside her stroking her cheek. "But I was never on your side. I was always working for myself." He rammed his blade into the side of her neck, splattering blood on the marble floor. Humarya lay limp and lifeless on the ground. His free hand grasped the two dark stones around her neck and yanked them snapping the chain.

"No," I said running at him engulfed in light sparks ready to fly but I was too late. The darkness that erupted from him was like nothing I had felt before. The power I had felt from Humarya just moments ago was nothing like what was coming from Kadon. The dark stones were truly at home with him. His grey eyes turned completely black. He turned to me and grinned. He slashed his arms down. Shadow spikes flew at me. I pushed light up towards them, but the spikes went straight through it. A body forced me to the ground. I screamed as the spikes pierced Harkura's back. Dark lines splintered across Kadon's face as he lifted his hand. A wind so strong it cut my cheeks as it burst through the room. Water gushed down on us. Dark magic exploded from him. Kadon flew up crashing through the ceiling. A roar some bang rumbled through the building as it collapsed.

I threw Harkura off me and sprung to action almost on instinct. My magic burst out of me latching onto every pierce of rock, dirt and rubble in the area. Sweat dripped down my back as I held the collapsing building up with my magic. My ears were ringing, and my lungs burned as I inhaled brick dust. My arms shook under the pressure. Harkura was laid by my feet, blood seeping out of his wounds. I hoped I hadn't hurt him further when I pushed him away, but I hadn't had time to be gentle. The rise and fall of his chest told me he was alive, but I didn't know how long he would last in that condition. El knelt beside Radius putting pressure on his wound as he deflected the water seeping through the rubble away from us. He looked ghastly pale and his breathing was ragged.

El's pink skin dripped with sweat. "How long can you hold that?"

"I don't know," I tensed my body pushing my power up through the rubble. Everything above us shook causing me to freeze.

El screeched as Radius collapsed on her. "Your majesty," She yelled holding him tight. Water quickly began to rise around us. I gritted my teeth. We needed to get out of here fast.

"Everyone to me," I said. Lady Gabrielle supported Yuko as they walked over to me. El staggered to my side dragging Radius with her. Once everyone was close enough, I took a wide stance. A drip of sweat blurred my eyesight. Gritting my teeth, I refocused my magic on the immediate area. Everything around us crumbled. My hands burned with power as I pushed the rubble above us. The Heart crystal glowed frantically around my neck as a dome of light formed around us. With one final shove, the rubble above us flew up into the sky creating a tunnel upwards. I pressed my fingers to the floor latching my magic into it and pushed us up on a disc of marble above the destroyed building.

Screams echoed around us. The capital was in ruins. Fires had broken out all over the city. Smoke and smog filled the skies. Lady Gabrielle gently rubbed my shoulder. "You have fought hard but there isn't anything else we can do right now."

I clenched my fists. "I can still fight."

"You cannot go after Kadon alone he is far too strong."

"I know but I can slow him down while the people escape."

I pushed her behind me as the air distorted. Pulling the crystal from my neck I transformed it into staff form and pointed it at the portal in front of us. Out stepped a man with dark brown skin, broad shoulders, and golden wings. "Rowan," I said.

He bowed. "Queen Mellissa. Our master has sent us to help your people evacuate." As I looked at the sky my jaw dropped. Portals were popping up everywhere. Hawklings flew out of them and were taking the people of the city back through. He held his hand out to me. "Come with me now."

I shook my head and turned to the others. "Take them first. Come find me when the city is clear."

Harkura pushed up off the ground. Sweat dripped from his forehead. "I'm coming with you."

I wrapped my arm around him as he tried to stand. I hadn't realised he was conscious. "Not this time Harkura." He opened his mouth to talk but I placed my finger on his lips. "No arguments. You are too injured. I need you to recover because if I fall, you will have to continue this fight."

His eyes filled with tears. "I will never stop fighting." He hugged me tightly. I breathed in his unique scent of ember for what may be the last time. "You will not fall," he whispered before letting me go. Rowan supported Harkura as he took him through the portal. My mouth was dry and my throat sore. With my staff in hand, I ran to where I knew Kadon would be.

Time to Wake

Gregory

Everything was grey. The sky was grey, as were the trees, bushes, and grass. Even the birds that flew past were grey. Greg had lost track of how long he had been walking in this strange grey wood. It could have been mere minutes, or it could have been months. Something inside him was broken and it had caused him to get lost. He didn't know what was wrong with him, but he couldn't find his way back. There had been glimmers of colour when he had heard her voice. Mellissa whispered to him in the distance but now her voice was gone. He hadn't heard it in a while. There wasn't anything else Greg could do but continue his walk in the quiet.

He stopped moving as something glistened in front of him. The trees around him distorted and the whole scene around him changed. No longer was in the sad grey wood but he was standing in one of the courtyards in the council building. To be exact the one where the tree of time stood. Greg's brow creased as he walked up to it. He placed his hand on it wondering if the tree could show him the way back. He jumped and spun around as someone said his name.

A young blond man similar in height to himself stood in the courtyard. He had his hands tucked in the pockets of his surfer shorts. "Matt, how are you here?" Greg asked, "You should be in the tree."

"I am in the tree." Matt gave him a crooked smile and shrugged. "For now."

Greg ran his fingers through his hair. He looked at his hands. They were responding to his commands. Why hadn't he noticed before? Matt grinned. "So you've finally realised he's gone."

Greg's jaw hung ajar as he stared at Matt. "How did I get rid of him?"

"You didn't. Mellissa forced him out, but Kadon fought to stay. The trauma of it put you in a coma."

Greg's heart pounded in his chest. He rubbed his forehead. How could he have forgotten what had happened? "Was Mellissa hurt?" he asked.

"Not yet." Matt looked to the sky placing one finger up in the air. "I believe she is still fighting at the moment." Matt looked back at Greg; his blue eyes solemn. "Greg, you need to go back now."

Greg rubbed the sides of his temple. "If I'm in a coma then this is a dream. None of this is real. I'm not really talking to you."

Matt grasped his shoulders. "I know this is confusing. You are right this is a dream but it's also real. Mellissa will need you. It's time for you to wake."

"I don't know how."

"Just follow your heart, it will lead you to her."
Greg spun around on the spot. Matt was gone and he was back in the grey forest. His chest tightened as his breath became sharp. Mellissa was in danger, and he was stuck inside his head. He cried out as he dropped to his knees.

Greg shut his eyes taking slow breaths. Matt had said to follow his heart, so that's what he did. Pushing out thoughts of everything else he thought only of Mellissa and let her light lead him out of the wood.

Greg opened his eyes. Everything was sore. A high-pitched siren rang, and everything seemed to be in chaos. He winced as he sat up. "Oh my God you're awake," said Victoria running to his side. He was on a small hospital bed surrounded by medical equipment. He tugged at the wires connected to him, pulling them off. Greg ran his fingers over the bandages on his arm, face, and neck. Victoria pulled his hand from the bandages as he began yanking them off. "What are you doing? You need those."

"I need to find Mellissa," he said.

"She is fighting Humarya. We have to stay put and evacuate with everyone else."

He clutched his side as he stood. Lifting his top, he looked at his wounds. Either the healer assigned to him wasn't very good or his injuries had been severe. As it was Kadon's doing, the latter was most likely. Victoria marched round the bed and tried to force him back in it. "Sit back down. You need to be checked over by a healer."

"I can check myself over." His hand glowed yellow and he ran it over his body. He was scarred inside and out. No wonder the healer had struggled. "Sanum quod fit." His hand went from yellow to green. He placed his hand on his side and sighed as the pain ceased. Moving his hand to his neck, he tried the same, but nothing happened. He moved on to his arm but again it wouldn't heal. His arm and neck weren't hurting him, but his arm was still red and blotchy from where his skin had peeled from being burned. He pushed past Victoria, heading over to the mirror.

Victoria grabbed his uninjured arm. She grimaced. "I wouldn't look if I was you." He yanked his arm free and looked in the mirror. The left side of his neck was covered in burns. The red swelling went all the way up to his cheek. He pressed his fingers to the line where his wound met the unharmed skin on his face. "This won't heal." He said. Victoria's gaze dropped to the floor as she shook her head. Kadon had scarred him. This mark on his face would be a constant reminder of how Kadon had abused and used him. He clenched his fists. Now wasn't the time for self-pity. "We need to find Mellissa."

"No, my only task was to protect you. I wouldn't be doing my job very well if I let you run out into a battlefield."

"Victoria, you don't understand." Greg grasped her hands. "I saw inside Kadon's mind. Humarya is the least of our worries."

"What are you talking about?" Her eyes scanned him up and down. "Maybe a second opinion is needed on your health."

She walked towards the door. He ran his finger through his hair. He needed to make her understand. "Kadon may have been the one in control, but I could also see his thoughts. His plans. Mellissa is in danger."

Victoria stopped at the door turning back to him. Her face seemed conflicted. She scowled. "Mellissa knew the danger she would be in when she left."

Greg shook his head. "NO, she didn't. I highly doubt it is Humarya she is fighting. Kadon planned to betray Humarya and take the dark stones for himself."

Victoria clenched her fists as her hands began to glow with magic. An icy wind grew around her. "I need to go help, Mellissa." She looked at him her eyes serious. "You stay put and evacuate with everyone else here."

"I'm going with you." She pointed at him and opened her mouth, but he cut her off before she could say anything. "I didn't wake up on my own. Matt helped me. He said Mellissa needed me."

"That's crazy, my brother is trapped in the tree of time. Are you sure it wasn't some weird coma dream?"

"I would still be asleep if it wasn't for Matt. He woke me for a reason."

She rubbed her chin and frowned. "Mellissa said she dreamed of Matt as well. Maybe he has been communicating from the tree." She tilted her head looking him up and down. "This is too dangerous for you in your current condition."

Greg pulled on his shoes and found a jacket in the cupboard. "I'm going no matter what you say."

Victoria flung her arms in the air. "Fine. Stay close and don't get yourself killed." She lead the way out of the infirmary. Greg followed her closely. He needed her protection right now as he was still weak from his ordeal. But Mellissa needed him and he couldn't let her down. He had been so stupid before thinking he needed to leave to be useful when really, he should have been at her side the whole time. He just prayed to whichever god was listening that it wasn't too late.

As they stepped outside. The grand white building that was the council was rubble. Smoke and dust covered the city. The dark power oozing over the area was stomach churning. How much had he missed in his coma? He ran with Victoria following the small glimmer of light aglow in this sea of darkness.

The Tree of Time

Mellissa

I skidded to a halt beside the tree of time. The tree was the only thing still standing amongst the destruction of the council building. I had seen the tree's branches swaying in the breeze when we burst out of the rubble. With what the tree represented, the fact it still stood wouldn't sit well with Kadon. Shadows thundered down from above. I dived and rolled to the side. The area where I had just stood exploded. Kadon floated softly to the ground. "Oh, little elf-ling I thought those hawklings had stolen you away from me, but it seems you can't resist my charms."

I aimed my staff at him. "I'm here to stop you."

He cackled loudly. "You can't stop me. You're alone little queen and I'm the most powerful being in existence." His eyes turned black. In a blink, he was right in front of me his hand wrapped around my neck. My throat constricted as his grip tightened. My eyes widened as I struggled to breathe. Kadon smirked as he tilted his head. "How is dear old Greg?"

My blood boiled. Crossing my wrists I pushed up at his arm breaking his grip on me. Kicking up at him I fired lightning toward his face. He put his hand up catching the lightning fizzling it out. With a flick of his wrist, I was thrown in the air by a gust of wind. He swiped his arm down and the gust changed direction smashing me into the ground. A metallic taste filled my mouth as my lip split open. I screamed as I dug my hands into the earth sending tremors toward Kadon. As the ground shook Kadon flew up off the ground. Vines shot up wrapping around him and pulling him back down. My vines fell limply to the ground as he slashed through them with water whips. He twirled a water whip round, swiping it down at me. I rolled out the way, but he whipped another one round. It caught hold of my staff. I held on tight to it, releasing a ray of light. Water splashed onto my face as the whips dispersed.

Spinning my staff, I fired reels of light at him. With barely any effort he snuffed out my light. I yelped as something burnt my ankle, shadows snaked round my feet. I yelled as my legs were yanked out from under me. I hit the ground, my head slamming into rock blurring my vision. My staff flew up out of my grip as I was wrenched across the ground. Kadon chuckled as I struggled against the shadow that slithered around my body. He pulled me up to my knees and stroked my cheek. I shuddered at his touch. "I must thank you for coming to me elf-ling, it saved me having to find you." He pushed my hair from my face. I thrashed towards him causing the shadows to tighten and cut into my skin. "Now, now I don't want to kill you. At least not yet. You will have a front-row seat as I destroy this world."

"You're a monster," I spat.

He grinned at me. "You say that like it's a bad thing." He turned to the tree of time his stare turning dark. He snarled at it. "First things first. This tree has to go." Both the air and sea stone around his neck glowed intensely. Shadows danced around his body as he fired a combination of air, water, and shadow magic at the tree. The bang echoed all around me. My ears were ringing, and smoke blurred my vision. I dropped back to the floor as I struggled against my binds. I shut my eyes tight engulfing myself in light. The shadows disintegrated. I jumped up calling to the heart. My staff flew into my hand.

As the smoke cleared, I gasped at what I saw. Kadon was cackling jumping around manically in front of the tree. The tree of time was split down the middle. "No," I whispered.

Kadon's eyes narrowed on me. "Oh yes." He swung his arm to the side striking the tree again. I felt the thud of the tree hitting the ground vibrate through the earth. My heart cracked in two. Matt had been sealed inside that tree and now he was truly gone. Any hope I had of getting him back was lost.

A heavyweight dove into the side of me. Shadows shot over me. The air was forced out of my lungs as a person landed on top of me. "Mellissa," said Lady Gabrielle from above me, "You have to snap out of it."

She got to her feet and pulled me up. "What are you doing here?" I asked, "You should have evacuated with the others."

"I will not abandon the city until all the people are out." Kadon clapped slowly. Lady Gabrielle stepped forward, taking a wide stance, and putting her arm out in front of me.

"This is amusing. It's like you lot all have a death wish." He shrugged. "Well, I will be happy to oblige you." Kadon launched shadows at us. I put up a barrier of light and the shadows sizzled away taking my barrier with them. I looked at Lady Gabrielle, we needed to get out of here. I threw up another barrier as Kadon attacked again. A funnel of water hit my barrier shattering it. The force of the water slammed us against some rocks. Lady Gabrielle was yanked forward by shadows. I dove forward reaching out, just missing her hand. Kadon pulled her into his arms. Lady Gabrielle fired plasma blasts at him. He wriggled as he let out a laugh. "Stop that, it tickles." He spun her round so she was facing me holding her tightly to his body. His eyes narrowed on me and a wide smile spread across his face. "You can watch me destroy the world you love, starting with this warlock."

It happened all too quickly. Kadon produced a dagger out of nowhere and slit Lady Gabrielle's throat tossing her body towards me. I launched forward pressing my hands to her neck. Her breaths were gurgled. Pushing firmly on the wound I tried to stop the bleeding, but it was no use. Blood kept seeping from under my fingers. My eyes filled with tears. "No," I said to myself over and over. Lady Gabrielle placed her hand on my cheek. I looked into her eyes. She didn't look scared or regretful, it was almost as if she was willing me to run. Her hand slipped from my face and flopped onto her body as she went still. "Lady Gabrielle," I shook her by the shoulders, but she didn't respond. "Gabrielle," I shouted. She was unresponsive. My stomach churned and I thought I might hurl. My whole body was shaking. She shouldn't have been here. She had stayed behind to make sure everyone got out of the city, which included me. The ground shook as I rose up to standing.

"Oh, darling don't look at me like that." Kadon said. He placed his hand over his chest and stuck his bottom lip out. "I was kind enough to give her a quick death. When I'm done with you, you'll wish I did the same for you."

I screamed as lightning sizzled through my body striking Kadon. He went flying across the old courtyard, landing amongst the rubble with a thud. He pushed up off the ground. Wiping the blood from a scratch on his cheek he smirked. "That actually hurt."

He ran at me, but I was also running. Power radiated from both of us. We collided with a bang. I went flying landing on my back on the hard ground, whereas Kadon just skidded back, never losing his footing, his arms over his face. He looked at me almost inviting me to attack again. He flew up and I followed suit. As I brought down the lightning, he summoned the rain. Between us, we created an all-mighty storm. As shadows and light collided, we both dropped to the ground. He landed gracefully on his feet, while I spun round and landed on my face. His eyebrow rose as he licked his lips. "I must say angry Mellissa is rather attractive." His grey eyes shone with something dark. I clasped my staff tight and ran at him radiating light. Pain exploded from my shoulder, I froze as I processed the shadow sticking out of it. I hadn't even seen him attack. I screamed as another shadow went through my left leg and I dropped to my knees. Kadon stood over me, a bored look on his face. "I grow tired of this." He flicked his wrist and shadows bound me. He balled his hand into a fist and the shadows tightened slicing into my skin. I crumbled to the floor my body shaking uncontrollably. "Now stay here like a good girl as I plummet the world into chaos." He flew up into the air. Up he went until I could barely see him. I needed to do something. Engulfing myself in light I pushed against my binds, but nothing happened. He had just been playing with me before. My left leg was numb. I couldn't just lay here while he did this. Something above exploded. The force was so strong it sent ripples deep into the earth. I thrashed about trying to free myself, but nothing happened. Everything began to shake. This wasn't right. The earth ached in pain. The scenery began to distort and fold in on itself. My eyes widened. Kadon landed beside me. He grabbed arm and yanked me up to my feet. Placing his arm round my shoulders he sighed. "It's beautiful isn't it".

My heart pounded in my head. I was left speechless as the veil crumbled in front of my eyes. I screamed as Kadon pressed his fingers into the wound on my shoulder. Blood ran down my arm. Kadon looked at me his eyes black again. "Now what to do with you." He flipped me over and I slammed onto the craggy ground. I cried out as glass shards pinned me in place. Kadon lifted his hand forming a shadow sword. I winced bracing myself for the impact. But the blow never came. My jaw dropped as he stopped moving. He appeared to be frozen like a statue. I tried to push away from him with my good leg, but I was stuck, still bound in shadow. He still didn't move. I looked around everything had stopped. The earth wasn't shaking, the distortion had frozen. It was like someone had hit pause on the world.

I flinched as someone clasped my shoulders. My eyes widened at the sight of Matt. "What's happening?" I asked.

He stroked my head. "Shh don't talk, just know help is on its way. I have slowed things down so they can reach you."

My eyes stung. "I thought you were dead."

"The tree of time can't be killed. We are a constant." Matt's ears twitched and he stood. He looked out into the distance. "They are here." He smiled at someone I couldn't see. Matt knelt back beside me and touched my binds and the shadow slithered away. "I will find you again." I blinked and he was gone.

I was pulled up into a warm set of arms. My hair was pushed from my face and Greg's green eyes were looking down at me. I went to talk but all that came out was a sob. "Sanum quad fit," muttered Greg. I took in a sharp breath as the sensation returned to my shoulder and left leg.

Vitoria stood behind Greg. "We need to get out of here," she said.

Kadon yelled from behind them. "How did you get over there?" His eyes bulged as he threw his shadow sword at us. Victoria put up a wall of ice. I shuddered as the sword became wedged in it. Shadows burst through the wall sending ice raining down on us.

A portal appeared beside us and a deep roar thundered through it. Fire burst out toward Kadon. Rowan ran through. "Quickly through here. You are the last people left in the city." Greg pulled me into his arms, and we all went through the portal. Kadon threw shadows after us but the portal closed before they could make it through. Greg jumped back and Victoria's arms went up ice at the ready. Stood before we were a scaly, tall, and broad, golden dragon.

"Wait," I said to the two of them. The Heart crystal hummed in recognition. I pushed away from Greg and walked toward the dragon. "You're the lizard, aren't you?"

The dragon nodded. I held my hand out to him and he rested his head on it.
"My name is Ignis," said the dragon, "and I am the keeper of the Sun crystal."

40

Broken

Mellissa

The earth continued to shake. I could feel it shuddering deep down to the core. I stood on the cliff edge looking out at the horizon. The night sky was twisted with the full spectrum of colour as day shifted to night and back again. The world was breaking apart and readjusting itself to something else. To something new but old. It was going back to how it used to be before the veil had been created. A chasm had formed inside me. I had failed to protect this world. This would be pure chaos.

Heavy footsteps rumbled the earth behind me. A puff of smoke drifted past my shoulder. "Queen Mellissa," said Ignis, "I realise the fall of the veil troubles you, but we must talk."

I ran my fingers across the Heart crystal. It hummed in response. "What is there to talk about? You were too late. We have lost."

"We can still stop Kadon if we work together." He replied.

I whirled round staring at the dragon in his big auburn eyes. "Now you want to work together. You wouldn't even see me when I was here before."

"The time was not yet right."

"So, the time is right now that the world is plunging into chaos?" I pressed my fingers to my forehead. "Your ancestor told Freya the same thing. Maybe if he had helped her back then we wouldn't be in this mess."

Ignis lowered his head. His grand size made me shudder. He could squash me like a bug just by taking a step forward. I stood tall tensing my body. "I thank you for rescuing us, but I can't help feeling if you had intervened sooner, we wouldn't have lost this badly."

"You are right young queen." He looked out at the horizon. "There has been a prophecy that each Sun crystal keeper has had a vision of. We always knew the darkness would come but the vision showed us that the light of hope would beat it back. It gave us a false sense of security that allowed us to sit up here in our cave detached from the world."

I stood beside him looking to the horizon as well. The sky was a swirl of pink, blues and yellow. "Didn't you ever think maybe you could have used your visions to try to stop the darkness from ever taking hold?"

"Prophecy has a way of making itself come true. If I had intervened earlier maybe fewer lives would have been lost but the darkness would've still come."

"How do you know that? You didn't even try."

"I fought Humarya when she first appeared and lost badly. When I told her the prophecy, I thought it would put her off knowing her mission would fail. Instead, she tried to stop the prophecy from happening, but she failed." He lowered his head. "Humarya and I both unknowingly played our roles in bringing about the darkness. It is what fate willed us to do." I felt a plume of warm air billow down on me as he turned towards me. "But we also helped find the light of hope."

"Where did you find the light of hope?" I asked.

"I didn't find it. A changeling boy, sent by the council did. The council became desperate to find the new keeper of the heart after Humarya loosened the seal on Kadon. Something she did to try to wipe out the elf royals because of a prophecy I told her." His eyes glowed red as he blinked. "You see how this chain of events brought you here. The light of hope."

I ran my fingers through my hair shaking my head. "I'm not the light of hope. I thought maybe the light had been a combination of Freya and me, but Kadon wiped the floor with me. I can't beat him."

Ignis' eyes glazed over as if could see something I couldn't. "You will find a way to win, as I have foreseen it."

I rubbed my chin as I thought of my dream where Freya had confronted the Sun crystal keeper. "Your ancestor said that part of the vision was unclear."

"It used to be but as time went on it became clearer. I believe that was because you weren't yet born."

"I still don't see how I can be the light of hope. If it hadn't been for Matt, Kadon would have killed me." My chest tightened as I said Matt's name. I'm sure it had been him, but I had been badly hurt at the time. I could have been hallucinating.

Ignis grumbled beside me. His large nostrils flaring. "But you didn't die because you had help. I believe that is what I've gotten wrong and my predecessors before me. You may be the light of hope, but you do not have to do this alone."

I looked up at him. His big scaly jaw looked like he could swallow me hole, but his auburn eyes were gentle. I tilted my head. "You really believe I'm the light of hope?" He nodded. "What about Freya? She believed she was this light but look what happened. What if you're wrong?"

"I don't believe Freya thought she was the light of hope. If she had, she would never have made the veil. I believe she was another pawn of the fates made to bring the prophecy into existence."

"I wish I could control my dreams. To pick what parts of her life I saw."

I tensed as Ignis lifted his front leg and pointed a claw at the Heart crystal. "All the previous keepers are with you always. All you have to do is ask your crystal the right questions." Ignis turned and began to walk away. "You should see to your people, and we can speak again soon."

My jaw hung open in awe as he flapped his massive golden wings and flew up through the mountains. I wrapped my hand around the Heart looking down at it. It still had secrets I didn't know. How was I meant to know what the right question was?

My limbs ached as I walked through the recently put-up campsite, full of the people from the capital. The hawklings had provided us with tents, bedding, and food. They had been very welcoming and helped heal anyone who was injured. My heart felt heavy as I took in the distraught faces of the people. It didn't matter how nice the hawklings were, these people's homes in the capital were lost. The city had fallen to Kadon's power along with the veil. Their lives would never be the same and it had all happened so quickly. We may currently be safe here, but I had no idea how long it would last. The mountains were shifting just like everything else. The magic and human worlds were becoming one. There was no way to know how the world would look once the land had finished adjusting. I had no idea where we would end up in relation to the rest of the world. Urbem Folium could be in a completely different country. I had no idea how long it would take me to find the elves again once things settled.

"Mellissa," said Victoria waving to me from in front of a tent. I made my way over to her. Her jaw was tense, and her brow furrowed. "How was your meeting with the dragon?"

"Ignis was regretful." I pressed my fingers to my forehead; a headache was already forming. "I don't want to talk about crystal keeper stuff. Where's Greg and Harkura?"

She nodded at the tent we were standing beside. "Harkura is in there. One of the hawk healers is still with him." A shadow covered her face as she looked away. "The shadows that pierced his skin left a residue."

My stomach churned. The memory of Harkura diving in front of me and taking that blow made me feel queasy. His injuries were my fault. I wrapped my arms around myself. "And Greg?"

She shrugged. "I don't know where he is. He disappeared shortly after you went to talk with Ignis."

"I'll go find him."

I turned to leave but she placed her hand on my

shoulder. She looked from side to side and drew closer to me. "Back in the capital when we came to find you. I saw_" She lowered her gaze as her voice became a whisper. "Matt. He was beside you. It looked like he spoke to you."

"You saw him too?" I asked. She nodded. A wave of relief swept over me. "I thought I had imagined it."

"What happened? How was Matt there?"

"Kadon destroyed the tree. Then when things were looking bad everything froze and Matt appeared. He claimed to have slowed everything down so help had time to arrive. He disappeared when you and Greg showed up."

Victoria pushed stray pieces of hair, that had fallen out her ponytail, off her face. Her forehead scrunched. "Our surroundings also went funny just before we found you. Do you think that was Matt too?"

"I think being in the tree of time did something to him. It gave him new abilities that allowed him to survive the destruction of the tree and help us."

"Why didn't the tree change Kadon?" asked Victoria.

"Maybe because Kadon fought it. He saw it as his prison, but Matt accepted his fate." My heart sank. Matt had accepted his new reality in the tree, but he shouldn't have had to. But the tree seemed to have made him stronger. I was glad Kadon never managed to tap into the tree of time's power. He was already dangerous enough without adding whatever new abilities Matt had on top. I shuddered at the thought.

Victoria untied the cloak she was wearing and held it out to me. "Here, I don't need it."

"Thanks." I took the cloak and wrapped it around my shoulders. The fleece lining was soft against my skin. It smelled sweet like Victoria's perfume. I looked down at my outfit. It was in ruins. "So much for my armour. Do we have a tent to stay in?"

She pointed to the one next to the one we were standing by. "That one is for you. There is a change of clothes inside from the Hawks. I'm going to stay with Harkura so I can keep an eye on him once the healer is done."

That's when I realised, she was in a fresh set of clothes.

She was wearing brown trousers and a cream tunic. I pulled the cloak tighter around myself. "We could all stay together. I'll get changed and come back."

Victoria waved her hand dismissively. "I'd rather not stay in the same tent as you and Greg."

I looked to the ground as I felt my face heat. "I'm still coming back after changing." I stomped towards the other tent but froze before I reached it. A weird jolt of power shot through me. Something felt off. The hole in my heart felt like it had widened. I needed to find Greg. Guilt stung me in the gut. We had barely spoken since he woke up from his coma.

"What's wrong?" asked Victoria.

"I don't know where Greg is," I said.

"I'm sure he will turn up."

My sight blurred as my eyes filled with tears. Something was different. I could feel it in the pit of my stomach. I had to find Greg. The last time I had ignored my gut feeling things had gone wrong. I put my head in my hands as heat radiated through my limbs. My magic swirled around inside me making my head spin. Bright lights sparkled around me as I was tugged forward.

I fell face first into the dirt. My heart pounded in my ears. Pushing up onto my hands and knees I took slow breaths trying to calm myself. The change I had felt hadn't been something bad. It had been the return of the power I had lost.

"Mellissa," said Greg. Strong hands wrapped around me, and I was pulled to my feet. "Where did you come from?"

I brushed dirt from my face. My head was swimming as what had just happened settled in. "I teleported," I said. "I wanted to find you and then I teleported." I threw my arms around him and hugged him tightly. Kadon's betrayal of Humarya had us on the brink of destruction but it had also given me back my teleporting. This would help navigate the new world that was forming a lot easier. I pulled back from Greg. My brief moment of excitement zapped away as I realised, he hadn't hugged me back. He was wearing a thick cloak with the hood up. I could just make out his green eyes and a tuft of red hair. I looked around the area. We were in a different part of the mountains. It was quiet here. We were far from the hawkling's home and our campsite. "What are you doing out here?" I asked.

"Walking," he said.

"Walking where?" I couldn't see his facial features under the hood, but I could feel the tension in the air. He hadn't planned on me appearing out of nowhere. He had been under the impression that I couldn't. "Why are you so far away from the campsite?" I asked.

"It was too loud there," he said, "I needed to think."

"To think about what?" He turned his back on me and didn't answer. I said his name, but he still didn't respond. Anger flared through me. I grabbed his arm making him turn and yanked his hood down. I gasped.

He jerked away from me. "I get it my face is hideous."

"No, it's not." I shook my head to stop myself from crying. How hadn't I noticed when he'd healed me? He still had angry red burns on his skin. They ran up from his neck to the left side of his face. "I did that to you. Is that why you're leaving?"

"I never said I was leaving."

"I'm not stupid. Why else would you be this far out?" He looked out at the horizon. I dug my fingernails into my palms as I clenched my fists. "I'm sorry. I should have found another way to free you." I placed my hand gently on his forearm. "Please don't go."

"That's not why I'm going? You saved me."

"Then why?"

He whirled around causing me to take a step back. His brow was furrowed and eyes wide. "I am leaving because I hurt you," he shouted. It felt like my heart had stopped as I saw the pain and anger burning in his eyes.

"No, you didn't," I said.

"Mellissa, I stabbed you," he said.

"That wasn't you. It was Kadon."

"It was my memories that allowed him to stab you where he did." He grabbed my wrist pulling me towards him. "They struggled to heal you didn't they." I looked down at the floor. His grip on me tightened. "You'll now have a scar." I didn't say anything. As he yanked at my top, I tried to twist away but I wasn't fast enough. He lifted my top just enough to expose my stomach brushing his fingers over the scar I now had. "I did that," he whispered.

I pushed my top down and grasped his hand. "Kadon is the one who stabbed me."

"He used my face to lower your guard." His gaze lowered as darkness covered his features. "I wasn't strong enough. I should have fought against his control harder. I deserved to be burned." He pointed to his wounded face. "This scar on my face is a reminder of my failure."

"Greg no. You can't think like that."

He stepped back releasing himself from my touch. "I'm doing this for you. If I leave, I can't be used against you again. You'll be safer without me."

"You're an idiot if you believe that. Do you think just because you aren't with me, I would suddenly stop loving you?" His jaw tensed as he clenched his fists, but he didn't say anything. "Kadon knows what you mean to me. You are in more danger wandering around alone and if anything happened to you." My voice broke as tears rolled down my cheeks. "I would be truly broken, and I don't think there would be any coming back for me this time." I dried my eyes with the cloak I was wearing. I stood tall, squaring my shoulders and locked my gaze on him. "Go if you must but don't tell me you're doing it for me."

His stance wobbled. He pressed his hand to his forehead. "I hate myself for what happened." I opened my mouth to talk but he cut me off. "It was my hand on the blade."

I slowly closed the gap between us. "You also saved me not that long ago."

He shook his head, his red hair falling into his eyes. "That was Matt."

"You saw him too?"

"He woke me from my coma so I could heal you. I couldn't even save you without someone else's input. You are better off without me."

"No, I'm not." I stroked his right cheek. He closed his eyes as he leaned into my touch. I ran my other hand down his burn. He flinched but didn't pull away. "I won't forgive myself for what I did either but as I told you before, you're mine." I went up on my tip toes and brushed my lips against his. "I'm never letting you go. Even if you leave. Even if you stop loving me. My feelings won't change."

He held me tight around my waist resting his forehead on mine. "I'm conflicted. I think my scars run deeper than just what is on my skin." He let out a long breath as his shoulders sagged. "What I do know is I love you and that will never change. Even if I do crappy stuff, like try to leave without telling you."

I snorted. "Yeah that was pretty crappy."

The side of his face twitched into a small smile. "It's a good thing you got your teleporting back. It stopped me from doing something I would've regretted."

He leaned into me and our lips met. I felt his pain as he kissed me. The longing and the confliction of his heart. Something was broken in him. We would get through this. He had been there for me when I had broken and fallen into despair and I would do the same for him. It didn't matter how long it took; I would never give up on him.

Two Wars

Mellissa

I look into the mirror but it's not my reflection I see. Freya's face stares back at me. It is uncanny the resemblance between us. She had the same long curls as me and the shape of her eyes matched mine. However, her skin was a darker brown and she is older than me. She looks weary and her eyes are creased at the side. The heart crystal hangs around her neck from a silver chain just like it does with me. Freya looks down at the Heart a sad smile on her face.

"I am doing this for you." She said, "I am sending this message with the Heart, so you understand why I did this. Why I made the sacrifices I did. So that you will know what to do next."

She looks up and our eyes meet. "I am not the light of hope this world needs you are, my child. You will bring peace to this world in a way I never could."

The image in the mirror twists and blurs. Freya's voice becomes muffled. I try to hear her words. I need to know what the full message was she left for her daughter. What her plan had been? "I love you, Marissa." Whispers Freya's voice as everything becomes a cloud of smoke.

I woke with a start. My head was pounding. Sitting up I threw my blanket off. I clasped the Heart crystal in my hand. Ignis said I had access to the other keepers if I asked the right questions. "Show me the rest of that memory," I said to the Heart, but it didn't respond. I gritted my teeth. Maybe I wasn't asking it correctly. It hadn't really been a question. "Can you show me the message Freya left for her daughter?" The crystal still didn't respond. "Please," I added. Silence. Letting out a frustrated groan I turned in my camp bed and froze. Greg was gone. He had been here when I fell asleep. My stomach twisted into knots. I jumped up and grabbed a cloak. Wrapping it around me tightly I headed out to find Greg, hoping he hadn't revisited his plan to leave.

The sun was high in the sky and plenty of people were out walking. I didn't have to look far as someone soon pointed Greg out to me. He was standing at the edge of the camp looking out at the scenery. "Greg," I said as I approached from behind.

His hands were clenched, and his body looked tense. "Lady Gabrielle's dead," he said. My heart stopped as a lump formed in my throat. His back was to me, but I could tell by the rasp of his voice he was holding back tears. "The hawklings found her body in the ruins by the tree of time, her throat slit." He lifted his hands looking down at his fingers spread wide. "I was there and I didn't notice."

I slowly walked to stand beside him. I clasped my hands together over my heart. "I'm sorry. I didn't realize you didn't know."

He turned to me. I flinched at his glare. "You knew."

Forcing the lump in my throat down, I nodded. "I told her to evacuate with the others when I went to confront Kadon, but she didn't. She stayed in the city to make sure everyone got out." My voice caught, and my throat felt dry. "Including me. Kadon had already wiped the floor with me but she still tried to fight. He slit her throat right in front of me and I was powerless to stop him."

"Why didn't you say anything at the time?" he yelled, "I might have been able to help her. I could have healed her."

My eyes filled with tears as I recalled Lady Gabrielle's last moments. She hadn't feared her death. As she lie there dying, she only seemed concerned about me getting away. "She died in my arms. It was really quick. There wouldn't have been anything you could have done."

He threw his arm out to the side. "You don't know that. You're not a healer."

The chasm inside my soul grew wider. I stared up at him blankly. "I have seen dead bodies before Greg."

Greg's chest heaved and his breathing became harsh. "But she's Lady Gabrielle. She can't be gone." Tears rolled down his cheeks. "She just can't."

I pulled him into my arms. Hugging him tight. "I'm sorry." He nuzzled his face into my neck. A wet patch formed on my shoulder as he cried. I gently circled my hand on his back in a soothing manner. I took slow breaths as I held back my own tears. It wouldn't be fair for me to cry. The pain I felt was nothing compared to what Greg was going through right now.

"What are we meant to do now?" asked Kai. "Without Lady Gabrielle, this all seems hopeless." His dark hair was a mess and his eyes puffy. He looked like he hadn't been up long. Lee had called an emergency council meeting to discuss Lady Gabrielle's passing. We had gathered in a small clearing near the camp and sat on rocks. Hardly the grand chambers of the council building. The timing of this meeting didn't seem right. Everyone was shaken by the news of Lady Gabrielle's passing. But as Lee had stated 'Any member of the council had the right to call a meeting and we all had to respond to the summons.' Kai's dishevelled appearance was shared by many of the others.

Lee stepped forward thumping his hand to his chest. "We need to vote for a new chairman. If we are to make it through this current crisis the council needs a leader."

"Now is hardly the time to be trying to replace Gabrielle," said Yuko. Her lips curled in disgust. "She hasn't even been buried yet."

"It may seem crass, but we must move forward. Kadon isn't going to pause his plans to allow us time to grieve."

I hated to admit it, but Lee was right. Kadon wouldn't halt his plans. It was likely he would use our grief to his advantage. We didn't have time to spend mourning. "I agree with Lee," I said. Everyone turned to look at me. Their shock was written all over their faces.

Lee's eyes were wide and his eyebrows looked like they were about to topple off his face. "You do?"

"Sort of." I pushed my hair behind my ear. "Kadon will be pushing on with whatever he has planned. I don't think now is the time for a vote, but I do think we need to move forward. We should have a quick funeral for Lady Gabrielle. Pay our respects by doing what she would have and protect our people."

"We still need a chairman." Lee crossed his arms and jut his chin out. "Someone to make the final decision when we cannot agree."

I rolled my eyes. "I suppose you nominate yourself, Lee."

He straightened his jacket and stood tall. "Well, I don't see anyone else volunteering. I think I would be the perfect candidate."

Greg snickered. "We're all doomed then."

Lee narrowed his eyes on Greg. The vein in his forehead bulged. "You almost got yourself killed the last time you oversaw a mission." said Lee, "So I think I would be a better choice than you."

"I don't want the job." Greg launched forward so he was right in Lee's personal space. Making Lee shudder as he loomed over him, illuminating their height difference. Greg narrowed his eyes as he looked down at Lee. "Lady Gabrielle's body has only just been discovered and you are already trying to weasel your way into her job. You will never be fit to replace her. Nobody is." Lee stepped back from Greg's glare. Greg clenched his fists. For a moment I thought he was going to hit Lee. Instead, he turned on his heel and stormed off. I stood watching him walk away. His reaction had been so unlike him. The events of the last few days had hit him hard. He was acting rash, too emotional. My heart sank. He was acting like me. Which meant if he was being emotional, I had to take on his role as the logical one but that was a lot harder said than done.

"I nominate Queen Mellissa," Hogan said.

"What?" I said.

I spun around to see him standing his hand braced against his chest. He walked over to me taking my hand. "You have always cared more about doing what is right than the politics of the council. You are the perfect person to lead us now." He turned round looking at the rest of the council. "I nominate Queen Mellissa to be our new chairwoman."

Yuko stepped forward also placing her hand over her chest. "I second that nomination."

Lee's jaw dropped. He walked into the middle of everyone waving his hands. "You can't be serious. She has the least amount of experience on the council and is always disregarding our rules."

Brandon, leader of the leprechauns stepped forward. "Actually, I have the least amount of experience on this council. In my short amount of time, Queen Mellissa is one of the few that has cared about what happens to my people. So, I also support her nomination."

Not so long ago the leprechauns had been denied representation on the council. Something I had fought to change after I became a council member. The wrong deeds of Kadon were not that of every leprechaun. Even if I wasn't the least experienced, I still hadn't been on the council long. My head was spinning. This wasn't what I wanted. I didn't want to chair the council; I wasn't sure if I could. Lee shoved Brandon. "Leprechauns don't get a vote when it is your king that is the current threat."

Anger flared through me. Lee's prejudice was something my temper never could handle. Brandon stared him down. He rolled his shoulders and held his head high. "Kadon is not the Leprechauns king anymore. We will never follow him again. He has never cared about us. All he ever cared about was power, similar to you." Lee's nostrils flared as Brandon turned his back on him. Brandon knelt in front of me bowing his head. "The leprechauns will follow Queen Mellissa if you will have us."

The three water nymphs knelt beside Brandon. Yuko looked up her ocean eyes locking onto mine. "The water nymphs have always seen you as our queen and we will continue to follow you."

"So will the dwarfs," shouted Hogan from the back.

I blinked a few times unsure of what had just happened. Three nations had just vowed to follow me as Queen. My mind raced as panic built up inside me. This was more than just acting as the chair of the council. but there was still three nations undeclared. The witches would back Lee. I didn't know Lord Cole well, but he was now the only leader the warlocks had. He could go either way. The fairies leader Ping wasn't here and was another wild card in the pack. Ping didn't like Lee but wasn't exactly a fan of mine either. As for the changelings, their vote would be split. Greg wouldn't want me to lead but he would never vote for Lee. It was likely Lee would try to get Greg's vote thrown out. However, both changeling leaders' votes could be seen as biased, due to Greg's relationship with me and Beatrice's relationship with Lee. I pressed my fingers to the sides of my head. This was too confusing. I didn't want to be thinking about how people would vote. " I thank you for your loyalty but right now this vote isn't what's important. We need to focus on the best way to protect everyone and navigate this new world that is forming without the veil."

The water nymphs and Brandon stood. Yuko looked Lee straight in the eye her brow raised. "See Lee that is a true leader, focused on keeping us all safe."

Lee's eyes looked like they were about to pop out of his head. "You are all ridiculous if you plan to follow that girl." He turned his nose up at us and stomped away. Kate of the witches and Beatrice, the other changeling leader followed him closely.

Yuko turned to me. "Do you still wish for us to have a funeral for Lady Gabrielle?"

"Yes. Everyone needs to have a chance to mourn her. We can do it this afternoon. I assume you and the priestesses have ceremonies for this sort of thing."

"Yes, we do. I will sort everything." Yuko curtsied while bowing her head at the same time. This change in dynamic was unsettling.

"What will we do next?" asked Brandon.

Everyone that hadn't stormed off was looking to me to lead and I didn't know what the correct thing to do was. I rubbed my chin. "I need to meet with the other crystal keepers. Kadon is a problem that we will have to tackle together."

This answer appeared to satisfy them as they all either bowed or curtsied and left. I let out a long breath, that meeting had taken an unexpected turn. I now needed to find Greg to see if he was all right and inform him of the funeral that was going to take place. He of all people needed the chance to say goodbye to Lady Gabrielle. I didn't think a funeral would settle the turmoil he was feeling. There was a lot more going on inside his head than I think even he understood.

I stamped my foot opening a wide, deep hole in the ground. Stepping back, I made room for Yuko and the other priestesses. They led us in prayer. Everyone was sombre as we watched Lady Gabriele's body lowered into the ground. The news of her death had spread fast through the camp. It was decided a quick funeral would be best. To allow the people to mourn and pay their respects. The hawklings brought her body back so we could lay her to rest. It still didn't feel real. So much had happened in the last few days. I had only been speaking to her yesterday. She had been alive only a day ago. I held back my tears, forcing myself to stand strong. Once the prayers were over and respects paid, I stepped forward sealing the hole up. I knelt laying my hand over the stone. The earth was harsh here, but I couldn't leave her grave unmarked. Sending waves of magic deep into the ground, a rose bush sprouted from the rock. As I stood it grew into full bloom.

Yuko placed her hand on my shoulder and gave me a weak smile. "A pink rose bush. She would have liked that."

I nodded and let her take the lead of the ceremony again. I made my way to Greg's side now that my contribution was over. I interlaced my fingers with his and gave his hand a squeeze. Yuko sang a song in another language. It was beautiful and warmed my heart. "What language is that?" I asked.

"Mandarin," replied Greg, "It's the native language of the water nymphs. It's a song meant to guide the soul into the next life."

I tilted my head. "You can understand them."

He nodded his face grim. When the song finished, Yuko blessed everyone, and the crowd broke up into small groups. Victoria and Harkura stood to the right of us leaving a respectful distance between us. Harkura nodded in the direction of Radius and Ignis. It seemed I was wanted. I looked up at Greg, not wanting to leave him yet.

He took my hand placing a rock in it. "Can you reshape it, into a heart and carve her initials in it."

I closed my fist round the rock and when I opened my hand again it was shaped like a heart. Looking down at it I shook my head. "I can do better." I walked over to a high wall that led further up the mountain. Running my finger over the stone wall in a heart shape I pulled a much bigger stone heart out of it. I staggered under the weight of it. Pushing my magic against it I hovered it over the grave gently laying it in front of the rose bush.

With my finger, I engraved Lady Gabrielle's full name at the top of the stone. I turned to Greg. "Take some time to think about what you want it to say, and I will add to it later."

He took my hand and kissed my knuckles. "Thank you." He nodded behind us to where my guardians and the other crystal keepers stood. "Now go. You are needed."

"Are you sure you'll be all right?"

He looked down at the stone heart I had created. "A moment alone will help me think of the right words."

I reluctantly let go of his hand and headed over to where the others waited. Ignis with his golden body shimmered in the winter sun. Radius looked tiny and stood beside him. The dragon's features were unreadable, but Radius's brow was drawn in and his body tense. "What's wrong?" I asked.

"There is a mass of soldiers gathering at the south end of

the mountains," said Radius.

"Is it Kadon? How has he managed to gather soldiers already?"

Radius shook his head his neck muscles tight. "I do not believe it is Kadon."

I knelt placing my hand on the ground sending out vibrations of magic. The earth responded. Why hadn't I noticed sooner? The earth had settled. It was no longer shifting.

"What do you feel?" asked Ignis.

I stood looking up into his enormous dragon eyes. "The earth is done being remade and its inhabitants have noticed."

Ignis went tense as he looked into the sky. "There is a disturbance in the winds. We are being attacked." He flapped his mighty wings and shot into the sky.

I turned to Radius. "Put a protection barrier up round the people and be prepared for impact. I'll go help Ignis." Radius nodded and called to his guardians as well as mine to assist him. I flew up following Ignis. I searched the sky not seeing anything, he was obviously feeling something I couldn't. "What is coming?" I asked.

"I don't know," he said, "I have never felt anything like this before. It is not a living being. It is an object moving at a fast speed. A cylinder shape with a point." Ignis tilted his head back. "Get on my back and hold tight. We are going to intercept these things."

I did as he requested. His back was rough and scaly, I dug my hands into his back holding on the best I could. My hands were clammy making it even harder. Ignis flapped his wingers forcefully and fast. With a twitch of his head, a portal opened, and he dove on through.

Three missiles whizzed past us. Ignis flipped mid-air raining fire down on them. One of the missiles exploded. I clung tightly to his back as he flew after the other two. The wind whooshed in my ears and my hair whipped violently at my back. "Attack with me," yelled Ignis.

I stood on his back wobbling as I tried to keep balance. I pushed my arms up creating a light barrier in front of the missiles. Ignis pulled his head back breathing fire at them. The fire smashed the missiles into my barrier exploding them.

"We did it," I shouted over the loud explosion.

"Not yet. There are two more ahead. Hold tight." Ignis commanded. I laid flat on his back holding onto his scales. Ignis tucked his legs in and lowered his head, flapping his wings at high speed. We shot through another portal coming out much closer to where the hawkling settlement was. "I don't know if I can catch them in time," yelled Ignis.

Radius' barrier glimmered around the settlement, but I didn't want to risk testing it out. Pushing off of Ignis' back I launched forward. I hurtled forward at high speed. The wind snapped at my face. As soon as I contacted a missile, I slammed light energy into it. As it exploded, I teleported to the next one. I placed my hand firmly on it. We were too close to the barrier. I teleported with the missile higher into the sky and released a mass of light energy, exploding it. I let myself free fall for a moment the wind whipping at my back. My broken heart wanted to stay here in the air falling. It would be easier than dealing with what was to come next. I had buried too many people recently. I didn't think my heart could take the battle that was coming for us, but I had to fight. There were still things left that I had to fight for. People I loved. I twisted round mid-air and teleported myself to the ground.

Ignis landed beside me. His eyes seemed to look into my soul. "This world needs the keeper of the Heart." I looked at the ground my arms shaking.

"Mellissa," shouted Greg running towards us. Victoria, Harkura and Radius followed behind him. Greg hugged me tightly. "What happened?" He held me at arm's length looking me over. "You're not hurt."

I pushed my windswept hair from my face. "I'm fine."

Victoria skidded to a halt beside us. She gave Ignis a sidelong glance looking weary. "Was it Kadon?" she asked, "How did you fight him off so easily."

"It wasn't Kadon," Ignis' deep voice boomed, "It was the humans."

The two of them gawked at Ignis like he had spoken a foreign language. Radius approached looking at me cautiously.

"This is what we feared. What I was trying to tell you earlier. The soldiers gathering, I believe them to be human."

I wrapped my hands around my shoulders. My heart sank. The humans were just scared. They attacked because they didn't understand what was happening. "I can talk to them. Once they realise, we aren't a threat, they will stop."

"And what if they don't," asked Victoria. Trust her to ask the hard question. The one I didn't want to answer.

I looked at them all. Taking a wide stance and standing tall, I tried to look as queenly as possible. "If not, we will have two wars to fight."

Epilogue

Courtney

Courtney strolled through the offices her stilettos clicking on the tiled floor. Her arms were full of files. As she rounded the corner back to her desk the ground shook. Papers were scattered across the floor. "Oh no, these are going to take forever to reorganise." She knelt and grabbed the papers closest to her.

"Let me help." Said Stan kneeling beside them and handing her some papers.

Courtney blushed. "Thanks." She took the papers.

Stan was six feet tall, with dark hair and chiselled features. He picked up the remaining papers and gave them to Courtney. "If you need help organising them back into the correct files, I am happy to help.

Courtney went to respond when the ground shook again. The whole building began to shake. The desks shuddered across the slick tiles. Country toppled forward. Stan caught her in his arms. She looked up at him. "What's happening? We don't get earthquakes here."

Screams erupted in the office. Courtney turned to see her co-workers running for the exit. Stan took her hand. "I have no idea what happening but maybe we should get out of here too."

Courtney nodded and they headed towards the door. As

she stepped forward the shaking got worse, and she fell to the floor. A tree burst through the tiled floor. It shot up and rammed its way threw the ceiling. Water scattered all over Courtney as the building's pipes burst. Stan pulled her back as the ceiling collapsed above them.

Courtney's heart raced and Stan panted as he fell to the ground. Trees continued to spread through the office. No, it was more like a forest was growing at a rapid pace and tearing the building in half. The earth itself was shifting apart as if to make space for these plants. Stan was on his feet again and tugged Courtney up. "We need to move."
They ran with their remaining co-workers as far away from the emerging trees as they could. There was no way out. They were trapped in a half-destroyed building by what appeared to be a magical forest.

Courtney looked out the window. They were too high up to climb out. As she looked at the sky she gasped. It was as if it was distorted. Like night and day were happening at the same time. But what shocked her the most was the figure of a man floating in the sky. Shadows danced around him, and his eyes were jet black. The sight of the creature made her blood run cold. What on earth was happening and what was that thing?

ABOUT THE AUTHOR

Whitney Morris has always had a passion for storytelling. Growing up she loved to escape to into the fantasy worlds of magic from her stories. She is a cat lover with one of her own, is crazy about owls, and is addicted to chocolate.

Whitney loves books, and she and her husband are raising their four children to be fellow bookworms in South Yorkshire, England.

The Life Crystal Chronicles is her first YA fantasy series.

Find Whitney on social media

Instagram   @wrlmorris_author

Facebook,
BookBub
Twitter &   @wrlmorris
Pinterest

Other books in the series:
Crystal Heart
Glowing Heart
Final Heart